An Opened Grave

SHERLOCK HOLMES INVESTIGATES HIS ULTIMATE CASE

An Opened Grave

SHERLOCK HOLMES INVESTIGATES HIS ULTIMATE CASE

L. FRANK JAMES

The Salt Works
a division of
PUBLISHERS DESIGN GROUP, INC.
ROSEVILLE, CA 95678
1.800.587.6666

Copyright © 2006 L. Frank James

No part of this book may be reproduced or transmitted in any form or by any means, electronic or mechanical, including photocopying, recording, or by an information storage and retrieval system—except by a reviewer who may quote brief passages in a review to be printed in a magazine, newspaper, or on the Web—without permission in writing from the publisher.

ISBN: 1-93408000-4

ISBN 13: 978-1-93408000-9

Library of Congress Control Number 2006929261

Creative Director: Robert Brekke

Cover Designer: Chuck Donald

Editor: Lyn Walker

Published by

The Salt Works

a division of

PUBLISHERS DESIGN GROUP, INC

Roseville, California

1.800.587.6666

www.publishersdesign.com

Dedicated to the memory of my beloved father,
L. Frank James, Sr.
(1918 – 2003)

Contents

Preface ix

1 An Early-Morning Vigil 1

2 The Intruder 13

3 The Mystery of the *Eye-of-God* 27

4 The Midnight Raid 55

5 A Breach in Time 73

6 The First Century 103

7 A Dead End 133

8 Separated and Lost 159

9 The Scene of the Crime 173

10 The Pursuit 181

11 The Effect 195

About the Author 226

Selected Bibliography 229

Preface

Dear Devoted Reader:

It is with a cautious yet resolute hand that I pick up my pen in order to relate to you this most remarkable episode in the extraordinary life of the world's most famous consulting detective, Mr. Sherlock Holmes. Knowing full well that the scope and magnitude of the following account is likely to arouse skepticism in the mind of the reader, I can only call upon the indisputable eyewitness by stating quite simply that I was there. I saw and actually participated in the unfolding of the entire adventure. Admittedly, the idea of engaging in a face-to-face meeting with Jesus of Nazareth is a concept that, even now, is difficult to completely accept.

Due to the seemingly unbelievable nature of the following investigation, I lean heavily upon the reputation of the writer, myself, as being honest and forthright regarding the retelling of many such strange cases in the life of Mr. Sherlock Holmes. I run the risk of repeating myself when I say, without doubt, that this adventure is unique. May history and time be my greatest judges.

Allowing for the fact that some period of time has passed since the events of this plot have taken place, they can now be written down. I assure those interested in such things that a certain amount of objectivity has replaced the initial passion related to the chain of events about to be recounted. Although, to date, this is the most important chapter in the exploits of Sherlock Holmes, it is probably not the last due to the ongoing and renewed life which was affected by the events of this study, this study in truth, if you will.

Upon occasion, my companion has reprimanded me for recounting his adventures with more than purely scientific intent. He has often prohibited me from documenting his efforts because of, as he refers to it, my tendency to sensationalize them. Looking through my notebook, I can easily find a dozen intriguing cases that justify the time and effort it would take to commit them to paper. There is the unique case of the Howard Stage, where Mr. Holmes' acting ability earned him the praise of the entire West End artistic community. Artificial intelligence was advanced with the incident of the Mechanical Man. The notable adventure of the Missing Topper made him the object of conversation around every breakfast table on the continent. However, all of these impressive triumphs pale by comparison to the incident I am about to unfold. Because of the unusual nature of the subject of investigation and the impact it enjoyed upon my cohort and me, Mr. Sherlock Holmes heartily encouraged its communication.

I lay this adventure at the feet of the devoted followers of the great detective and request only that opinions be withheld until the last word is read and the final intention is understood. Avoiding the notoriety of exaggeration, I seek only the solace of truth and reason, something that my leading man has always insisted upon. With these reservations issued, may it please the reader to accept the offering of this strange yet wonderful mystery.

Sincerely,

DR. J. H. WATSON

1

Upon arriving at the appointed place I received,
instead of clarity, more mystery.

—Dr. J. H. Watson

It was the autumn of 1908 that found me busy in the Great City with my medical practice. The cesspool of mankind, known as London, had grown in size and stature as well as human need. Being a doctor, I was continually occupied with individual suffering.

On a daily basis, my office was filled with patients claiming to have every conceivable disorder known to man, both real and imagined. For a medical practice, I am not sure which is worse: a hypochondriac who pays his bills or an authentically ill person who does not. One might speculate that the pace of urban life, the rapid changes of industrialization, and the advent of psychology in the new twentieth century had impacted both body and soul to the degradation of all the citizens of the vast metropolis. But I will defer to the social critics to make that determination. At any rate, the idea of leaving behind my medical practice was well worth a daydream. Indeed, I was envious of my former partner in adventure, Sherlock Holmes, who was now retired. I remember thinking to myself that there must be something beyond this humdrum work-a-day existence.

Not having had, for some time, any word from my distinguished former roommate and friend, the world's foremost consulting detective, Mr. Sherlock Holmes, I fancied him quietly and contentedly at leisure pursuing his bee-keeping activities in the Sussex Downs country. Knowing him to be a showman by nature yet deprived of the audience attendant to the solution of a front-page murder, it was hard for me to imagine him satisfied with this type of rural lifestyle over a long period of time. He possessed a need for an odd mixture of intellectual as well as physical activity. However, I presumed him to be contentedly resigned to a secluded and retired existence looking after his apiaries and perhaps writing an essay or two about some unusual investigative subject matter. I readily envisioned Sherlock Holmes happily scraping away on his violin until all hours of the morning, no doubt, plumbing the depths of a Mozart sonata or some such thing. I assumed, at any rate, that he was gladly occupying himself with the pastimes of his new life. Unfortunately, such was not the case.

It was a particularly damp October day in London. The gray fog had pushed its way into every chink and hole in the armor of the city to the extent that visibility beyond one's own hand, stretched out in front, was a challenge worthy of the greatest practitioner of the deductive arts. Busy at my daily tasks, I was interrupted by the arrival of a cryptic telegram from my former landlady, Mrs. Hudson, requesting my immediate presence at my old lodgings, 221b Baker

Street. No explanation was given.

It was past the hour of eight o'clock when at last the lamps were extinguished, the door was locked behind me and a sigh of relief escaped my lips. I hailed a hansom cab and sat back with my eyes closed, trying to imagine what possible situation could have caused this most recent communication from the accommodating, yet always concerned, Mrs. Hudson. Upon arriving at the appointed place, I received, instead of clarity, more mystery.

The Landlady seemed pleased to see me, yet was preoccupied and jittery; with what, I could not say. I ascribed her nervousness to the anxiety of old age. She always appeared to tolerate her tenants rather than to enjoy them.

"...And the rooms have not been occupied since?" I asked.

"I should say not," she replied, "they remain as yourself and Mr. Holmes left them, that very night...some years ago."

"Why have you not rented them?"

"I'd got no chance...no one seems to take a liking to the place, for some unbeknownst reason...maybe it's the smell of chemicals, Mr. Holmes and his experiments...and the like, what makes people disinterested," she said, not quite believing her own explanation.

Mrs. Hudson led the way up a darkened staircase. With a pleasingly familiar seventeen treads, we arrived at the top of a well-acquainted landing. She handed me the lamp while unlocking the door. Once unbolted, the heavy door slowly swung open of its own accord, as it was always wont to do, into a vast dark place which appeared to have grown considerably in size. I thought at the time this was due to the reduction of its contents.

She was indeed correct. The rooms seemed to be exactly as they were when we left. I stood for a moment at the threshold, with the lamp projecting dancing images onto the scant covered furniture and bare walls. Instantly a flood of memories, pouring through my mind, evoked emotions that must have been easy to read on my countenance.

I noticed Mrs. Hudson off to one side, staring at me with a tolerant expectation. That caused me to turn to her. We shared a visual connection that did not last long but was wordlessly heavy. She said nothing, but after a moment, with trepidation, she turned away and entered the room as I followed.

"It could be too..." she said, after a silence, glancing at me and then back again into the spaciousness of the room, "that people sense the mood of the rooms and what was left behind...if you take my meaning."

"I am afraid I do not," I said, pausing before I spoke again, "I do, however, recognize the smell a faint mixture of formaldehyde and hydrochloric acid. But that might be merely rooted in my memory." I trailed off.

"That's not my meaning, Dr. Watson...it's something, what I've thought about and can't quite pinch." She waited. "Can you feel it, Doctor?"

I took a silent moment to absorb the full impact of her words and the substance of the room we were in. Still, I could sense nothing. Holmes often accused me of not having much of an imagination. But, slowly as I stood there in anticipation of the next move, there was a growing awareness of a perceptible 'something.' What it was continued to escape me.

"I've come up here many a' time in the past years only to find the feeling that this flat of rooms have...," she hesitated, "never been empty."

It was at that instant that the vague notion I had felt crystallized into a specific realization. That was indeed the feeling. Mrs. Hudson had articulated it with piercing simplicity. A shuddering chill went down my spine. There was an unmistakable feeling that the room was not vacant. Not only this, but the idea that it had been recently used crossed my mind. What could possibly be the origin of this strange impression? I could not say. In fact, at the time, I briskly dismissed the feeling, putting it down to familiarity, personal history, and a 'nostalgia' surrounding the room and its erstwhile inhabitants.

"Nonsense!" I exclaimed, taking the lamp and walking through the rooms resolutely.

As the obscured areas of the premises became lit one by one with the dull amber light of the single flame, the feeling of occupation dwindled. Checking the various nooks, the windows, the fireplace, and the closets, I found them all to be secure and empty. Except for some random, vaguely familiar covered furniture that left a ghostly impression as shadows flickered and stretched according to the moving flame I held in my hand, I could find nothing. Because of my denial regarding this whole notion and my scientific bent, I was immediately inclined to write the impression off to the mental make-up of an old woman. There is often a vague line between reality and fantasy that age sometimes evokes.

"You are imagining this thing, Mrs. Hudson."

"I am, am I?" she shot back. "'Afore you speak, don't be so quick to put it down to the wild dreamings of an old woman, Doctor. I 'ear noises up here, I tells you...mostly in the middle of the night."

"Noises? What kinds of noises?"

"The kind 'o noises, what is unearthly, Doctor...," she paused for a full rest, "Moanings and mumblings that are not of this world. Strange muffled talking and creakings, the likes of which I never heard afore...and yet somehow familiar."

There was a silence. I found I was shivering.

"Poppycock," I stated.

"It's been going on more regular lately. Almost every night," she insisted. "One day last week, on Wednesday morning it was, I unlocked the door only to find the window, there, opened a bit and a distinct smell of tobacco smoke a lingering in the air, I did, Doctor." She stopped in her narrative to test my response.

"Is anything missing?"

"Not a bit of it. Everything's the same as you left it, long ago, and what of it, just some old furniture and an empty set of rooms."

"Did you alert the authorities?" I wanted to know.

"They thought I were a daft old lady, Dr. Watson...lost me senses, they says, wild fantasies they says. Humph!" she snorted. "But I knows what I 'ear and I knows what I knows!"

"Why did you contact me?"

"You're the good Doctor," she said assuredly. "They'll believe you."

As she nodded her head, the reason for her summons became clear. "What do you want me to do?" I asked, secretly knowing the answer.

"Why, Doctor, I want you to spend the night here to see and 'ear for yourself the terrible comings and goings of the place."

The idea of holding vigil for a night in my former set of rooms initially held very little fascination for me. There was, upon reflection, something compelling about the assignment that drew me. What it was, I could not say. There must be some logical explanation to the odd occurrences described by my former landlady. I tried to apply the methods used to such a successful conclusion on so many occasions by my friend and teacher. What would Holmes deduce from the given facts? No immediate theory came to mind that would explain all of the circumstances. Could it be an old client or maybe an adversary of the famous Mr. Holmes risking all to jimmy the window high above Baker Street in the middle of the night, perhaps looking for something or someone? I suppose it was possible to climb up the outside drainpipe or drop down from the roof to effect an entrance into the room, but why? Could it be an admiring devoted follower looking for the thrill of being at the place where so many adventures had unfolded? It can only be assumed that my experiences with my friend, Mr. Sherlock Holmes, had made me intensely interested in crime and certain intrigues, of which this was obviously one. I knew, of course, what he would have done. If he were in an active mood and adequately motivated, he would eagerly take up the course of action suggested by Mrs. Hudson. He would have requested my presence, naturally, along with my service revolver in accompanying his late night, perhaps early morning, vigil. I knew what had to be done.

Being otherwise engaged that night, it was arranged with Mrs. Hudson that I should be an overnight guest upon the following evening at the notable 221b Baker Street. I was preoccupied the entire day with the upcoming night's anticipated watch. Little of what I could imagine would explain the unusual happenings at my appointed location. "Not enough data," as my distinguished friend would say. I finally resigned myself to the position that I could find out what was going on only by direct empirical observation. That said, I prepared myself for what I presumed to be an intriguing overnight stay.

Again, I closed up my surgical office with a constrained but expectant enthusiasm. Checking, more than once, for the presence of my service revolver in the right pocket of my dark gray Ulster, I partook of a somber and thoughtful evening meal at a local establishment often patronized by my companion and myself in the days of our collaborations.

The people of London had not seen the sun for several days. In the twilight of the windless eventide, the brown fog seemed to hang upon the city and its inhabitants, not unlike a heavy eiderdown blanket hugging the contours of an occupied bed, making movement laborious and thought filled with effort. The dank mist made everything appear otherworldly and oddly out of joint. There is something about fog that makes one feel out of touch and separated from the reality of the surroundings. Things that are familiar and clear in the light of day become strange and spectral in the gloom of the dense stuff. I have often thought of what it would be like to grope about without the advantage of sight. How different life would be.

The fog seemed to make the blackness of the night even blacker. Any vestige of day vanished as time plodded ahead. The gaslights placed at even intervals along the various roads of the great city were almost ineffective. Although most of the streetlights had been converted to electric bulbs, there were still some pockets within the metropolis where gas lamps were to be found. This was welcome progress in keeping with a new age. I wondered how the lamplighters could even find their way to do their illuminating duty. Perhaps the dullness of the evening or the business of the upcoming watch made my thoughts dreary. I did not enjoy the prospect of spending the night in my former lodgings. It would be cold and lonely. But I also knew full well that the assignment at hand was an essential piece to solving the mysterious puzzle.

Upon my arrival, Mrs. Hudson and I shared a pot of Earl Grey and a long conversation. For some reason, the subject of the upper room and the reason for my being there were never mentioned. I went upstairs by myself and settled into the largest of the suite of subject rooms with the words of the Landlady still reverberating in my ears. "May God be with you tonight, Doctor." The thought that my maker was somehow overseeing my visit afforded me little comfort. I made the observation to myself that I would rather have the indomitable presence of my cohort, Mr. Sherlock Holmes.

Upon orienting an upholstered chair toward the window that I suspected to be the entrance portal of the intruder, I settled into the room, extracting my pistol from my pocket and resting it upon my lap. I noticed that the chair in which I sat was the very one most usually reserved and occupied by my companion. The arms were rough and cut from various experiments or unconscious fiddling with sharp objects in which my friend would often engage. It exuded the acrid odor of tobacco and chemicals. Morbidly, I reflected on Holmes' intermittent bouts with morphine and cocaine.

At this point let me divulge to the reader, in the form of a brief note, the meaning of the previous sentence. Mr. Sherlock Holmes' brain was of such a constitution that it required almost constant stimulation. When crime was afoot and the trail was still warm, he was unexcelled in his energy and initiative. The man would leave no stone unturned, regardless of the hour, to solve the mystery; the more chilling the felony, the better. However, when there was nothing of interest to pique his appetite for such things, he would languish about for days in a somewhat desultory fashion steeped in inactivity. It was during these times that the temptation to use opiates or cocaine was greatest. I would see him laying on the settee, crumpled up in an artificially stimulated state waiting for the next adventure. Although I usually said nothing, this feckless behavior was most alarming. I attempted, more than once, to dissuade him from his participation in such activities; it was of little use. The drugs, he felt, were essential to keep his brain alive and help the time pass.

Mrs. Hudson had closed the door behind me without locking it. She had promised herself and me to keep a sharp ear out for any disturbances during the blackness of the night. After a few moments of welcome quiet, I could hear, in the distance, the tolling of the formidable timepiece known as the heartbeat of the great metropolis. Big Ben sounded out, after its usual hourly signal, twelve evenly round gongs, indicating, of course, the midnight hour. Beyond that, it rested for a short time in its appointed duty of regulating the pulse of the city.

Sitting there, my thoughts wandered to many intriguing nights, at various locations, of similar surveillance I had spent with my companion. Mrs. Hudson had, thankfully, provided for me a small carafe of coffee, which I placed on the floor in front of my feet, making it accessible and helpful on my watch. Also placed beside the chair was an oil lamp and matches should the need arise. There was nothing left to do but to wait in the darkness.

Time, of course, moves so much more slowly under these circumstances. The seconds dragged into minutes. My thoughts ranged from shoes and ships and sealing wax to cabbages and kings and everything in between. Each sound magnified the importance of the moment and seemed to make something out of nothing. But still, time waged on. I thought of *A Study in Scarlet* and the first time I met my friend, the first time we entered the residence in which I currently found myself waiting. Silence. The one o'clock gong, more random imaginings. The two o'clock gong, still nothing. The mist of the outside world seemed to mingle with a certain fog that slowly overcame my attentiveness.

I thought at one point, with surprising vividness, about my next-door neighbor's cat scratching incessantly at my window, as it is wont to do when desiring attention. The scratching became an irritation as I realized I had been dreaming. Suddenly I snapped awake to the scratching noise at the window directly in front of me.

I sat bolt upright, inadvertently kicking over the carafe of coffee and spilling what was left inside the container onto the wood floor in front of me. Chiding myself for the blunder, I simultaneously reached for my revolver as the scratching sound persisted. Now, being fully awake, I noticed the faint image of a figure outside the apartment apparently trying to pry open the window while dangling down on some sort of tether. The source of the drab light that illuminated this eerie scene escaped me. Frozen in time while watching this picture unfold, I fought to steady my nerves against the increased heartbeat rate within. Slowly but deftly, the intruder forced opened the window and raised the sash to make his entrance into the room. The thought bolted through my mind, at this late juncture, that I should have at least attempted to contact my friend to seek his counsel before launching into this desperate confrontation. I regretfully determined it was too late for that now.

I felt a push of cold damp air. Deliberately, and I remember thinking to myself, rather clumsily, the figure struggled through the window and into the room. Barely being able to discern his shape, I guessed he was working to untie the rope that was about his waist. I groped for and found the matches and oil lamp at my side. Awkwardly, I attempted to strike one of the matches. My hands were shaking. Again I haltingly tried to light the lamp, striking match after match, as I could hear the intruder scuffling and mumbling to himself in a lumbering voice I found strangely familiar. While he wrestled with the rope, he conveyed the impression that he was not aware of my presence in the room. This was to my advantage, I thought, as I finally lit the lamp, transferring it to my left hand while occupying my right with the pistol. I stood up.

Dazzled by the brightness and huddled forward to spy more clearly, I saw the figure of a man who had finally solved the knotted rope. My foot nudged the overturned coffee carafe in front of me and pushed it aside, clearing the path. By this time, he had made the effort to lower the window sash as much as the thickness of rope would allow, leaving the tail end of the hemp laying inside on the floor carelessly. I made an obvious sound, clearing my throat, to attract his attention. This noise, coupled with the preceding explosion of light, jarred him stiffly upright and turned him slowly toward me. Even though the lamp shed but a single flame of yellow light, compared to the previous blackness, it appeared to flood the room. The man turned around to face me. Leading with his sharp chin, his visage, although awkwardly distorted with something I could not define, became perfectly distinct. I was astounded to discover that it was my old friend and former roommate, Mr. Sherlock Holmes.

2

THE INTRUDER

We are lost, Watson. Lost...hopeless...

—MR. S. HOLMES

There was a stunned silence before I blurted out his name, "Holmes!?" Let me clarify myself. I would not swear to having said that word out loud with the intensity indicated. But if I did not say his name, at that time and in that way, I certainly should have because I knew it was he immediately. Placing his hand between his eye and the light source, he paused for a moment of pondering thought and shouted back in disbelief, "Watson?" I distinctly remember the latter name being uttered audibly.

The reader will, at this point in the narrative, notice that within the previous paragraph the singular 'eye' was employed by the author instead of the assumed plural 'eyes'. There is a good reason for that. Only one eye was available to the illumination. Mr. Sherlock Holmes had over the other eye a patch that I can only imagine afforded my friend some sort of disguise suggestive of a pirate's appearance. This nautical theme was obvious because other seafaring accessories were evident, including a false nose and whiskers. A bogus wart as well as a feeble attempt at a brigand sailor's costume gave an entire picture which added up to what could only be described as comical. It struck me oddly because the detective was known for being distinctively expert in his ability to mask his identity. These various additions to his person were so badly executed that I was confused and consequently torn between laughter and pity. There was also, I noted upon a full vertical scan of the man, an apparent 'pegged leg' that he wrestled with to the point of distraction. He also sported upon his left shoulder a stuffed parrot. How and why he would manage his entrance into this particular room with such an awkward burden was beyond me.

"Hello, is that indeed you, Holmes?" I definitely remember saying out loud, unable to avoid coloring my voice with raw disbelief.

"Arrr and how did ye know it were me, Matey?" he asked, genuinely surprised.

"Well, I think it is quite obvious, is it not?" I rebutted, laughing.

"It is?" he halted, and then continued without an answer. "The parrot, I thought was a subtle yet effective touch, don't you think?"

"It is absurdly out of keeping with anything but a juvenile masquerade party," I ridiculed, thinking that my friend was putting me on.

"The wooden leg and the eye patch?" he inquired, offering an expectant expression, which was oddly shiny due to the greasy makeup that covered his face. He effected the appearance of some sort of circus performer. The makeup looked like a rank amateur had applied it.

"Some sort of prank or childish charade," I shot back in derision.

"Why on earth would you be dressed as a pirate of all things?"

After a deep sigh, he responded blankly, "I do not know or remember...the truth, Watson...the truth."

As he delayed speaking, I could see behind the clownish facade an authentically pained and wounded soul that was exceedingly sad, to the extent of being pathetic. It was at this point that I noticed something in the man that I had seldom, if ever, seen before. He was quite human. It struck me that he seemed to be totally lost and confused in his current circumstance. This was odd. I paused to think of the very nature of the man. I had always placed him and his extraordinary abilities to a large measure above mortal standards and therefore invincible. Now I saw, for the first time, he was vulnerable.

"Do you think...?" he finally trailed off sheepishly, looking at himself with renewed interest.

"Well, I would say that it is not entirely in keeping with the 'disguise' standards you yourself have established and maintained over the course of our association," I regrouped, trying to soften my previous statement. "But it is certainly, distractedly, effective for a pirate, if I may use those words in this instant."

A silence ensued.

"Distractedly...effective?" he aped, finding the positive in my words. "That's not bad, not bad at all. It would certainly, then, throw my nemesis off guard long enough to afford me the time to devise my next move, eh, Watson?"

"Yes, of course," I responded, not knowing what else to say.

I was about to ask him who he believed his nemesis to be when my thoughts and the silence were broken by the distant sound of Big Ben indicating the three o'clock hour had arrived. Time was inevitably plodding along.

"How was Paris, old man?" he asked, randomly triumphant.

"What the deuce are you talking about?"

"I can readily infer by the odor of tobacco in the air that you have recently returned from France! It's as plain as the nose on your face!"

"That is absurd; I have not been to France for years." I could clearly see that his mind was a blur with bewilderment.

He was visibly crestfallen. "Well then, Watson, what does bring you to this particular locale at this time of day or rather night, as it were?" he said, starting to move aimlessly.

"I was about to ask you the same question," was my comeback. It was now a cat-and-mouse game.

"The Moriarty gang is after me! The Devil himself..." he whispered, with wide paranoid eyes. "I must remain incognito." Skulking to the door to listen, he paused.

Satisfied, he continued. "How have you been? I haven't seen you for some time. How is your practice—saving lives on a daily basis, are you?" he quickly asked, abruptly changing the subject while he fumbled in his pocket for something. I took note of the fact that he was apparently moving about the room in order to avoid my piercing gaze.

"I can see, of course, that you have recently performed brain surgery to relieve cranial pressure on a lieutenant of the Guard, eh, Watson. Well done! Successful, no doubt?" he said, as he finally pulled his pipe and tobacco from his leather seaman's pouch.

Nothing about his observation could have been further from the truth. Not only had I not performed any such surgery recently but also I do not remember ever having done so for any lieutenant of the Guard. I asked suspiciously, "Wrong again! What on earth would lead you to draw such a conclusion?"

He was devastated. "Well, I thought...just a hunch," he replied, merely dismissing the question with a slight smirk on his absurd face, "simple deduction, Watson, the old gray matter."

The man was a shell of his former self. His shadow danced nervously on the surface behind him. I thought of *The Adventure of the Dancing Men*. The image was one of a grotesque, exaggerated figure of a man, out of perspective, projected in erratic movement onto the wall separating the outside mist from the interior theatrical scene. He fumbled to pack and light his briar. As the shadowy play continued, he struck a match.

"What sort of a hunch?" I continued my side of the dialogue as I watched him closely.

A quick intake of breath; he stopped short. "Quiet, Man!" he whispered out loud, as he pressed his left forefinger to his lips while cowering in a corner.

"Your behavior is bordering on paranoia."

"It is not paranoia if people are really out to get you, my dear fellow."

He listened to the empty air for a while and then, being content, turned his glassy gaze back to me. Before he could speak, he let out an involuntary yelp as the flame of the match he was holding burnt down to the thumb and first finger of his other hand.

Diverted from his rambling train of thought and trying to minimize his painful mistake, he made the observation: "I believe you may put away your service revolver now, Watson. I am not much of a threat, am I?"

"Oh, yes, of course." Being focused on my friend's odd behavior, I had forgotten my pistol. I replaced it into my right pocket.

There was a pause while I tried to think of where I should go with the conversation. What took me aback regarding this present encounter with Mr. Sherlock Holmes was the disjointed nature of his movements and thoughts. His sunken eyes and heavy limbs rendered him old and tired. Had you asked me beforehand about what I would reminisce with my former roommate, I should have told you it would not be this confusing subject matter at hand.

At once, he blurted out in a vicious manner, "Stupid, Watson. Stupid, fat, Doctor Watson!" He laughed, jeeringly.

Never before having heard such a comment from my friend, I was quite naturally stunned by this random insult. I said nothing, but earnestly cannot deny that great pain coursed through my soul. Direct slanders were extremely out of keeping with his nature.

In the next moment, he dramatically transformed and began to finger, joyfully, an invisible violin. The detective hopped about on his 'wooden' leg, humming a familiar strain and looking around the premises, dully unaware of the absurdity of the picture he presented.

The thought dawned on me that he was basking in the haze of some sort of drug.

"We progress, my dear Watson, we progress!" he said out of the air, jubilantly.

I approached him, as he seemed to be in some sort of reverie. Suddenly, without the smallest inkling of a warning, his mood changed, instantaneously, to a pained and sour expression. "I am lost, Watson...what can it be, what is the answer?" He reached for me. "I want to believe but I can't...It cannot be true...I need more data."

Deliberately moving toward him, I held out my hand, inviting him to give me his arm so that I could investigate any possible evidence of drug use. "I am not sure what you mean..." I queried, trying to continue the thread of conversation.

At first he pulled his arm away but then resigning himself while dropping his unlit pipe, he allowed me to observe the needle marks left by the clumsy hand of a desperate victim; a victim of self-imposed drug usage. As his emotions suddenly shifted, he looked at me longing for help and shaking with fear. Placing his other hand on my shoulder, he reached down to loosen the brace that held the pegged extension. Then bending his knee and putting weight on the foot that had been bound to his thigh, he collapsed into a crumpled pile on the floor.

"We are lost, Watson. Damned and lost...hopeless...It goes against everything I've ever..." he muttered again. I knew, of course from my experience, that this sort of drug use could cause violent and unpredictable mood swings, of which this example was a textbook case.

"It isn't possible, Doctor...none of it," he rambled on, as he curled up into a ball.

I will have permanently fixed on my brain the image of the great detective and my friend helplessly astray, writhing and weeping in a fetal position on the hard, wood floor of 221b Baker Street.

"Rest, merciful heavens...why cannot I have some rest and clarity..." he trailed off.

As he fell, I heard the weighty thud of something that was in his other pocket. Reaching in, I found a small medical box that included a hypodermic and two vials of clear liquid. It took but an instant to open the glass containers. In one I noticed the acrid smell of morphine and in the other that of cocaine, a dangerous combination. Casting them aside, I hurriedly ran to the door and down the stairs only to find a wide-eyed old woman in a nightgown, unable to sleep, clutching her shawl about her shoulders and holding a lamp. After informing her of the identity of the intruder, Mrs. Hudson, shaking her head and complaining that she "knew it would come to no good," busied herself with making coffee and something to eat. She seemed to be relieved, however, at having the mystery explained.

I knew, most certainly, that the drugs alone could not have evoked such a tumultuous response from my companion. There had to be another reason for this exaggerated emotional reaction from the famously competent detective. Mr. Sherlock Holmes, as I have briefly alluded to before, has been known, to indulge in drugs in order to relieve the boredom of inactivity. He sometimes did this for weeks on end. He would lounge around indifferently without eating or moving, with his eyes closed, waiting. Although I am sure he was fully aware of my disapproval of his drug use, he would nonetheless ignore my watchful eye and proceed with his self-assured injections. I would simply put up with his abusive behavior until it passed with the advent of the next new and interesting case. Never had I seen him, however, in this extreme condition. I instinctively knew that something of monumental importance must have transpired to cause such a mental breakdown.

I placed the lamp down on the floor and proceeded to lift my thin companion up onto the sofa where he lay in uneasy repose, mumbling to himself, with his eyes closed. He was speaking in a language that I, honestly, could not understand. Exhausted, he soon fell into a fitful sleep.

Unable to sleep and wanting to occupy myself while he lay there, I was determined to make the premises habitable. Retrieving the rope and closing the window seemed to instantly help the atmosphere of the room. Fetching some kindling and coal from downstairs and reactivating the fireplace worked wonders to brighten the dank, oppressive quarters.

Mrs. Hudson brought up a tray as I settled into the task of completing my watch. Soon, a faint dawn came where Mr. Sherlock Holmes and I were reunited at our familiar former residence under extremely unusual circumstances.

Time, however, was relentlessly moving forward, punctuated only by my friend's deep, even breathing.

In the morning, Mrs. Hudson was eager to have me stay. I sent word to Dr. Bender to cover my appointments for at least a few days, as I was indisposed. He was more than willing to do so, as I have helped him out on many a similar emergency in the past.

That next day of dreary weather outside was marked, inside, by Holmes' sleeping soundly on the settee and me dozing off in the overstuffed wing chair to which I have already alluded. I knew that shortly ahead lay a terrible time of recuperation for my friend. Withdrawing from habitual drug use was never easy. Because of past loyalties and an unwillingness to open my friend up to public exposure, I was determined to accomplish the self-appointed task without external interference. I knew it would not be a pretty sight.

Between naps that day, I carefully removed his disguise, noting that my colleague looked pale and gaunt under the grease paint and false whiskers. He appeared to be dehydrated and malnourished. Sporadically he would awaken, and I would, at that point, take the opportunity to get him to eat or drink something.

Afterwards he would, being greatly fatigued, fall back again into a restless sleep. During that time, he mumbled many things to himself that I did not fathom. I presumed these ramblings to be terribly important to him, due to the impact they had upon his expression. He seemed to be uttering bothersome things in different fragmented languages I could not interpret, although I did recognize some random Latin. I observed him closely.

The following night was one of the longest of my life.

Although, in the past, I had never been able to discourage my friend from the usage of artificial stimulants and opiates, because of his current state, which was now as low as I had ever seen, I was determined to see the whole business through. You may recall previous episodes where, with help from various quarters, I was able to temporarily remove the man from his addictions. But that success was, unfortunately, short-lived. You have, no doubt, heard it said, "Once an addict, always an addict." This may or may not be true, but in view of this particular incident, I allow the reader to draw his own conclusion.

Neither my companion nor I have ever been of a religious bent. Being a doctor and scientist by nature, I have learned to rely exclusively on the material world for guidance as opposed to the intangible or unseen spiritual realm. Because of the nature of my profession, I concern myself only with the body rather than the soul of mankind. Mr. Sherlock Holmes, of course being the quintessential practitioner of the deductive arts, has always leaned on his own powers of reason and logic to accomplish his goals. Although he has never denied the existence of God per se, he has never embraced the notion either, not having much interest in the subject matter. The reader will recall a question raised by my friend during the conclusion of the case I dubbed *The Adventure of the Cardboard Box*:

> *"What is the meaning of it Watson?" said Holmes, solemnly, as he laid down the paper. "What object is served by this circle of misery and violence and fear? It must tend to some end, or else our universe is ruled by chance, which is unthinkable. But what end? There is the great, standing, perennial problem to which human reason is as far from an answer as ever."*

I suppose one would have labeled Holmes an agnostic. Perceiving the suffering, depravity, and chaos of the world and yet at the same time suspecting some just creative force behind it all, one might conjecture that he believed there to be no rational proof for either the existence or non-existence of God. Not willing to ascribe all of existence to chance yet equally reticent to give a benevolent God the honor for all creation, he simply was, heretofore, not interested in religious matters. He concerned himself with the physical, not the metaphysical.

Begging the reader to forgive me for what might be presumed a digression, the issue of God is brought up at this particular point in the narrative for a specific reason. The length of the night referred to above was interminable and riddled with appeals to the Creator from both of us. The need to evoke the assistance of a higher power in helping the great detective rid himself of the insidious hold, which shackled him to these chemical substances, was obvious. Never have I had the occasion to feel so helpless in my effort to aid a fellow human being. For those of you who have never experienced the unspeakable physical and emotional trauma brought on by the withholding of addictive opiates from the victim, words, especially mine, are inadequate. The imaginings of the brain plus the resistance of the body to the lack of the vital substance is overwhelming. Time and time again he pleaded with me for relief from his misery, but I was resolute. More than once during the night did I look heavenward to ask for aid while the man in front of me writhed in physical pain and deluded torment. He, too, in his delirious state called upon the name of God.

"...my bones are on fire...burning...make it stop dear God, make it stop!" he screamed, during spasmodic intervals. "...it can't be...the Devil...investigate, verify the truth...what case is there, old man...the Devil is out to get me..."

At one point he felt as if he were being attacked by a pack of relentless dogs set upon his eternal destruction. Uncontrollable fits of shaking racked his body. I held him tightly, as a father would hold a frightened child awoken by some sort of dreadful nightmare.

"...that hound, Watson, be it from heaven or hell, haunts

me...Let me be!" he agonized, reaching out his hand into space.

Alternately tortured, then at ease for a while, he rambled on a long, nonsensical monologue about some woman of remarkable insight and character asking him a question for which he had no answer. Next, he was off on another tangent, where he was lifted up out of a river by some inexplicable force. This tirade was interrupted by yet another awful mirage of mental distraction in which nondescript insects were ceaselessly swarming him, setting off another fit of writhing convulsions. It seemed to be an endless cycle of actual physical pain followed by imagined invasions of fiends from infernal regions. Being his friend and colleague made it especially unbearable to watch.

"...the truth, God...it can't be possible...why?" he mumbled, time and time again. "Use your head, man...no more water...help me reason...make it be true...please God..."

On and on it went before he finally succumbed to exhaustion.

The following day saw the complete opposite. Holmes showed a surprisingly calm and restful manner. Indulging in regular meals, provided by our landlady, and strong coffee consumed with firmness of spirit, Holmes began to come to his senses. It was difficult. But slowly, over the course of the ensuing week, he began to recover, as did I. When filled with determination, my friend can have the strongest of constitutions.

Day by day, Mr. Sherlock Holmes increasingly returned to his old self. Agreeing with Mrs. Hudson and myself to, at least temporarily, take up residence at 221b Baker Street, he set about a new task with ferocious energy, as if born anew. He was always at his best when beset with activity and interest. I continued to check on him regularly and consistently discovered him to be engrossed in what appeared to be some sort of research project. It was wonderful to see him so occupied. It was reminiscent of so many past occasions when he became totally consumed by the task at hand. He had soon surrounded himself with what appeared to be volumes of serious historical and linguistic significance. His acumen, when it came to absorbing such scholarly material, was remarkable. At this point in his recovery, I thought, the object of his studies was not as important as the very act of studying; he needed some focus upon which to expend his energy.

It was a dank, late winter evening when, upon my arriving at the premises, he heartily invited me to sit down. A roaring fire marked the room, as a clock in his chambers tolled the hour of nine. The days were spinning onward.

"Watson, my dear fellow, have some tea and fill your pipe. I am of a talkative disposition," he said cheerily. I settled down, pleased to see him in such a state of mind.

It has never been my method to pry information from my friend. In former days we would walk for hours at a time without exchanging a word, as two friends on intimate terms are wont to do. I knew he would tell me the cause of his current concern when he was ready to do so.

"It has occurred to me," he said keenly, "that I owe you a great deal." I started to protest, but at that point he stopped me and continued. "No, Watson, you have been, as it were, the catalyst necessary to cause in me a renewed and vigorous reaction. I do not wish to dwell in the past by reminiscing over my successes. Neither do I wish to ponder and regret my involvement with chemical stimulants from which your efforts, Doctor, to save me have been admirable. I am thankful. And not to minimize what you have done, my dear fellow, by putting it behind us, I urgently insist that we look forward. The game is afoot, Watson, and time is of the essence!"

Needless to say, I was intrigued.

"As you are aware, it has been my life's desire to make a name for myself as the world's foremost consulting detective. My efforts in this area, thanks to your compulsion to document a few cases with minor points of interest, have been successful. I have been pleased, up until now, to occupy myself with the stemming of local as well as international criminal activity and to dwell on the satisfaction it has brought. What I am about to tell you involves a decision I have made. This decision at which I have arrived is pursuant to a rather careful deliberation on my part. It is a choice that has cataclysmic implications. I would be remiss, my dear fellow, if I told you that I did not need your help in solving what most would believe to be the greatest mystery of all time. The past, present, and future of mankind could all come to bear on this singular conundrum, the significance of which cannot be overstated."

There I sat, in rigid anticipation, as my companion hesitated. I knew, of course, that he was not wont to exaggeration. He looked at me as if to test the magnitude of his statement and the potential effect it had. Attempting to determine exactly where he should continue, he drew a large breath.

"Where should I begin?"

3

THE MYSTERY OF THE *EYE-OF-GOD*

This is how it would all end: a soggy grave and a
cold quiet passing. —MR. S. HOLMES

ome eight months ago, as one often says it seems like only yes-
terday, upon an unusually clear spring morning, my research was
interrupted by the receipt of a telegram," Holmes said.

"As you know I had taken up residence in the Sussex Downs dis-
trict, where I was enjoying a semi-restful existence while indulging in
various pastimes of no great consequence. I was occupying myself,
that morning, by writing a paper on the value of blood types in
tracking suspects of unsolved crimes. The telegram was from a Miss
Elizabeth Hackberry requesting an audience with me regarding some
sort of a personal mystery that needed solving. She failed to go into
the details of the matter. Not having been engaged in any case for a
time, I eagerly agreed to meet with her."

As he paused, Holmes allowed a look of more than admiration

to pass over his features. He fleetingly glowed like an infatuated schoolboy in a dreamy haze. This was most out of keeping with his character. Quickly then, pulling himself back together, he went on.

"I am not in the habit, as are you, to describe potential clients in terms of fashion or beauty, but in this instance let me state my undeniable observations." Holmes hesitated again before he pressed on. "Upon her entrance into my little home, I noted she was simply and demurely dressed. She had an indefinable sparkling radiance about her that was singular. Never have I met a woman, in her late twenties, who had such a presence of maturity and intelligence coupled with stunning beauty reflected both outward and within. It is difficult to describe this immediate effect upon my perception because of the intuitive nature of the impression. She possessed, at one and the same time, an unmistakable brilliance, as well as a careworn preoccupation that I could only presume was the cause of her desire to avail herself of my consultation."

His faraway look betrayed him. I interjected impishly, "Why, Holmes, I do believe I detect a note of adoration on your visage. I am of the opinion that such a hint of fondness on your part is inconsistent with what I know of your attitude toward the other gender."

"Ah, yes, but, Watson, I cannot deny my impressions. Please permit me some room to muse in my dotage." He shook his head.

Gathering himself, he continued, "I invited her to sit down in a chair by the hearth, but instead she proceeded to pace to the other side of my country parlor, placing herself in the window seat where she was showered by early afternoon sunlight.

"I thought to myself, at the time, that she was the type of person who enjoyed the clear light of truth as opposed to the arms-length dullness of questions that have no genuine answers. As I have often told you, Watson, a little imagination and fancy can be used to promote a wide range of helpful theories when it comes to analyzing people."

My companion often accused me of having very little creativity when it came to my problem-solving ability. He slyly looked at me out of the corner of his eye as he began to relate his conversation with the young lady, which went like this:

"May I open the window?" I inquired of young Miss Hackberry.

"Please do, Mr. Holmes."

"How can I be of service?" was the question I asked, as I lifted the window sash.

"I need your help, Mr. Holmes, in finding my father," she responded resolutely.

"Your father?" I said with disappointment, asking myself how I had become the Missing-Person's Bureau.

"He's been missing for over two weeks."

"I should think that the local constabulary would be the avenue of quickest results for you, then." I responded.

"I have tried that. Because of Mr. Hopkins' inability to locate the whereabouts of my father, due, I suppose, to the rather unusual circumstances and potential international complications surrounding his disappearance, the Official Force suggested my best course of action was to contact you, Mr. Holmes. Apparently you specialize in solving insoluble mysteries, and I am at my wit's end."

"I became intrigued and must admit, Watson, that her ignorance of my reputation was disarming." Holmes interrupted his own narration before he continued.

"What are those circumstances, if I might ask, Miss Hackberry?" was my rejoinder.

"Well, Mr. Holmes, my father was, rather is, a long-time public servant being attached to the Foreign Office, posted to overseas as well as domestic assignments. He was pleased to attain the position of official attaché to more than one Middle Eastern Arab Emirate. In working with these delegations, he was afforded a unique opportunity that was, he felt, in keeping with his public duty as well as his private conviction. A conviction for which he took advantage according to the opportunities which providence provided."

There was a silence at this point. She looked at me as I began to light my pipe. "May I smoke?" I inquired.

"Forgive me, but I would prefer you wouldn't. I am enjoying, so, your beautiful country day and the fresh air it extends," she said politely.

I snuffed out the match as I prompted her, "Please continue."

"My father is, at this time, the primary go-between for the London Office to several of the Palestine Arabic sheikdoms. As I said, I have not heard from him for over a fortnight. When in town, he lives in a small flat south of Battersea Park near Clapham."

"And yourself?" I interjected.

"I live not far from Regent's Park; I reside at a boarding house off Portland Place and maintain a modest but adequate living as a translator. I have an acumen for languages."

"Was he regular in his communications with you?"

"Extremely. When Mother died five years ago, he and I were left alone. I am unmarried. We are family and, as such, very close. His current assignment found him to be in this country most of the time, although occasionally he would make forays into the Middle East as needed for diplomatic purposes. But he would always inform me as to his whereabouts or if he would be gone for any length of time. He was very conscientious about that."

"Has he been heard from by his office?" I asked.

"No, they have also initiated inquiries, both officially and unofficially. But to date they have not received a word." There was a silence.

"Curious," I commented.

"This is the last communication I received from him." She pulled from her handbag a small envelope out of which she produced a slip of paper and proceeded to read the contents:

"Liz, I hope this note finds you well. Something has come up which requires my immediate attention. Please, do not worry. I will be in touch. Pray that God may speed our efforts. Pray with all your heart. With great love, Father."

"May I?" I asked. She handed me the note. I could glean nothing from the correspondence except that the writer was attempting to hide a great agitation. It was posted in Clapham two and a half weeks earlier. The paper was of common British stock.

"You spoke, before, of his private conviction."

"Yes, I did. My father's faith is extremely important to him, as mine is to me. Being both members of the Church of England, we have been inspired by the efforts of world outreach and mission organizations that have been successful in distributing the good news of Christianity to international locations. We do the same.

"The devoted followers of other religions, for example, are certainly free and open to distribute their beliefs to England and have done so for years," she added.

"It has always been our desire, Mr. Holmes, to encourage and indeed aid in the introduction of such material as the Bible to those in other countries, who would benefit from receiving it. Indeed we are implored by our Savior to spread the Word of God into...Judea, Samaria, and the uttermost parts of the earth. This is merely a small step of obedience to our Lord in which we engage."

"And exactly how does your father take that small step?" I inquired.

"My father has made a practice of conveying bundles of Bibles, or portions thereof, into the areas of his assignment for the enlightenment of those who are interested. With the aid of a few local believers, the Books are then distributed, and the Spirit of God is able to move on the hearts and souls of those who received them. My father's purpose has been, simply, to make available and understandable the Christian word of God to people in their native languages. Because of his position with the British government, he has always felt it improper to directly proselytize the locals within his area of responsibility. But he has continued to be comfortable with his engagement in the efforts I have mentioned. May I have some water, Mr. Holmes?"

"Yes, of course." I fetched her some of our invigorating country water.

"Thank you. The water here is quite refreshing." After a brief thought, she voiced, "I suppose this type of effort has been going on since the Crusades and Richard the Lion-Hearted, has it not?"

"You are quite right. Historically, the British have had a keen interest in that part of the world," I confirmed.

She continued, "Let me add this, Mr. Holmes. Although there is nothing precisely illegal in what my father is doing, it is, needless to say, a sensitive area of practice. While the overwhelming majority of people in the Middle East are encouraged by or at the very least indifferent to the availability of such Christian literature, there is a small but vocal minority who consider the presence of such material to be extremely offensive to Islam. I do not know if this is important, but there is even a select faction that is openly belligerent toward my father's practice and has threatened him on more than one occasion.

They call him an infidel."

"Most intriguing. But surely your father, as an official of the British Foreign Office, would have been disposed to curb his engagement in such practices when the stakes wagered had risen to these new heights? A member of the delegation could scarcely be involved in stirring up such hostile religious fervor among the people who are in his area of duty?"

"My father's struggle with such a dilemma caused him to seek the council of the Almighty on a continuous basis. After much prayer and introspection, he was convinced that the benefits derived by his actions outweighed the deficits. He is a very sincere man."

She hesitated and looked at me with clear and penetrating eyes. "Mr. Holmes, you have never found that the practice of a questionable deed which was on the borderline between lawful and criminal, turned out to be in the ultimate best interest of those concerned?"

"I thought to myself, Watson, of the several occasions upon which you and I were free, unlike the Official Force, to illegally jimmy a lock and look behind what were thought to be secured doors in order to solve the mystery. We did this, of course, at some risk and damage to ourselves and to the law, but in order to bring about justice."

Holmes was, of course, correct, and his relating of the conversation continued.

"Yes, I see your point," I admitted to Miss Hackberry.

"Mr. Holmes, I am terribly concerned about the disposition of my father and I have been praying to God that He would send me an Angel of Hope to locate my father's whereabouts." She continued to look at me with a piercing gaze. "I am convinced he is still alive and that you are that angel."

Well, after a moment of thought, I succumbed to the inevitable. Being summoned by the Creator himself and elevated to a heavenly rank, I could hardly refuse.

"I believe we have time to make the four-fifteen to the London Bridge Station if we do not hesitate. I shall, of course, be required to investigate your father's set of rooms, in Clapham, first thing tomorrow morning. We can take the seven o'clock A.M. from Waterloo, upstream. I should also like to step into a telegraph office along the way."

"Mr. Holmes," she said rising, "I do not know how much a person in your business charges for his services, but I do have some little amount saved up against the advent of an unforeseen need."

"Miss Hackberry, never having received a divine calling before, I could hardly be expected to know what to charge, could I? Please, let us work on a contingency basis while allowing the Almighty to figure out the compensation. Agreed?"

"Agreed." She smiled and shook my hand.

"After a very pleasant trip and an overnight stay in the City, we proceeded the following morning to Clapham to do a little on-site investigating. Although I had little or no reason, at first, to suspect that foul play had transpired with Mr. Hackberry, upon conversing at length with my traveling companion, his daughter, my conviction altered. Based on what I learned about the character of the man and his history of uninterrupted communication with his daughter, I grew to the opinion that something untoward had indeed happened to him. My working hypothesis was, for lack of additional data, simple enough. Some, or one, of these Islamic religious sects had made good on threats to harm the attaché. While hoping for the best, I thought to myself that the worst was always possible; would we finally discover that we were too late and the threats of the fanatics had been realized? I hesitated to speculate any further. As I have often warned you, Watson, unfettered conjecture without fundamental tangible evidence can engender as much harm as good in any detective work.

"The apartment of Mr. Hackberry was small but functional. There were numerous items of potential interest, including Palestinian and southern Syrian artifacts and several packets of communications in Arabic, ranging from personal to official in nature. Upon investigation, Miss Hackberry remembered her father telling her of a secret locked cupboard where he kept documents of sensitive content. In her initial consternation over the disappearance of her father, she had forgotten to inform the police of the existence of the hiding place but had since remembered it; she did not, however, know the exact location within the premises. We took a good deal of time probing the walls and floors, as well as the furniture, for possible hiding places. While testing the integrity of the floor near the hearth, I noticed a hollow sound beneath the front edge of the carpet. Upon closer inspection, I found what seemed to be an almost imperceptibly loose floor board that, when forced with a small pry, popped out, revealing a locked metal box below. I recollected seeing a key in the top right drawer of the desk. Upon retrieving it and turning the key in the lock of the box, I was able to open it.

"The contents laid out on the table, revealed some official communications between governments about contested land. There were other documents regarding the sharing of special information that was not for general consumption, but I noticed one handwritten note that was particularly compelling. It was scribed in an ancient Aramaic style, so my companion told me, and had a large wax seal with the image of a single eye emblazoned, which reminded me of something I had just seen. The piece of paper was of a rough type, certainly not English, and had a distinct odor, a pungent smell that was Middle Eastern in origin. She took the note and as she eagerly pored over it, she was able to pick out a few select words. Some of the important words she could decipher were 'Allah,' 'Infidel,' 'Homeland,' 'Revenge,' and 'Nabul.' She told me that most of the writing was stylized to the point of being incomprehensible. It was dated, she said, the day before her father's communication to her.

"Proceeding quickly and hoping we were not too late, I was afraid time was not on our side. As we left the flat, it caught my attention. The same seal that was on the note in wax was fixed in bronze on the centerpiece of a large amulet that was lying on the table by the sofa. That is where I had seen it, an hour earlier. The seal and amulet both had the double crescent swords in a field of stars with a single eye in the middle; quite distinctive. Picking up the amulet, we ran from the room to hail a trap for the train station where we would head back to Waterloo and then Charing Cross posthaste. While awaiting the train, I picked up a *Times* and took note of the ship movements for the last three weeks. I discovered a brace of possibilities.

"Upon arriving at the hotel, I found a response to my telegram. My sources told me (in reality it was my brother Mycroft, who continues to keep his finger on the pulse of English International affairs) of a particularly violent and active Sheik with British business dealings in the Southern Palestine area, who controls a gang of loyalists he calls the 'Eye of God.' Apparently this band is not directly associated with Islam but is more or less a sort of self-proclaimed vigilante group of fanatics; very difficult to control.

"You remember Toby, I believe?" he asked, interrupting his

narrative and looking directly at me for a response.

"Why yes, of course, the greatest canine detective of all time," I chimed in.

"Well, he is dead, Watson."

"Oh, what happened?"

"Old age, my dear fellow, it happens to us all eventually, you know."

I did not have anything to say to that.

"But, I am glad to inform you of the fact that Toby has left among his posterity a son of surpassing skills in the olfactory arts. Toby the Second proves the old axiom that 'the acorn falls not far from the tree.' I know that he is a dog of unequalled abilities," Holmes continued.

"Being uncertain of the potential resistance I might encounter, as well as the unfortunate possibility of tragic and startling news, I asked Miss Hackberry to stay behind and wait for me at her Portland Place boarding house. I persuaded her that her assistance was not needed. This was an admonition I later found out she ignored. Before I left, however, she assured me that she would be praying for me and bade me Godspeed. I remember saying to myself, at the time, that I would certainly appreciate the presence of the Almighty at my side, but if He was otherwise engaged, I would settle for the attendance of my faithful friend, the good Doctor Watson and his enthusiastic, rather more substantial spirit.

Reaching into the pocket of my Ulster, I braced myself with the solid companionship of my pistol. I then picked up Toby the Second and took a hansom to the waterfront area. I arrived at the wharf some time after dusk and welcomed the cover of darkness to hide my movements.

"Alighting from the cab, I started my walk along the wharf with

Toby the Second on a short tether lagging behind. While looking for the ships I had identified earlier as being suspicious, I was surprised to see few people and little activity on the docks. The fog was starting to form on the river, as it is wont to do at that time of night. I allowed Toby the Second to whiff the 'Mr. Hackberry' note and the 'Eye of God' amulet. After that he hesitated, and then, snorting, he proceeded to drag me further down the wharf toward the gloomy darkness. I eagerly followed, trusting his nose.

"After a while, Toby the Second stopped to sniff around as if he were lost. I gave him some leash, and he wandered aimlessly until he hit upon something and started to pull me perpendicular to the dock. We ran into a crude gangplank attached to a moored clipper ship that, after a closer inspection, I noticed bore the name *Nabul*. It was the very boat I recognized from the newspaper as being scheduled to depart back to its Middle Eastern point of origin the following morning. Tying off Toby the Second to a dock cleat, I proceeded up the rickety plank. It was strangely quiet. In the dim light of the ship's passageway, I heard some slight commotion originating from what I thought to be the lower depths of the vessel. I followed the sound down a corridor of stairs, where the noise became louder. I drew my pistol, Watson, not knowing what to expect. At the end of a long dim hall, voices were emanating from behind a closed door. As I got closer, I heard at least two men talking in Arabic. Taking a deep breath and hoping for the element of surprise, I flung open the door to reveal a couple of swarthy men standing in front of a bound, gagged and blindfolded fellow, whom I presumed to be Mr. Hackberry. The brace of men turned toward me and, after seeing my revolver, drew slightly backwards.

"I must be falling down in my dotage, Watson, but no sooner did I begin to feel in control, than the door came flying back my way, no doubt due to the efforts of an unaccounted for third individual behind it, knocking the pistol from my hand and rendering me unarmed. I was immediately beset by three able-bodied men, overpowered, and knocked solidly in the head to the point of unconsciousness."

Mr. Sherlock Holmes paused at this point in his narrative to thoughtfully relight his briar, which had grown cold due to neglect. He continued.

"When I awoke, I discovered myself to be securely bound, both hand and foot, lying face down in a small launch en route to somewhere. My head was throbbing. Turning it from one side to the other, I observed the gentleman I had come to rescue, with his blindfold and gag removed, in a similar attitude and looking somewhat expectantly to me. He seemed to be rather serene and calm, considering our current situation. I also noticed by the facial wounds that he had been abused rather badly at the hands of his captors.

"There was an unspoken moment between us. As a slight smile crossed his face he whispered to me, 'Mr. Rodford Hackberry, at your service.'

"To which I responded, 'Mr. Sherlock Holmes, at yours.'

"The launch stopped. There was some little bit of an argument on board regarding what I could only surmise was a problem with the engine or boiler or something. I heard some scurrying about and more discussion in their native tongue, then a command was given, after which I was immediately rolled over the starboard gunwale, followed by my co-captive, who was tossed over the port side. In the darkness, I could but hear the muffled splash of his entrance into the dank Thames River shortly after mine."

The detective sighed deeply before restarting.

"The skiff drifted on, leaving us to struggle in the water. This is it, I thought. This is how it would all end: a soggy grave and a cold quiet passing. Time seemed to stand still. The liquid filled my ears, closing me in and making me feel distinctly alone. My bonds were well constructed and inescapable, leaving me resigned to my fate. I thought of Toby the Second tied up on the dock and perhaps wondering as to my whereabouts. I thought of you, my friend, Doctor Watson.

"As I went down, writhing in helplessness, I closed my eyes and suddenly saw a vision; yes, Watson, a vision. It was the visage of Miss Hackberry entreating her God on my behalf. The vision was more real than a daydream—and less real than if she were actually present. It seemed substantial and full somehow, not abstracted. Immediately I grew calm; a bright wonderful light flashed before my eyes and lingered. Inexplicably, as if by some sort of mighty hand or power or something, I began to rise up out of the depths of the river. Through no capacity of my own, the ropes binding my feet and hands were suddenly loosed.

"I cannot explain it, my dear fellow, even though I have thought about it a hundred times since. A reasonable, logical interpretation eludes me.

"As you know, Watson, rarely do I describe an event as inexplicable," he went on. "Being predisposed to attribute the things of reason and logic to their proper order, I avoid the inclination to admit as supernatural the cause of such enigma. Let us not forget, Watson, the incident of the great hound of Baskerville Hall. Where everyone else was convinced of the ghostly nature of the beast, I was persuaded of the opposite view. The reasonable answer turned out to be the correct one. I believe the animal was, after all, nothing more than flesh and bones decorated with phosphorus, eh, Watson?" A grin crossed his face as he looked at me out of the side of his eye.

Mr. Sherlock Holmes, not unlike some sort of magician or sleight of hand artist, delighted in allowing others, including myself, to wildly theorize over the bizarre and strange aspects of a peculiar mystery. I remembered commenting, during the telling of the above referenced Hound of the Baskervilles, about this defect my friend had. The defect, to which I refer, is my companion's proclivity to keep those around him in the dark regarding the solution of a brain twister until the last possible instant. This pattern offered him a gleeful satisfaction that he particularly savored. Because of his masterful nature, he enjoyed the sudden gasping reaction that such a revelation recorded upon the countenance of the onlookers; a very disturbing habit.

His expression turned from slyness to wonder.

"But this one, Watson...this one is different." He looked upward. "This one seems miraculous. I can think of no other explanation. There is no other explanation."

Holmes continued his story.

"I located Mr. Hackberry straightaway, brought him to the surface, and without thinking, untied his hands and feet. I still do not know precisely how I did it. But, it is no mean trick in the deep water of the ancient river, Watson, I can assure you. I pulled him to the nearest wharf, where we both struggled to climb up. Upon the platform, I looked over the dark liquid strip that flows through the metropolis and wondered how the Thames felt about being cheated out of two victims by an unknown power.

"The running lamp of the craft, manned by the kidnappers, betrayed the fact that it was adrift. One could see by the dim light of its single yellow lamp that the small crew onboard was scrambling about, attempting to reactivate the motor. I noticed another launch coming hard down the river. Judging by the green gaslight on board, one could discern that it was one of the Official forces, which regularly patrol the waterway. Making no pretense at good manners, the boat, filled with constables, came alongside the drifting craft and boarded her with great fervor. After a brief melee the police prevailed, subduing the rascals."

Mr. Sherlock Holmes' facial expression softened; after a turn and a pause, he restarted his remarkable statement. "Standing on the dock and observing the *deus ex machina*, I felt a strange draw over my right shoulder. I turned to discover the noble and unflappable person of Miss Hackberry moving from the shadows toward her father with outstretched arms. The affection between them was obvious.

"After their reunion, Mr. Rodford Hackberry swung around and administered a hearty thanks to me. I found myself feeling somewhat uninvolved. You will be pleased to learn, Watson, I was uncharacteristically humble. I looked down at my wet shoes and mumbled, 'It was nothing.' And I meant it.

"Miss Hackberry came to me and congratulated yours truly for everything I had done. I then told her, 'I am afraid I did more to undermine the effort than help, Miss Hackberry. I was a bit clumsy; off my game, I suppose.' I confessed, attempting some small bit of bravado."

"I, too, must apologize. I am afraid your admonition to remain behind fell on deaf ears, Mr. Holmes. Following you at a distance, I finally sensed the need for the involvement of the police. I became worried when you were so long on board the clipper."

"You were quite right, of course, to summon the Official Force. I seemed to have been in need of police assistance tonight. I was not quite up to the task," I observed.

"You made yourself accessible, Mr. Holmes." She looked at me squarely, "Besides, it was not your doing, anyway. I am a Christian, Mr. Holmes, and as such I was praying for you constantly. It was God and his son, my Savior, Jesus Christ, and His Holy Spirit that were with you, Mr. Holmes. I am sure of it. How can we repay you for making yourself available?"

Holmes broke off the story.

"I did not know what to say, Watson. Never having been under the aegis of the Trinity, I found myself at a loss."

He continued. "The work is its own reward, Miss Hackberry. But I assure you that there must be some other logical explanation to it all. Something quite unexpected was about here. I cannot believe that God would bother with me and this little mystery," I responded.

She paused. "God was here, Mr. Holmes. If you seek Him with all your being, you will find Him. He cares."

"At that point she reached out and gently took hold of my soggy hands. She drew me closer to her and whispered earnestly to me. 'Well, I thank you, Mr. Sherlock Holmes. And I thank Our Lord.' I could feel her warm sweet breath and sense her sincerity. Then, she turned and walked away, holding the wet, left arm of her father."

Here the story ended.

"A remarkable woman of faith, Watson. I would be telling less than the truth if I were to deny having dreams of her since. Ah, what one would give to be young again.

"I took Toby the Second home, but my thoughts were elsewhere. The scoundrels were eventually convicted and imprisoned or deported, so justice was served. It was not reported in the newspapers, at the insistence of the Foreign Office. All in all, it was an unqualified success, but not because of me, Doctor."

There was a long silence as both of us allowed this singular story to permeate our minds. Never have I heard such a recounting as this that defied reason. My old friend seemed completely baffled.

"I know what you are thinking, my dear fellow," said Holmes, leveling me with his gaze. "There has got to be some logical explanation to this strange and seemingly unfathomable mystery. There are so many questions that need answers. What are the simple deductions? How did I escape? Were the ropes, perhaps, loosed by the impact into the Thames? Was there some sort of low water mark on the river itself that afforded me the luxury of pushing myself to the surface, thus giving me the time I would need to break the bonds? Why did the engine on the launch suddenly stop working? What was that bright light that flashed before my eyes when I was bound in that watery grave? Was it all just one large fluke of nature, a random happenstance?"

He was correct, of course. Those were the very same questions that were racing through my mind.

Holmes continued to unpack his thoughts. "I have dwelled on these things continuously. I have relived the incident a thousand times, and still I have no concrete answers.

"I can assure you that the rope ties were formidable and well executed. The Thames at that sounding is deep and dark. There would be no reason to assume the motor aboard the craft was anything but seaworthy. I did not black out. I remember everything distinctly. No, the only explanation, Watson, the only interpretation I can come up with is divine intervention."

"Divine intervention?" I echoed involuntarily.

"Yes, Miss Hackberry must be right. God, our maker, does exist. He was there. And even though I find it somewhat difficult to believe, I was helped...supernaturally."

There was another silent pause while we both pondered the previous statement and permitted the notion to seep in. If, however, I was honest with myself, I had to admit that those were the very inklings going through my head. I stopped myself and said, "Let me make sure I properly understand you. Are you then claiming as a reality the very existence of God, a Creator? And that he, indeed, is interested in our affairs?"

"I have given much thought to the ideology and doctrines of our age, Watson."

"The detective turns deist?" I scoffed. "I have never known you to be interested in such things. You are a man of reason and deduction not religion."

"I am not keen on religion, old man; I am concerned with logic. That is what makes the rational cognition of a God all the more vital."

"How so?" was my reaction.

"The idea of deity is not illogical." He studied me. "I insist that it is not unreasonable to believe in a Creator–God."

I finally spoke, "What? Knowing you as I do my dear fellow, and I suspect I know you better than almost anyone, I find that last statement of yours very difficult to swallow," I commented directly.

"I must aver that it is valid to assent to a God who created all that we see," Holmes insisted.

I shook my head before I restarted, "Surely we have moved beyond thinking that a Creator started all of this." I looped my left hand through the air. "Our scientists and great thinkers have given us the logical explanations we need to account for what we see and are. After all, old man, we are in the age of reason. This concept of a Creator–God has been all but rendered invalid or at least irrelevant. We have the scientific community's logical explanation for the origins of the species. We now know that life can self-assemble. We do not need God."

Holmes perked up, "On the issue of the evolution of the species as offered by Mr. Darwin, I remain an unprejudiced doubter. There is simply not enough data to assess the conclusions he draws. There are certainly enough mental leapfrogs in the theory that would allow one to be a healthy detractor of his determinations. A concise look at the numbers alone and the odds of such a random happenstance of life as we know it to be, self-assembling would stretch the bounds of reason for even the most liberal scientist. The jury is still out on that one, Doctor, and time and research will tell."

I mulled over this hefty topic as I surveyed him with diffidence.

He looked back at me with half-closed eyelids but said not a word. I halted to collect my thoughts and then proceeded onward, brazenly plying my gray matter. "Well, you would assuredly have to agree that there is enough data to conclude that our eminent thinkers have the principles firmly in place for a man-made social structure that would bring about a virtual Utopian society. Let me add this, dear fellow. We obviously do not live in a perfect world, but our greatest philosophers indicate that man's own ingenuity is the best solution to the troubles and depravity around us."

"Your argument loses me here. How did you get from the topic of evolution theory to Utopian society?" he asked.

"Well, is this not the logical end to the evolutionary spiral? Do not we all desire the eventual end of trouble, crime, illness, and suffering; mankind on his own striving to achieve the best of all possible worlds?" I asked in return.

"I am not so sure, Watson; this is, indeed, weighty subject matter. The notion that you have just described, that there is trouble about and that it needs to be addressed, would contradict the very random meaninglessness that an accidental, purposeless universe would seem to require."

"I don't quite follow you."

"You appeal, as every person does, to some sort of higher good; for instance, the need and desire for a Utopian society. You have a value system that is not chaotic but moral. Why? How did you come by that ability to discriminate and make judgments regarding good and evil? Some would call it a conscience. Logic would seem to assert that design and morality begets design and morality. And, so, conversely chaos and randomness begets chaos and randomness. Why do you demand order and decency if we exist in a disordered and indifferent environment?"

"Well, I am not sure I could say," I tossed my head vaguely.

He went on, "How can I attribute what I see as the grand design of the universe, the laws of mathematics and physics, to the result of random chance and self-fabricated evolution? How do I account for the very nature of the heart of man; the desire for meaning, purpose, truth and significance? What of the need for justice and social structure that permeates the very essence of progressive ideals? Why does mankind strive for betterment? Every culture, inevitably, has some embedded sense of right and wrong. What is the source of that consciousness? How can I embrace all this," Holmes whirled his hand as he underscored his point, "that I see and know to be true, if I am left with the conviction that it is all accidental and arbitrary? Where is the hope, Watson? A Creator–God concept is the most viable explanation for such self-evident realities."

We, again, each thought privately.

I doggedly spoke forth, "I cannot for the life of me imagine how a brilliant logician like you would care to entertain such notions as this. You have always insisted on not filling your head with such extraneous matters if they did not directly bear on the solving of your precious crimes and mysteries. You have insisted on that repeatedly. Why are you presently occupied with such lofty thoughts?"

"Ah, yes, Doctor, but these issues do, decidedly, have a great deal to do with this very mystery I have lately experienced."

My friend absentmindedly fumbled with the poker at the embers in the fireplace before he resumed.

"What have I told you time and time again, Doctor? Systematically remove every impossible explanation to the puzzle until you come to the possible, no matter how improbable it might be, and continue from there.

"Since the advent of this recent adventure, Watson, I have been obsessed by the thought of finding the answers to these many questions. I have also been racked by my inability to materially account for the Eye of God mystery, itself. As you yourself witnessed, it has almost driven me mad. Because of my failure to explain the facts of the case, I sought to find solace in the drugs from which your intervening hand has saved me.

"Now I am left to face the greatest question. I have thought about my past, my present, and its impact upon my future. If I insist that the existence of a Creator–God is the best working theory that explains the universal circumstances around me, does this God actually want to engage in the lives of men? Miss Hackberry is a Christian. Is it possible for her to be correct in her belief? Are Christians, if I understand them correctly, precise in their view that God did come down to earth in the form of a man? Is this God–man, indeed, Jesus? Why did he come? Is Jesus Christ truly the only Son of God, or is he merely one god among many? Is there such a thing as the Holy Spirit? Is the Holy Spirit actually afoot performing earthly tasks? Is he," Holmes said pointing upward, "disposed to a personal relationship with his creatures? Does he actually desire to interact with us, and how so? If there was an historical Jesus and if his claims about life and himself are true, to what purpose do they pertain? Is he now alive or dead? Are there actually higher spiritual planes of unseen reality, which reflect upon the seen world? Is there an after-life? Questions, questions..."

He looked at me, keenly, and supplemented, "Did God, like the watchmaker metaphor explains, create the universe, fling it out into the cosmos, and let it wind down on its own, leaving us to figure things out for ourselves? Or is he constantly or intermittently involved in our daily lives; and if so, to what extent? Why use deduction, logic, impartial investigation, Doctor, if there is nothing to it?"

I quickly pondered the possible impact that such exhaustive brainpower would have on the issues of metaphysics and ontology.

"To glean the truth, I have studied every source I could lay my hands on, current and past, both Holy Writ and secular histories. While poring over ancient languages and mores, as well as contemporary philosophies and theologies both occidental and oriental, I have now focused my energy and gray matter on but one subject, Watson, the truth. I must leave no stone unturned to disprove or verify the truth of Christ: his belief, his religion, and his claims."

"But truth? What is the truth?" I interjected. "It is certainly one thing to uncover the facts in a recent criminal investigation but quite another to probe the ancient realm of the metaphysical."

"Indeed, Watson, I am torn, vacillating between trust and suspicion. After careful consideration, one specific issue lays at the fulcrum of the debate: Is Jesus speaking the truth? And one particular incident is at the center of that discussion. The Christian assertion of a resurrected Christ, can that be true?"

"Why is it so important that that be true? What difference does it make that the resurrection of Jesus really happened? God can exist, God can interfere in the lives of men without Christ rising from the dead, my dear fellow," I asserted taking the opposite side of the argument.

"Ah, Doctor, but here is the nub of it all. If the Biblical accounts are accurate, Jesus stated ahead of time that he would die and rise from the dead three days later. If this bold prediction turned out to be true, then logic would dictate that we must add a great deal of credence to his other statements, several of which have him claiming equality with God Almighty. Permit me to offer an analogy. The structure of the entire house depends on the firmness of the first cornerstone. The existence of a substantial building makes certain the unseen foundation below and, conversely, the entire edifice can be extrapolated from the foundation. The cornerstone is then an essential first step to determining the solidity of the house. In this case the cornerstone is Jesus. Is it possible? In my opinion, everything hangs in the balance. I am an open-minded skeptic, Doctor. Christ's own prediction of his coming back to life after his execution on a cross at the hands of the Roman authorities, did it happen? Were the eyewitness accounts reliable? Were the soldiers guarding the tomb steadfast? Did the followers of Jesus take his body? Are the answers to these questions obscured by two thousand years of myth and translation errors? Is it an *a priori* argument to assert, 'No one can rise from the dead; Christ was someone; therefore, Christ did not rise from the dead'? Is that the long and the short of it, Watson? Was Jesus as mad as a March Hare or as designing as Machiavelli himself, or neither? Was Christ merely one genuinely blessed oracle of God among many, or was he something else?"

There was once again a silence. I found myself uncomfortable regarding the subject of the present conversation. I have always felt that religious matters were best left to those who are religious. I am not.

"You vill remember, uf coorse," Holmes reminded me, as he stood to full height and adopted the compelling character of the eccentric Norwegian explorer Sigerson, a role he played to the hilt some years earlier in order to disguise himself, "as I refer to dee case you called Dee Empty House, ven you explained my two-yeer absence from England."

I pondered the remarkable narrative to which he presently referred and to which I listened on an April evening in the year 1894. As I reflected upon his self-imposed exile for a brace of years from Britain just prior to the case of *The Empty House*, I wondered why he had seldom made allusion to it during those intervening years.

Holmes abandoned his Norwegian dialect to continue. "Believed to be dead, I was free to travel to Tibet and other regions. Being more than a bit discomforted by the acquittal of certain dangerously vindictive members of the Moriarty gang, I was able to take advantage of my reported demise. I was at liberty to visit Lhasha and spend some days with the Grand Lama there. Also, on that sojourn, I had opportunities to pass through Mecca, Persia, and the Khalifa at the Khartoum. Although I found the exposure to alternative religions to be interesting, in the long run, they produced no substantive epiphany. The Eastern art of meditating, by emptying one's head of anything and everything, I discovered to be particularly repugnant to my basic mental constitution. Activity and engagement, my friend, that is what the brain requires. All of those farflung experiences ultimately found no home in my heart or mind, Watson," he hesitated, "...but this Miss Hackberry, *Eye-of-*

God business is different. I now see myself as a man driven, if you will allow, driven to refute or verify the falsehood or truth of Christ."

Holmes confessed, "Forgive me, my dear fellow, if I seem to be rambling, but I am quite at a crossroads. All of these issues must be addressed. Knowing me the way you do, you realize that I will be fully satisfied only by acquiring firsthand, on-site empirical evidence. This must be done in order to construct a cogent conclusion. The Christian claim of Jesus' resurrection from death is of the utmost importance. It is like the very first calculation in a series of many. If you do not get the first one right all the others that follow, no matter how correct they might be individually, will be wrong. There must be a logical explanation. I could conjecture all life-long but there is nothing like a fresh trail, eh, Doctor; the scene of the crime?"

"Well, of course," I reasoned, wondering what he meant by a 'fresh trail', "but what good is an on-sight investigation going to be to you after the passage of almost two thousand years? I doubt very much you will be able to discern the footprints of Jesus now, my dear fellow, even with the use of your ever-present magnifying glass, much less actually find the exact location of the event after all these years. It is absurd to think so."

"No, no, Watson, you misunderstand," he protested. "I am not proposing to investigate the scene now, I am suggesting going back to the actual event in question when it occurred, then and there. This is something I must do if ever I am to have peace about this whole affair."

"You are talking nonsense," I laughed. "What a ridiculous idea."

"And I want you, my faithful friend, to go with me." He looked at me with another roguish grin.

I returned his look with one of my own. In stunned silence, I gawked at him as if he were daft. He was sincere. "How on earth can you go back in time as an eyewitness to an incident that happened half a continent away and nineteen hundred years ago? It is unthinkable!" I said, not realizing I had stood up to make my point.

"Please sit down, old fellow. What I am about to tell you will take some imagination to completely comprehend."

4

THE MIDNIGHT RAID

*"Here we go, Watson!" Holmes moved the right
lever forward.* —DR. J. H. WATSON

As I have said before, my companion has often accused me of having very little imagination. I sat down looking at him as if he were a poached egg.

Holmes continued, "This is not a decision that I have arrived at lightly. But it is, rather, an opportunity of which I must, without hesitation, avail myself." He studied me for a moment. "Do I notice a distinct look of incredulity on your face?"

After a short moment, I shot forth, "'Incredulity' is hardly an adequate word; if a sufficient word exists. The whole idea is beyond preposterous, even approaching insanity! Perhaps a notion more closely associated with one housed in the southeast of London at St. Mary of Bethlehem." He did not flinch but continued his annoying sardonic glare. I strode on, "Bedlam, I suppose you have heard of it?"

"Yes, my dear fellow, I have heard of it. But I assure you that the idea of this little concept, as it were, does not have its origin in the bowels of that institution but rather in the mind of a terribly clever scientist. A fellow, I might add, with a unique notion of time and the potential ability to conceive of things and actualize them with creative fancy."

"What on earth are you talking about?" I inquired.

"Well, suppose that time is not linear or static as we might normally conceive it but rather fluid," he speculated.

"Fluid?" I knitted my brow.

"Yes. Suppose, Watson, that time exists in all its aspects concurrently. In other words, all periods of time happen together at once and yet, in a sense, apart and at differing moments. You see?" I continued to stare at him blankly.

"Perhaps the only thing necessary," he proceeded, "is a device which would transcend the thread of continuous duration and thus enable the possessor of such a contraption to access any moment in time, at will."

"Rubbish!" I responded.

"Is it?" he rejoined. "What if time were like a parade? You and I are in the parade, moving forward. We can see the passing scenery as well as a little ahead and a little behind. That is the only point of view we have. But, supposing there is an entity outside the parade looking down, having equal access to any portion of the passing occasion. Some may call him God. That entity might be able to see the entire parade at once and yet have the ability to interpose itself at any juncture therein. And now, conjecture that an inspired scientist could come up with a machine that went beyond the bounds of a particular rank in formation and could, indeed, jump from place to place within the parade, or, perhaps stand on the fringe, watching the entire event unfold without being a participant. What then?"

I gave the parade analogy some thought. The clock tolled eleven.

My friend continued. "What if time played out like a path before and behind, and one needed only a means of transportation that understood the unique ways of the course, the ruts and the windings, the ups and downs of the twisting highway. Would that not relieve the driver from completely understanding the roadway and enable him to rely on the 'horse' to draw the unique carriage onward or backward, as it were? Leaving the traveler to concentrate on the destination?"

"But...time is...," I thought out loud.

"Is what?" my friend quizzed.

I remained deep in thought. "Time is solid, concrete," I finally said, unable to continue my sentence. After he looked at me, as if to test the effect of the previous statement, he proceeded onward.

"I am not so sure, Doctor, what if it is fluid?"

The detective plowed forward. "A few weeks ago, old man, I was spending time with my brother Mycroft at the Diogenes Club when he was collared by a government official and subsequently engaged in some sort of esoteric dialogue about the current affairs of state, leaving me, quite to my own devices. I happened to overhear a nearby conversation between a chap named Filby and another named Hugart, which revolved around a certain scientist. This Filby fellow referred to the scientist only as the Time Traveler. That, of course, caught my attention. By eavesdropping on their exchange, I gleaned just enough information regarding the nature and possible location of the scientist's laboratory. Filby insisted this Time Traveler had concocted a machine that could actually transport a person, or persons, back and forth through time."

I laughed, involuntarily, as my friend hesitated, looking at me squarely. He seemed to be wholeheartedly sincere, so I asked, "How on earth could a machine possibly do that?"

"Without seeing the thing or testing its mettle, I could not say. Not enough data."

"It is absurd!"

"Maybe yes and maybe no," he responded, and then after a beat, he went on. "This, of course, prodded me to investigate further. I have discerned from my inquiries that the reputation of this scientist, Time Traveler, spans the gamut from reliable to suspect and everything in between, more reliable than not. I also now know the location of his laboratory and his time-traveling device. I have been anxiously preparing for the journey, and to that end I have also been working under the presumption that the subject time machine will do what it purports to do."

"What journey?" I responded with my mouth open.

"Why, the journey of a lifetime," he said. "I intend, Watson, to commandeer this contraption and take it back in time to investigate, firsthand, the greatest mystery known to man and the very same conundrum, I might add, which has almost driven me mad—the death and resurrection of Jesus Christ. And I want you to go with me, Doctor."

I could say nothing.

Holmes went on, "I believe it is possible that this time traveling machine actually exists and is functional. If it does indeed do what it ought, this is an opportunity that cannot be ignored. It is a favorable moment that must be grasped. Do you see, Doctor?"

"I do not," I blurted. "How can you possibly believe such a thing?"

"Why not?" he enjoined.

"Time machine indeed! It is, of course, lunacy. And it is at odds with all the known scientific thinking, surely?"

"We shall discover for ourselves," he muttered, and reached for his pouch.

Could my companion be right? Could such a device actually exist? I shook off the notion as unbelievable. Reasoning to myself in silence, I came to my right mind realizing that he was not in his. Of course, I had heard about this sort of thing from other physicians and psychologists and have on occasion been in the presence of a deluded individual, but rarely one deluded to this extent. I took a moment to muse quietly over the career of the great man and allowed myself to consider how he could have fallen so far. As he took a minute to tend to his briar I plotted my response. In cases of this nature, I thought, it is usually best, at least initially, to humor the victim lest one stir the pot to a violent boil.

"How will you go about obtaining this vehicle, if it exists at all?" I inquired, playing along to see how far he would go.

"I, or rather we, would steal in, tomorrow night to be exact, shanghai the time machine, as it were, and be on our way," he said.

"Will not he, this scientist, notice that the thing is missing?" I wanted to know.

"Well, with any luck at all, my dear fellow, we will have the thing back before we took it, thus allaying any suspicion," he answered confidently.

"What if it is under lock and key? There are laws in this country, you know."

"Oh, I am painfully aware of the laws, Watson, but it is not as if we have never done anything like this in the past. It is quite within the scope of our experience and expertise," he insisted. "Anything, my dear fellow, to solve the mystery!"

His false mental state seemed to have gone beyond the bounds of reason and facts to the point of a self-deceiving lapse of conscience.

Being amazed at my friend's matter-of-fact attitude toward this bizarre concept, I was nonplused to say the least. The fact that my puzzlement led to my trying to speak and having nothing come out of my mouth was not surprising to me.

"Why are you so perplexed Watson? It is quite elementary."

I finally thought of something to say, in keeping with the conversation, while I secretly tried to devise a way to administer some sort of effective mental care on the poor fellow. "What will you say? How will you get around in the land of nineteen hundred years ago?"

"Oh, I have recently made quite a study of ancient Greek, Latin, and Aramaic, along with the written Sanskrit and a smattering of Hebrew. I have also familiarized myself with the history and mores of the cultures, as well as the Holy Scriptures. That coupled with a little improvisation and a few coins of the ancient Roman realm, which I acquired by bartering with a numismatist on Portobello Road near the Westbourne Grove area, should stand us good stead."

He produced, from a nearby valise, a hefty bag of archaic gold and silver pieces he poured out onto his palm.

"What about my practice?" I protested.

"You will not miss a day. In fact, you might be able to service some of your patients even better the second time around, if we come back a bit early," he chuckled.

I failed to see the humor. Unable to come up with any other reason for not accompanying him on his fantasy, I told him that I would be pleased to go.

Because of our friendship and history together, I thought to myself, it would be best that I should be there with him when he was confronted with his folly. If others somehow accidentally became involved, I, in my capacity as a doctor, could protect him, explain his delusional state, and assure them of the necessity of any inconvenience caused by his actions.

"What time tomorrow night?" I asked.

"Midnight. Be on time and do not bring your service revolver. It will not do in the first century."

"As you wish," I said, but because he was as mad as a hatter, I thought of bringing it just the same.

"Oh, and Watson, I am perfectly aware that you think me as mad as a hatter and in desperate need of professional mental care; perhaps you are correct. But, on the other hand, if you are not right and this time contraption actually does the trick, it will be revealing beyond comprehension. I simply must find out the truth about Christ. At any rate, my dear fellow, this is a compact between you and me alone, agreed? Without my consent there can be no communication of this adventure." He looked at me as I nodded.

"I also want it noted that I continue to have very real doubts about any claims of divinity espoused by Jesus of Nazareth or his followers. I remain an open-minded skeptic, Watson. There is, in all likelihood, some logical explanation to the whole affair. But I am resolved to plumb the depths of the matter to the fullest extent possible." He went back to his book. "Tomorrow night, then."

The next day, I could think of nothing but the approaching evening. My scientific curiosity getting the best of me, I was naturally inclined to wonder if time travel was indeed possible. What if it was actually so? It was an intriguing notion, to say the least. I shook my head and eventually convinced myself that my friend was a victim of an as yet unexplained phenomenon and, perhaps, was in possession of an emaciated brain caused by fatique and an overuse of drugs. What I felt he needed was a good long holiday in the country, coupled with peace and quiet, in order to recuperate his faculties. Upon reflection, I convinced myself that the best scenario that could possibly unfold during the course of the evening would be for Mr. Sherlock Holmes to be directly and realistically confronted with the absurdity of his wild speculations and jolted back into the rational world. I could not determine how much fantasy was steeped into this supposed overheard conversation, at the Diogenes Club and his subsequent investigation but it resonated, to my way of thinking, as a smacking big illusion; a self-deceiving false impression, as it were. A time traveling machine, an obscure, unnamed scientist, and divine intervention, what ideas! For the life of me, I could not comprehend how a man with such a reputable sense of logic and reason could have fallen so low. But at this juncture, I was certain that I must play along with him in order to bring him round. If he were to recover, it would be up to me. At any rate, being torn between curiosity and pity, I felt compelled to join him at the appointed hour.

When I arrived at his place at midnight, I found him to be in buoyant spirits, ready to depart and holding a medium-sized satchel filled with goodness knows what. For some reason, he must have felt as if he were going on a long trip. I supposed it was a dramatic prop for the sad theatre going on in his own mind; part of his mad charade, one would surmise.

"What have you got in there, Holmes? I asked.

"Oh, various and sundry potential necessities, my dear fellow; my bag of tricks as it were. One can never be too prepared for a journey of nineteen hundred years, I always say." He smiled and squinted at me.

As we climbed aboard a brougham, he asked, "Watson, have you your pocket watch attached to your fob this evening?"

"Well, yes, of course. Why?"

"I should very much like to learn the effect time traveling has on its workings."

"Myself as well," I said humoring him.

We trotted north through Hoxton and on into the Hackney, an area of London with which I was not familiar. In silence, and out of my peripheral vision, I monitored Holmes for erratic behavior. As he directed the cabby through a series of turns that, frankly, left me behind, he hummed, incessantly, a strain of Chopin with which I was familiar and that I knew him to often play with abandon on a summer's eve. I wondered if he had his violin in his bag of tricks. We finally arrived in a part of the city that was foreign to me.

"Stop here," he told the driver. We got out.

"We will walk the rest of the way," he said, peering through the darkness.

The street was deserted, being, by now just past one o'clock.

"Where are we going?' I murmured.

He said nothing but waved me forward with his right hand. He preceded me as we walked down the right side of the street before crossing left and turning onto a perpendicular roadway with looming brick houses of uniform construction. These structures were barely visible to me in the reflected light of a dull, moonless night. There was only an occasional street lamp to pierce the darkness. I am glad one of us knew where he was going.

At one point, Holmes stopped me by placing his hand on my chest and standing stock-still with his ear attuned to some sound I could not discern. After a slight pause, he grabbed me by the arm and we scurried to the left down a nearby staircase. It led to a basement door of one of the aforementioned brick houses. I could not see any singular features that would differentiate this domicile from one of the others on the same street.

I started to speak, but before I could utter a word, my friend had his hand over my mouth to inhibit such an action. We waited there for a spell before I heard the faint regulated tap of boots slowly approaching on the hard surface of the roadway. The metronomic constancy of a constable walking his beat while pacing out his duty was one familiar to my ear. We stood there like a classic carved stone frieze in the base of an ogee molding, motionless. The policeman continued his route, walking right above our position and then crossing the vacant street away from us only to stop for a time in his tracks. This interval of utter silence while the constable paused seemed interminable but once it was over, it was replaced by the continued tapping of his boots slowly fading away. We breathed again. Up the staircase and once again on the surface of the roadway, we continued our trek.

Holmes stopped me once more in front of a similar brick structure and pulled me downward to the basement entrance like the one previously mentioned. I could hear him extracting his jimmy and deftly solving the lock. Once inside the lower room, we stood awhile to accustom our eyes. He pulled me forward quietly, up an interior staircase, through a door and into what I could only assume was the first floor hallway. We heard a noise from upstairs as if someone was retiring, and then all was silent. Holmes was calm, and I could detect no form of mental agitation in him, something I was looking for. There was a dreary light coming from somewhere that helped us along. My friend stopped in front of a doorway to our left and fumbled for something in his pocket. He opened the door and after a beat I heard the scratch of a strike-on-box safety match that flashed the room to reveal a study of some sort, with books and scientific apparatus. My friend immediately blew out the match and closed the door without a sound. As we continued down the hall, I thought of the cunning craft of stealth and what it meant to a person in this kind of work. We stopped again in front of another door in the same hallway. There is, of course, an art to the building of suspense; an art that my companion enjoyed practicing. Once again he quietly opened the door and struck a match.

This time, the light revealed a laboratory with a vast array of chemical paraphernalia. Holmes immediately blew out the match and pulled me through the door, closing it gently behind. Once inside the large room, he hesitated as if listening for any movement within the house. He struck yet a third match, illuminating the contents of the room. It was indeed a laboratory of some extent and meant for the serious experimenter. The shelves on the walls held various vials of substances marked carefully and organized to a purpose. There were all kinds of logbooks and measuring devices that indicated not only the systematic approach but also the serious nature demonstrated by the inhabitant. I could not determine the area of study for which the laboratory was intended, but it was sophisticated. The side wall had two large windows that were curtained from floor to ceiling. Beyond the chemical equipment toward the back wall was a large round object covered with a tarpaulin. Upon its discovery, my companion was pulled toward it like a corrupt official to a bribe. He lit a small lamp he found on the countertop and then removed the tarp with his other hand.

Once the cover was removed, one could plainly see a glistening spherical metallic framework made up of bars of nickel, brass and ivory, orderly but not symmetrical in design. It was a good five feet tall at its apex. There appeared to be a large saddle inside the center of the device, directly behind two white levers and a control panel. The dashboard boasted an assortment of gauges that, I presumed, would indicate important information. What kind of information I could not fathom. One of the bars had an odd twinkling appearance about it, which was somewhat unreal. The surreal impression of the contraption was a result of its seeming to pulsate between translucence and solidity. It was, after a fashion, more hypnotic in its effect than any merely solid object would have been and gave one the vague notion that the device was more than three-dimensional.

There was also a small empty socket, which looked like a cylindrical magnet, amidships that would seemingly accommodate the insertion of some sort of an implement or structure, perhaps a tool or key. It was a curious item, indeed, and one that certainly warranted perusal.

I have thought repeatedly about the ensuing sequence of events. Time and again, I have considered the chronology of that which immediately followed our discovery of the device. For obvious reasons, the word 'sequence' is confusing. What occurred happened so quickly and at odds with conventional cause and effect that it melds into a single blur which needs to be organized and communicated to the reader. I suppose the word 'sequence' is the rub here. The word implies a chronologically ordered, or at least a systematic, progression of events. Because of the fabric of the stuff involved, that is time itself, my description of the events will tend to be woefully inadequate. At the risk of being scrutinized closely, I will tell of the 'sequence' from my point of view without reserve, as I am now obliged to do.

While we were standing there staring at the contraption, my friend turned his torso sharply toward the door. In the flickering light, I saw him cock his head as if to listen for any ambient noise. After a brief silence, we both heard a low thud from upstairs somewhere that indicated the household was awakened. He reacted posthaste.

"Quickly, Watson, climb aboard," he whispered urgently, as in one motion, he snuffed out the lamp, placed it back on the counter, and ducked his head to crawl through the framework in order to get into the device.

"What?" I asked, not knowing what to do.

"Now, Doctor, we have not a moment to lose!" he shot back, settling in and extending his hand toward me.

I hesitated, but only for a split second. Hearing another low thump coming from a falling foot on the upstairs floorboards caused me to react without thinking. I plunged into the machine, through the framework, with careless abandon, bumping my head slightly on one of the brass bars and causing my hat to fall off outside the contraption. I immediately turned to grope for it.

"Leave it, Watson. It will not do in the first century, anyway, my dear fellow," he said as he dragged me back into the sphere.

There was about enough room in the saddle of the device for one and a half people. The two of us and the satchel were crammed into the thing with barely enough room to breathe.

Holmes did not pause. "Here we go!" he said, as he pushed the first lever to the right.

We sat there waiting, poised in anticipation. Nothing happened. I could barely see in the dim room as he tried the same lever again to the left. Still nothing happened. He attempted the other lever. When that did nothing, he tried them both in combination: nothing. I had a fleeting thought of the absurdity and sadness of the man who sat so closely next to me.

The continuing movement from upstairs stirred my friend into unbridled action. "Out, Watson, quickly!"

We tumbled out of the framework and sprawled onto the floor of the laboratory. Holmes was up without a pause and had another match lit before I could recover my feet.

He was desperately looking around the room, for what I could not say. "Look, man, look! It has got to be here somewhere," he speculated.

"What am I looking for?" I wanted to know.

Before Holmes could answer, we heard the pounding of feet coming closer down the tread of each and every stair. Suddenly he stopped.

"Hello, what is this?" he asked, while lunging toward the workbench and grabbing hold of an eight-inch, roughly cylindrically shaped, crystalline structure. It appeared to be made of silver-white quartz or some such element with glimmering facets and a dull reflective gleam. One end was irregular in configuration while the other appeared to be a milled cylinder.

"This has got to be it!" he exclaimed triumphantly, holding the thing over his head as his match went out.

"Quickly, Watson, back in the machine!" he blasted. Holmes led the way back inside the framework as I followed. The room was dark as we fumbled our way by memory. I could not relocate my hat as I went stumbling over something.

I must admit that, at the time, I was caught up in the stream of action and I did not edit my behavior, but rather acquiesced to the commands of my companion. Although I was incredulous about this whole adventure, to say the least, I blindly followed. I supposed it was the years of experience and working with the great detective, coupled with the fact that he was rarely wrong and almost always knew the right thing to do at the right time. This caused me to automatically obey his orders without hesitation.

By the time I felt my way back into the device, my friend had somehow inserted the milled end of the crystal into the round magnetic receptacle in the middle of the machine. It apparently fit like a glove. At that moment I heard a click of a door latch and turned my head to see the door opening on the other side of the laboratory. Light from a hand-held lamp flooded the space as we saw in the doorway a wide-eyed, bearded man in a sleeping gown poking his night-capped head intently into the room. There was an instant when his eyes and ours met in astonishment.

"Here we go, Watson!" Holmes moved the right lever forward; the crystal emitted a faint glow.

I stumble to describe the sensation. All at once the room began to whirl clockwise with a rush of wind. The one gauge on the dash started to revolve, in the same direction, as the feeling of falling headlong through space overtook me. It was extremely discomfiting. I grabbed hold of the seat to stabilize myself as best I could. The laboratory became cloudy as I noticed the man at the door without hesitation accelerate with superhuman speed around the workbench and reach out his flailing arms and hands. He was upon us in no time. He shouted something that was uttered so quickly that I could not make it out. It sounded like the peep of a chick.

Holmes said something in response and immediately moved the other lever, stopping the progress of the needle on the gauge and the rush of wind in the room. The bearded man's grasping right hand was, by now, barely an inch away from the frame of the device when it came to an abrupt halt. There was an almost imperceptible frozen moment in time that stood totally still. The night-capped man with a wrenched look on his face was grasping the air for all he was worth. I, with what I am sure was a terrified expression and a white-knuckled grasp on the edge of the seat, was unable to move. Holmes was feverishly straining to move the levers to the left and backward. It was a ghostly scene, a tableau worthy of an absurd Jean Watteau rendering.

All at once, things outside the device started to happen in

reverse. With a rush of wind, the room and the needle on the one gauge began to revolve in the opposite direction. Although the misty room seemed to whirl with the wind, I was quite able to observe the goings-on around the laboratory.

The bearded man ran backwards around the workbench at a ridiculously accelerated speed. It was almost comical. Once again, but in reverse. I noticed him stop at the door, as if once again frozen in time, and as before, peer into the room with a shocked expression, with his oil lamp outstretched to illuminate the scene.

"Now, Watson, the satchel!" Holmes shouted in desperation as he manipulated the controls. "Grab it, quickly!"

I looked down on the floor to see the subject carpetbag that had, no doubt, fallen out of the machine when we scrambled to locate the crystal. At once I reached out to drag the bag back inside the contraption as quickly as I could, and without thinking, I also retrieved my hat that was lying right next to the satchel. During the effort, once again, the bearded man started to come forward as before, only to be reversed by my friend's management of the levers on the console.

Straightaway I noticed a tremendous pain in my left ankle. I looked down to discover my foot was outside the whirlwind that had surrounded the car. I had failed to bring myself fully back into the machine after retrieving the satchel. It took every effort I had as I struggled to pull my leg completely into the whirlwind around the parameter of the contraption. I quickly succeeded, only to feel a numb and tingling foot, now inside the machine, being tortured by a thousand needles. It was as if, somehow, there had been a tourniquet around my calf that had just been released.

As before, I felt the odd sensation of falling headlong, out of control through space. While my vision was partially obscured by the cloudy and windy haze, I watched the history of the room unfold in backward order.

I briefly saw my friend and myself staring in wonder at the glistening vehicle before the tarpaulin shrouded our view. It is a singular thing to see oneself in the flesh, I will avow. I had not realized how much weight I had acquired around the mid-section; at least a stone. I was beside myself with wonder. There was a moment of darkness, after which we saw the bearded man, now dressed in a laboratory coat, removing the tarp and accelerating backward through the scene while working his experiments and assembling the machine at an augmenting speed. We saw others, servants and what might be presumed to be acquaintances of the bearded scientist, racing through the room. The rate was nearing the edge of what I thought to be human perception, and yet we went on.

Day became night and night became day as we hurtled through history at an ever-mounting pace. I glanced at my friend to find him resolutely focused on the controls of the craft, eyeing the gauges that moved anti-clockwise at an increasing speed. He was intent upon the journey. One gauge was whirling so fast it was a blur, another not so quickly, the third slower still, while the fourth was barely moving.

My foot was awakening slowly.

After that short distraction, I found myself transfixed by the passing scene. The room was no longer a laboratory but a sitting room of some sort and then a parlor. But there was no opportunity to savor that scene before a new one appeared. Day and night were beginning to blend into one, causing a twilight type of diffused lighting to glow continuously.

Although my head was swimming, I started to get a sense of the seasons coming and going, the rhythm of summer giving way to autumn, to winter, and then spring, repeating itself until that too became a continuous drone. Movement within the room was an indistinct smear. Then the house fell, as if gone by some sort of cataclysmic happenstance. At that point the machine dropped a bit with a thump as if settling onto a slightly lower level. Another nondescript home appeared for an instant, only to fall with another accompanying bump of the machine.

The houses gave way to tilled, arable lands and a rustic village, and then to uninhabited forests. It was now possible to realize the rising and lowering of the sun and moon with regard to the horizon. Years melted away in quick succession. The countryside was beautiful as ancient trees, oak, larch, and elm, shrank rapidly before my eyes, only to give way to denser more unkempt foliage. I saw shooting glimpses of wild animals that used to roam the woodlands in herds before cities in this area were even dreamed of. Without showing any signs of slowing, in the least, time retreated faster and faster into the dark ages and before.

On and on we went, hurtling through time. Our speed into the past apparently multiplied. I noticed the slow dial now moving at a marked pace. I closed my eyes, feeling overcome with vertigo as I began to experience motion sickness, a light head, and an upset stomach. The falling sensation was now becoming too intense to endure. I did not know how much time had passed either inside or outside the machine when I reached the point of resignation, and still the contraption went on as if it might explode into a thousand pieces. The noise all about us was unbearable.

Without warning, the thing came to an abrupt stop.

I sat there for a suspended period with my eyes closed and my ears ringing. It was not quiet; there was a noise like many voices chanting in unison. I could feel myself shaking.

5

A Breach in Time

Do not forget, my dear fellow, we are on the brink of investigating firsthand one of the greatest mysteries of all time. The significance of this venture can scarcely be overstated.

—Mr. S. Holmes

I slowly opened my eyes to be greeted by the vague light of dusk and a variegated glow of yellow-red. Closing them quickly, I asked myself if it was not, rather, the first rays of the sun falling upon a new day. I opened them again after a few beats and recognized the source of the light. It was from some kind of stacked-wood fire that was dispensing smoke and a heat which was markedly intense on the right side of my face.

Craning my neck, I perceived that a clearing with a dense surrounding oak forest was barely visible, silhouetted in the deep violet-orange of evening twilight.

We were not alone.

Both of us sat there, unfocused, in frozen silence. As the ringing in my ears dissipated, the crackle of the bonfire became pronounced.

After an interminable wait I glanced at my friend to observe him with an open mouth, surveying the scene in speechless wonder. He had already moved the levers to the neutral position, causing our vehicle to come to a well-deserved rest.

We were nestled off center in a man-made round glade, bordered by a circle of intermittent large, erect stone monoliths connected on the top by capstones. These rock structures were spaced evenly around the perimeter of the clearing. Immediately under our vehicle, the hard packed ground was scorched in a narrow band. The log fire was in the center of the circle. Additional heat, in the form of what appeared to be steam vapors, was emanating from the framework of the device, which was exceedingly warm to the touch. Directly beyond the bonfire on the right side of us were fifty feet of packed bare dirt and beyond that was a compact thicket of forest undergrowth and stately large trees, the likes of which once blanketed southern England. The edge of the clearing on our left side was a scant few yards away and equally dense.

Also, I might add, I was immediately struck by the proximity of what I would estimate to be about one hundred people surrounding us and staring back in our direction with as much stunned incredulity as we must have displayed ourselves. One poor fellow was within a scant foot and a half of being squashed by the time machine and was fairly petrified with fear. We were being watched from all sides.

Holmes finally broke the silence with a whisper. "We have arrived."

"Yes, it would seem, but where?" Being petrified, I rejoined moving nothing but my lips.

"Not where, Watson, but when."

"I beg your pardon?"

"I strongly suspect we are exactly at the same place on the globe, as we were, my dear fellow, only at a different time than we were, if you get my meaning."

I did not. But after a thought I asked, in disbelief, the obvious question anyhow, "Well, then, when are we?"

"If my calculations are correct we are sometime late summer in the year of our Lord 29 AD. It is approximately six months before the celebration of the Hebrew Feast of Passover in the year 30, the time that the best scholarship would indicate the martyrdom of Jesus Christ will occur. This would seem to allow us ample time to make the journey to the Middle East, to Jerusalem to be exact, to witness the event."

I could not believe my ears. "Calculations! What calculations? This is absurd!" I spouted, trying to keep my voice under control. I was completely stunned.

"If I am not very much mistaken, this dial represents hours and days, this one years, this one tens of years, and this gauge here would indicate hundreds of years," he said, allowing his gestures to complement his comments as he pointed to the control panel in front of us. "Leap years are cleverly accounted for," he stated calmly. "As you are well aware, Watson, the leap year was first incorporated in the Gregorian calendar to compensate for the difference..."

For some strange reason, I found myself unwilling to endure a lecture on the present subject, so I clapped my ears and uttered an angry grunt, thus stopping my friend from going on. He summed up, anyway.

"Suffice it to say that comparing the present indication of the dials relative to where they were in the laboratory when we started, I would say that we have traveled some eighteen hundred seventy-nine years and about five months into the past, if I understand the gauges correctly," he concluded.

I looked at my watch and noticed, according to it, the time that had elapsed.

"But how can that be?" I voiced my observation, "Only eighteen minutes have transpired on my pocket watch."

"Interesting. That is what some might call a paradox, my dear fellow. The question is, are you eighteen minutes older or, indeed, eighteen hundred and seventy-nine years younger?" he added. "And five months."

"I am neither! This is perfectly ridiculous! It is a dream, or a nightmare." I pinched myself firmly on the thigh.

"Ouch!" Then, after a thought and a lowering of my voice to a whisper, in disbelief, I said, "Or, perhaps, some sort of illusion?" I paused. "Maybe we have been mysteriously transported to the dreadful Stonehenge?"

"It is neither, Watson. It is not imaginary, and I would estimate we are at least a good one hundred plus miles to the east and north of Salisbury Plains where the rocks of Stonehenge reside. Hundreds of years from now, this very spot will be occupied by the city of London. This ground upon which we find ourselves will support the foundation of a residence where a clever scientist will invent a time traveling device, the very one within which we sit at this very moment in time. Amazing, is it not?" He paused. "This place, however, at this time, might be similar to the area of those rocks of Stonehenge to which you referred," said Holmes, as he reached through the framework and fanned the air. "It is quite real, I assure you."

A nearby larch tree that stood in stately dark composure appeared to be unconcerned with our recent violent journey. I tried to observe the cloudless evening sky in order to reference some stars, but smoke from the fire obscured my line of sight. I also found it exceedingly difficult to turn my contemplation away from the crowd about us that continued to stare in our direction with rigid anticipation.

Then, following his example, I extended my hand to touch the atmosphere outside the machine and felt the warmth within arm's length. These gestures of ours seemed to enliven the locals. They started to move backwards. Discovering them to be quite material, my mind raced as the reality of our position slowly began to dawn upon me.

As they stirred, I noted that they were dressed in various hooded tunics with different colored sashes about their waists. Some of them wore green or brown knee-length robes and were clean-shaven with long hair. Others wore sky blue full-length cloaks and featured long beards with rather short hair. They appeared to be almost all males of various ages, as far as I could determine, but it was difficult to tell, given the dim light and the costumes worn. There were, distinctively, a small number of women holding what appeared to be bouquets of mistletoe. Most of the men held long walking sticks. A few older fellows in the full-length sky blue tunics had small scepter-like carved sticks that appeared to be both decorative and useful, perhaps as a weapon of some kind.

Because they were initially transfixed by our sudden appearance, I could note the form of their group structure. I assumed that we had apparently and inadvertently caught them in the middle of a ritual of some sort, because they appeared to be ordered and deliberate in their placement. The folks in the sky-blue robes were grouped in the mid-point of a large circle around the fire. To the left of them were the green-hoods and to the right were the brown-hoods. They were in three ranks of participants, with the tallest in the back. The women were scattered at even intervals around the circle holding the mistletoe in front of them. All the focus of attention, before our arrival, appeared to be on the blue-hoods, a few of whom were holding their golden colored short-stick scepters up toward the heavens. They seemed to be caught mid-ritual.

Those closest to us, after getting over the initial shock of our arrival, moved away in trepidation, and those farthest from us moved closer as we became the center of attention. We were indeed fortunate, if you want to call it that, to have arrived precisely when we did. A few moments one way or the other could have proved disastrous if one among the group had been occupying our present resting place.

While advancing on us out of curiosity, a couple of shorter blue-hoods changed their demeanor, for some reason, from inquisitive to hostile. Perhaps because of fear, they were waving their golden batons in an increasingly threatening manner. Holmes noticed this immediately, and standing to his full height, pulled the time machine crystal structure out of its receptacle. He held it up above and through the top of the time-travel vehicle, not unlike they had held their scepters. The facets of the crystal structure glinted most dramatically as they reflected the dancing flames of the great fire. This had the effect of giving pause to the two shorter blue-hoods, as there was an audible, collective gasp of awe and admiration from the entire ensemble.

However, this wide-eyed wonder was short lived. The brace of feisty blue-hoods, quickly collecting themselves and others, reclaimed their advance with renewed vigor. Uttering several verbal growls and hoots to rally the more timid among them, they began to lead a growing mob of selected brown- and green-hoods toward us with rising intensity.

As the surge of hooded worshippers gained momentum, Holmes rapidly inquired, "I do not suppose, my dear fellow, you have, quite predictably against my strictest orders, brought along your service revolver with you?"

"Well, yes, as a matter of fact, I have, but how did you know?" I remembered sheepishly, starting to pull it out of my pocket.

"Elementary, Watson! Hand it here, and posthaste, old fellow!" Holmes shouted over the din.

In my dispatch, I fumbled my Eley's No. 2 onto the floor of our transport and was forced to scramble after it. The noise of the crowd grew in volume and proximity.

"Hurry, man!"

Just before the leading blue-hoods got to the time machine, I handed my companion the pistol. Simultaneously, they raised their bludgeons, about to strike. At that precise moment, Holmes pulled the trigger at extremely close range and deftly shot the baton out of the hand of the nearest blue-hood, shattering it into a hundred splintery pieces. The ensuing explosive effect was instant and complete.

The loud report and effectiveness of the pistol shot echoed through the night air and caused the two blue-hoods to grab their ears and scramble back into the darkness like panicked sardines. The advancing mob instantaneously stopped cold and fell on their faces, prostrate before the two time travelers and their device. The majority of the people, who had held back from the mob, quickly followed suit and bowed down in solemn silence.

All was quiet. Holmes stood there in the machine with the crystal held high for the longest time, as the humble group remained all around in prone array.

At last Holmes spoke and, with an assured comportment, he stated, "Druids."

"Druids? How do you know?"

"Simple deduction, Watson, based on my recent historical research."

"You mean it is true? You are not daft? This contraption actually transports people through time?" I finally asked, with a start.

"Which one of those questions should I field first, my dear fellow?" He chuckled as he began to exit the vehicle.

"Why do you answer questions with another question?" I wanted to know his reasoning, and I was more than a little put out by his cavalier attitude.

"Quite frankly, Watson, I was a bit skeptical myself, but I do know that we are here and now," he stated firmly, pointing to the ground he was standing on. "And it should only take a short time to confirm our suspicions. As to whether I am daft or not, well, time will tell, eh?" he said continuing his smirk.

"You have purposefully deceived me!"

"I reported to you exactly what has transpired, my dear fellow."

"Yes, but who in his right mind would have believed such a ridiculous proposition?"

He looked at me blankly.

"I was merely humoring you because of your unbalanced mental state," I confessed.

He made no verbal comment.

I followed his example by exiting the machine. Once outside, it took me a while to find my feet, still being a bit affected by the trip. My foot was now completely revived. I should have been tired, considering the hour my modern London body thought it was, but in reality the opposite was true. I was quite alert.

Holmes took off his coat and pulled out of the satchel a couple of flowing tunics of rough looking cloth. Putting one on and tossing me another of the same ilk, he bade me to do likewise. We placed our twentieth century clothing into the bag along with the firearm. Because of our new outfits, we immediately appeared to fit into the scene.

He now turned to evaluate the clearing. With outstretched arms, crystal in hand, my companion orated, in Latin, a loud and friendly sounding phrase that caused one worshipful head from the back to pop up and respond. It was one taller blue-hood who had not been a party to the mob and seemed quite pleased to engage in Latin conversation with this stranger from another time. Holmes called to him to join in conversation. As they met halfway, they were required to step over the vigilant worshippers still frozen with fear on the ground.

As my friend and the blue-hood enjoyed a cordial conversation, I noticed on the fringe, in the shadows of a huge stone pillar, a new arrival. He was dressed in a rather ornate white full-length robe with gold trim. He wore a glistening headpiece and carried a golden mistletoe-studded sickle and a gold scepter of impressive richness. Besides the dress, the one striking thing about the white-robed man was his size. He was a giant of a man, head and shoulders above his contemporaries and nearly as massive side to side as one of the stone monoliths. The two, still skittish, shorter blue-hoods who had attempted to lead the mob were wildly informing the white-robe of recent events.

Observing how the two blue-hoods talked to him and how he comported himself, I could surmise that the white-robed man was used to being in authority and having others grovel before him. Being drawn to his sheer size, I could also see, in the light of the fire, his sallow eyes get big as the others were, no doubt, describing what had happened a few moments earlier in the clearing.

At the time, I did not fully realize my first impressions of the white-robed fellow. In retrospect, however, I gained clarity. There was a superior attitude behind those eyes that disquieted me; I detected a lustful intelligence that I had rarely seen before. He could not completely hide an unspoken treachery and a sense of wanton dissatisfaction. He seemed restless and opportunistic. His heavy, cunning gaze reminded me of someone I had seen before, someone I instantly struggled to remember. What did Shakespeare call it, 'a lean and hungry look'? This was but a momentary impression and how true it would later turn out to be I could not, then, imagine.

The dominating white-robed man strode over to the conversation going on between Holmes and the blue-hood. Upon his entering the dialogue, the blue-hood was unceremoniously dismissed and he then humbly bowed as he deferred to the newcomer. The white-robed man smoothly and diplomatically sounded out the time-traveling stranger. Having forgotten most of the Latin I had learnt at University of London in 1872, I was at a loss to understand what they were saying. And although I could not understand most of the words, after a lengthy repartee that built to a crescendo, I felt like I was observing a verbal fencing match; a fencing match that ended in a draw.

Mr. Sherlock Holmes peeled off toward the time travel device while the white-robed man ordered everyone on their feet and turned them all toward the detective. The bizarre competition which then took place almost defies description.

After the white-robed man spoke in his native tongue, he grew silent and then, slapping his mammoth hands together, he began a strange and eerie dance accompanied by rhythmic chanting. At a designated moment, he flicked his left hand over his head and it appeared as if he had magically produced a bright flame burning from the palm of the same hand. Quite impressive! The crowd concurred with appropriate 'oohs' and 'aahs'. Mr. White-robe blew out the fire while taking in the praise as if it were not new to him.

The great detective, in the meantime, took a moment to rummage through his satchel. He spun suddenly, and with a simple flick and a quick churning of both his hands, spontaneously conjured two flames, one atop the middle finger of each hand held high above his head. The crowd reacted with amazement. Mr. Sherlock Holmes, unable to resist an admiring throng, whiffed out the fires and offered a slight bow of gratitude.

Mr. White-robe was fuming. I could observe, now, a golden-colored bag hanging from his sash behind his back. The man once again closed his eyes and brought both hands together in front of his face. With a great deal of histrionics, he slowly worked himself into a trance-like state, complete with the proper sound and motion. At the height of his agony and abandonment, he pled with the stars and dropping down on his knees from exhaustion, he opened his hands to mysteriously reveal a beautiful, small, white, dove-like bird that flapped its wings to gain its balance as he perched it neatly on his right forefinger. Totally spent, he stood up, recovered his sickle, and transferred the bird so that it was high on top of the golden mistletoe staff for all to see. The crowd burst forth with hearty and boisterous approval in which Mr. White-robe beamed for the longest time. I noticed that the two smaller blue-hoods were clacking the crowd to take full advantage of the moment. Mr. White-robe raised one eyebrow and looked at my friend. A most satisfied coo could be heard from the dove.

Holmes reached into his satchel and pulled out the crystal structure and the pistol. Facing the Druid, he backed away from him as far as the clearing would allow. Directing the people to part so that he would have a clear line of fire, he turned an about-face so that his back was to Mr. White-robe and the dove. Placing the revolver barrel on his right shoulder and adjusting his right thumb to pull the trigger, he held the crystal in his left hand so that one of the particularly reflective facets could enable him to clearly see the image of the Druid and bird to his rear. Patiently he aimed the gun, and with the steadiest of hands, he squeezed off a loud round that splintered the night and annihilated the golden mistletoe top on the staff, sending leaves everywhere. The frightened bird took wing and flew off into the black sky, never to be seen again, while Mr. White-robe dropped what was left of his staff to stare in awed wonder at my companion. The throng roared their excitement and marveled at this great magic. Holmes was truly in his element and was savoring every laud to the utmost; this praise lasted even longer than the previous.

Recovered from his stunned amazement, Mr. White-robe was now furious. He gathered up all of his incantations, pronouncements, and spells of every kind. Leaving no gesture untried, he gyrated around the fire several times, hooting and agonizing with rising frenzy. Finally with the greatest of effort, he jumped high in the air and came down throwing something into the fire. There was a loud pop; extraordinary yellow-red flames shot impressively upward to an exuberant cheer of onlookers. They had rarely, if ever, seen a more stunning display of pyrotechnics then they witnessed that night. The greatest round of praise and admiration that night clearly belonged to Mr. White-robe, who reveled in every precious moment. He was at the top of his game; he could do no more.

The pressure was now mounting as all eyes turned to my friend. He had a perplexed look on his face, as expectations were running high. Looking into his bag of tricks, he seemed to be stumped. He rummaged around in the thing a second time before he stood up with a totally defeated look on his face. In his downcast state, he humbly started walking toward the victorious Druid. As Holmes passed by the fire he turned abruptly; looking heavenward and moaning he threw his arms back behind him, over his head and full-circle as he was twirling his hands, then down to the ground, allowing his whole body to follow and gently hit the earth in the prone position in front of the conflagration. These histrionics were breathtaking. All of a sudden there was an enormous boom as wood and fire exploded in all directions, driving the people backward. Then, a huge plume of brown-green flame followed. It shot up and managed to both last twice as long and rise twice as high as the Druid's did. There was an unbelieving, collective silence afterwards as the onlookers once again fell to their knees, out of fear, and worshipped the great detective. When Sherlock Holmes stood up, he turned and was pierced by the glare of the vanquished Mr. White-robe, who reluctantly kneeled down with the others. Would the stale saying 'If looks could kill' be true, indeed, the end of Mr. Sherlock Holmes should have been a certainty that evening. My companion had made a dangerous enemy.

Holmes did not stop there; no, he pulled out of the satchel some box matches and proceeded to ceremoniously light a series of them. And then, while warbling gibberish and gesticulating wildly, he placed the matches on the ground as an outside perimeter around the time machine. I could only presume that he was trying to convince all those within view that he was putting some sort of spell or hex around the vehicle to ward off any curious types.

My suspicions were correct. As an aside, Holmes muttered in a frenzied, ghoulish way, "I am doing this to discourage anyone from going near the thing."

He spoke some pronouncements in Latin that were translated into the vernacular. Apparently it worked, as people immediately shied away from the thing as if it were a poisonous snake.

When, after a few impromptu words by some leaders, my friend expressed a desire for some nourishment, we were royally escorted through a stone archway to a nearby hovel. The unfortunate owner of this convenient domicile was pressed into service to be our host and treated us as if we were gods on a casual visit to view our very own creation. The fatted calf was killed and consumed during a feast at which we, as honored yet mysterious guests, were the center of attention. Throughout the improvised banquet, the white-robed man was consulting in and ordering the affairs of all around. I felt his watchful and piercing gaze upon us as he retained a diplomatically pleasant smile in order to, I thought at the time, allay any concern we might have about our position. He was sizing us up like a cat keeping an eye on a couple of newly arrived fish in a bowl.

Except for the defeated white-robed man and his cronies, our Druidic hosts were most pleasant. The entire party of celebrants seemed to be authentically joyful and in tune with their surroundings. The Druids just readily fell into the nature of things as given. There was actually singing and laughing as each one took a stab at telling the tallest tale or singing the best song. Even though I did not understand their guttural dialect, which sounded to me like a primitive Welsh, I sensed the good-spirited nature of a contented people who blended with their environment.

My companion and the white-robe, not without polite discord, had quite another conversation over dinner. After this simple but eagerly welcomed meal was over, Holmes communicated our fatigue, and we were immediately escorted to the master suite. It was a round lath and mud hut with no ventilation, a thatched roof, and a raised threshold with a wooden door that barred shut from the inside. A hint of smoke bathed the interior as if it were common to have an inside fire; a small ashen fire pit in the middle of the floor confirmed this.

After we settled down a bit, we lit a single taper that was by the fire pit and paused to ponder recent events. I could not sleep. Finally, I voiced, "Druids! Unbelievable!"

"Yes, quite remarkable."

"How on earth does the bloody thing work?"

"I presume you mean the time-traveling machine?"

"Of course I do," I responded.

Calmly, he stated, "It would appear, after seeing it in action, that this device has the capability of creating, upon command, a limited vortex of temporal disruption."

"A what?" I asked and then added, "And please refrain from being pedantic."

"Apparently, the circular whirlwind we observed encompassing the machine during our trip was formed by energizing the crystalline–metallic framework. This would seem to have the effect of separating the inside of the sphere from the ambient time-sensitive exterior, and so making its contents independent of time as we conceive it. A 'shell', so to speak, protecting the inhabitants from the ravages of time; at least what we might call the strictures of time, when it comes to the dictates of the known laws regarding linear progression."

He could see that I still did not understand.

"Imagine a large, substantial bubble, as it were, about the same size as the time machine. Now envision yourself and me traveling in this bubble in an ocean of water, being pulled along by tidal and gravitational forces. It would encase the atmosphere required to temporarily sustain life and be independent of the surrounding environment." Sherlock Holmes allowed his gestures to accompany his words by making a broad circle in the air in front of him for my benefit. "Now, imagine having the ability to motivate this bubble, not unlike a submarine being energized through the liquid, impervious to the current and potentially harmful effects that the water outside the bubble might have on the limited ability of the human body to maneuver in such an environment," he mulled over.

"Yes, I understand the bubble analogy, but how would this time sphere be energized?"

"Not having had the time to fully investigate the orb, I would speculate that there would have to be, on board somewhere, perhaps under the seat, a small-voltage galvanic-electrical battery. This would merely be composed of a series of copper and zinc plates, inundated with water, enabling it to charge and discharge at least enough power to initiate the bubble effect. This crystal structure," my friend said, holding it up, "must, no doubt, act as a conduit or hub, if you will, to disperse a modest electromagnetic field to the framework, thus producing the shell. Quite simply, actually, the direction of motivation could easily be accomplished by creating a vacuum in the time line, either on the front or back side, causing the machine to move into the void, thus thrusting itself forward or backward, depending on the desired destination."

"A vacuum in the time line?"

"Yes, a short-lived, evacuated dimension devoid of the rigors of temporal duration...mathematically conceivable but very abstract and difficult to explain, old fellow," he concluded, making it sound elementary and esoteric at the same time.

As I silently spent several deep moments mulling the pithy topic of time travel, my friend abruptly changed the subject by shifting into a didactic mode. I so dislike it when he feels the compulsion to do that.

"The Druids were, rather are, quite influential in this time period. It will be interesting to learn about them firsthand. What is known of them in the twentieth century is highly speculative and drenched in legend as their influence fades. They were, are, ostensibly worshippers of the creation, the stars, the countryside, the nature of things, and the power of God. Although they are idolatrous, they have not abandoned the concept of a Supreme Being. They hold aloof and do not involve themselves in the petty day-to-day concerns of others. Equivalent to the Eastern Magi, the Druids are often referred to as wise men. Poets, bards, and philosopher–physicians make up the ranks of Druidism. We do know this, however: their religion does not stand the test of time. That is a very telling point, Watson."

My friend paused before he spoke again. "What do you think of the one giant fellow, my competitor with the white-robe?"

"It is quite fitting that you should ask. I entertained a very uneasy impression of him to say the least," I said. "I know quite well that he was not very pleased with his defeat at your hand. I saw hatred in his eyes. And how in the world did you accomplish those amazing magic tricks of yours, anyhow?"

"Yes, it was quite impressive, was it not? A good magician, however, never reveals his secrets, old man," he replied, as he languished over his recent victory.

Holmes continued, "I would hate to think that I have, so soon, created an adversary in this time period. I was hoping to go through this age unencumbered with foes, but I fear that enmity will follow me wherever, or whenever, I go." The detective was interrupted by a polite knock on the door. After a quick exchange of glances between us, he went to the door and opened it.

There, standing at the threshold, were four people including our host, the tall blue-hood translator, and two of the Druid women blushing and shyly clinging to their mistletoe bouquets. After a brief but pleasant, albeit awkward, exchange, my companion closed the door, sporting as bemused a grin on his face as I have ever seen.

"Well?" I inquired.

"In order to make our stay as pleasant as possible, we have just been offered the overnight companionship of two Druidesses," he replied. "Our host has four wives himself, and three hundred head of cattle; apparently, he is a very well-to-do fellow."

"Good heavens!"

"I politely declined, of course. What is of note, however, is that this proposed accommodation was at the behest of Drumb."

"Drumb?"

"Yes, the large white-robed fellow that I magically defeated around the bonfire earlier this evening; the one to whom I alluded just before the interruption at the door. Drumb is quite a remarkable person. He is an Arch Druid, as indicated by his white robe, visiting from the Isle of Man, well educated and very powerful, not just in religious circles, but in this society as a whole. He is also extremely intelligent, dare I say, crafty? Along with his massive shoulders, did you see the size of his frontal lobe? I am afraid I might have told him too much about our purpose here, and in doing so, inadvertently made a mistake by not giving him the credit he deserves. He acted as though he expected some sort of tribute from me but, I can assure you, none is forthcoming." My friend hesitated. "I see, now, his scheme. He is attempting to make our lives quite comfortable here, perhaps to delay us and buy himself more time."

"More time?"

"To formulate a plan. He knows of the crystal, the pistol, and the power they can wield. I told him that we are not gods but that I am a Greek scholar and you are my servant. The time machine is merely an elaborate vehicle that speeds up conventional travel. I am not so sure that he believed me. In fact, he looked rather skeptical."

"What does he believe?"

"Most of the people here are convinced that we are some type of supernatural beings on a holiday of sort. Drumb is not so easily taken in, however. His questions are probing and insightful. Yes, indeed, he is dangerous and influential; worse yet, he is ambitious. This is a combination needful of our highest attention."

My friend held up the crystal and looked at it for the longest time. He then placed it back into the bag. "Let us guard this carefully, with our very lives. We certainly do not want any Druids to come along and hurtle themselves into the twentieth century, do we?"

What a thought...a Druid wandering the streets of London. What would he think?

That night I dreamed that I heard an eerie chant of demonic proportions encircling the hut.

The next morning came dull and early. I felt sick to my stomach and wondered if Drumb had put some sort of curse on us.

When several local people, our host and Drumb included, implored us to stay on for at least a fortnight, we declined. Holmes insisted on staying only a couple of days.

"I want to delve into the Druid belief system to see if there is any substance to it," Holmes said.

He would leave with the Druids early in the morning and return late at night without a word. As he predicted, he allowed himself only two days of this regimen.

The next morning Holmes was up and eager to move on.

"Well?"

"Well, what?"

"What of the Druids?"

"Oh, they are nothing more than simple nature worshippers, very crude. Although they do believe in spirit places, the power of the gods, regeneration after death, and ancestor worship, they consider themselves to be directors of rituals more than mediators between the gods and man.

"Druidism is one of the ancient families of religions, which includes the recreation of Egyptian, Greek, Norse, Roman, and other Pagan belief systems. The Druids focus on the creation instead of the creator; they limit themselves to earthly idols, often trees, the animals, the sun, the moon, and stars."

"What's wrong with that?"

"Let me explain it this way. If a sculptor creates a beautiful statue or depiction, why would you insist on limiting your worship to the piece of art? I would think that you should rather idolize the artistic genius that created it."

"I do not, at all, see any harm in appreciating the world around us and enjoying beautiful pieces of art. I repeat my question, what is wrong with that?"

"Well, Watson, nothing is wrong with it, but it is limiting. You see, everywhere one looks one finds structured beauty, harmonious music, design, system, and organization."

"Go on." I crossed my arms.

"When I observe the meticulous design of mankind and nature and the orderly progression of seasons and the clever systems of procreation that have been put in place to sustain and advance the physical world, astronomy, biology, botany, and geology, I find it necessary to assume an intelligent creative force behind it all."

"Why is that?"

"If I were to happen upon any orderly arrangement, let us take the English alphabet for example, I would discover the system of letters and their combinations and I would be curious about them. Not unlike an anthropologist being naturally curious about cave paintings and the people that made them. I would investigate the use of letters and words in the development of language and the need for communication. I would find out that man contrived the alphabet for a purpose. I would be remiss in my natural predilection if I did not extrapolate from something such as the alphabet, the existence of an intelligent designer as the cause of it. Everywhere I see a design, I can conclude a designer; I have, then, cause and effect. As I ponder this concept further and venture up the scale of increasing complexity, I would advance until I came to the ultimate designer, the final cause; some would call him God."

I inserted quickly, "Yes, but who designed the ultimate designer?"

"When I contemplate an entity that is, in itself, totally independent, all powerful, all knowing, all seeing, everywhere and in every thing, always and forever, self-evidently creative, transcendent of time, and perfect, I have nowhere else to go. I have come to God, by definition, the infinite, irresistible, inescapable cause."

A new thought struck me. "Yes, but what about the other side of the coin, old man, what about disorder and unruliness? You and I have seen for ourselves the sometimes chaotic nature of the criminal mind. We have witnessed man's disregard for the structure of law and the contempt for order. In our adventures, we have occasionally been brutally shaken by the reckless inhumanity that perpetrators enact on their victims without regard for reason and common decency. How could a perfect God create a chaotic criminal creature?"

"That, my friend, is a paradox. What seems on the surface to be senseless, wanton chaos is not of necessity so. You and I have consistently dug deeply below the surface of a criminal's intent to ultimately unearth the reason for his unspeakable actions and found them to be, without fail, selfish, greedy, twisted, and quite intentional. An individual, very often, who possesses a deep-seated, inferiority, must adamantly prove himself to be better than others. A bully, in any culture, needs to constantly prove his superiority to those around him, quite frequently by acquiring their wealth or destroying them. That depravity speaks to the condition of the heart of man, not the nature of God, Doctor."

I brooded for a while. Becoming tired of waiting for me to respond, my companion announced, "The Druids are well meaning but primitive and ignorant. The one exception to that conclusion is Drumb, of course. I suspect very much that the Arch Druid is artful and insidious. We must be off right away."

Holmes would have it no other way. He did, however, allow the Arch Druid and his entourage to accompany us. There were five of us all together. "We can keep an eye on him this way," my friend said slyly.

Holmes pulled out a compass and after reconnoitering, headed in a resolute direction across a field. "Judging by the compass, and confirming the location of the sun and the moss on the trees, this way should be due south, toward the river and Londinium.

"Londinium?"

"Yes, the ancient Latin name for the future great city. If we are when I think we are, my dear fellow, we are in soon-to-be-occupied Britain, a good distance south of Wall of Hadrian which will be built some one hundred years from now in North England," he noted.

"Occupied?" I could, on this particular morning, utter only one-word questions.

"Yes, Watson, by the Roman Empire. Hopefully we will discover that, at this juncture in time, we are ruled by Tiberias, the adopted son of Caesar Augustus. The most important event in the reign of Tiberias is the life and crucifixion of Jesus Christ, whom the procurator of Judea, Pontius Pilate, will put to death at the insistence of the Jewish authorities; a significant event that history will someday note."

"I am not sure I am up for a history lesson this morning."

Ignoring my desire, he went on, "This is, of course, during the same time when the vast Mediterranean seaboard was, or rather is, controlled by an iron-like Roman grip. I keep forgetting when we are; I am mixing my tenses, Watson. Also during this period, the Romans desire to exploit all of Southern Britain for the tin deposits, natural resources, and lumber, which, as you can see, are abundant."

There was nothing left for me to say but to agree with him on that point. We walked through some tall grass and then started to fight our way among wild undergrowth and dense forest. It was not easy going.

"Mark this location carefully, Watson; we shall have to relocate it if we are to return to the future."

Drumb stopped us and with a quizzical look pointed to a crude path that was almost indistinguishable. We went the way he indicated.

"Does he know where we are going?" I asked.

"Yes, as I feared; I was anxious to get information and, regretfully, I told him too much of our plan. He told me, last night, they had never heard of a Jesus Christ in the eastern Roman Empire, or any sort of Messiah figure at all. But he said he was open to the idea of a new religious leader, and he said he wanted to come with us to see for himself."

"Are you sure that is wise?"

"He might be useful in the short term. What do they say, Doctor? 'Keep your friends close, and your enemies even closer.'"

As we went along, Drumb periodically spoke to my companion, who responded.

"He wants to know why we are walking and not taking the elaborate traveling vehicle instead," Holmes said, turning to me.

"A fair question," I affirmed.

"I told him that it makes you sick in the stomach to use it too much and you preferred to walk in the fresh air, anyway."

"Well, there is more than a modicum of truth in that."

Although, because of my scientific propensity, I was extremely excited about the whole concept of time travel, I refused to betray that thought to my friend. I conjured the idea that I was not being treated with the estimation I deserved. I vaguely felt that somehow I had been inadvertently misled. I pouted.

"Do you think the machine is safe there in the clearing during our absence?" I asked.

"Yes. That is Druid holy ground back there, and I think the fear of the gods is enough to keep it untouched," he explained. "How does it feel, Watson, to be a god?"

"I would not know," I retorted.

As the increasing reality of the situation continued to impact me, I spouted, "What about my twentieth-century practice?"

"Did you not tell your associate you would be gone for a while?"

"Of course not. I thought this whole idea was a figment of your imagination, a pipe dream, some sort of delusion!"

"A pipe dream? You have got to have a little more faith in me, my dear fellow," he replied with a smile.

"I have faith in you, I suppose, but not to the extent of traveling through time, for heaven's sake. You will admit it is a concept that is hard to swallow."

"Oh yes, Watson, I will admit it requires an adjustment in one's thinking."

"An adjustment? I do not see how you can take this thing so calmly, Holmes. This is unthinkable."

"We will have you back in your surgery before you know it, old fellow. You will not miss a patient."

I responded, "This entire investigation is absurd."

We walked down the path for a while in silence before Holmes said, "Do not forget, my dear fellow, we are on the brink of investigating firsthand one of the greatest mysteries of all time. The significance of this venture can scarcely be overstated. I must...I am driven to confirm or deny the truth of Christ."

In retrospect, I would concur with his assessment of our situation, but at the time I failed to be of one mind with him.

"It might be difficult to overstate the significance of this operation to you but not to me. I have no interest in religious matters. I am a bit upset that you have dragged me along on this excursion," I whined.

"For another reason, Watson, I am glad you are with me."

"And what reason would that be?"

"You are a witness, of course; you will be able to corroborate my story. You will concur, I am sure, that it is potentially difficult for the average mind to allow for such a pilgrimage. No doubt, you will be my faithful chronicler and ally, eh, Watson?"

I thought, at the time, it was a question that did not require an answer. I did not give him one.

It was getting warm. The reader will recall that we had already removed our twentieth-century garb and donned sandals and tunics.

We made our way down the intermittently shaded path, going in and out of the sparkling sunlight. At one point, Drumb insisted that we were going the wrong way and pointed in the direction of a perpendicular path. The great detective would have none of it and continued along the present course. The Druids reluctantly followed. Mr. Sherlock Holmes winked at me.

My traveling companion presently picked up a stick that lay by the way; breaking off some twigs, he fashioned for himself a sort of crude staff. This allowed the Druids to take the lead again. As he strode forward, he presented a picture of ancient Biblical description, the prophet of something or other on an epic quest of monumental importance.

I noted, after a time, that my tunic was scruffy-looking compared to Holmes'. Finally, I spoke up. "I say, why do you get the finer of the two robes and sandals?"

He did not answer the question but merely smiled his annoying smile.

"What else have you in your bag of tricks?" I pressed. "A silk caftan, perhaps?"

"Let me see." He paused, eyeing me with a critical look. "You look the perfect role of a humble servant accompanying a learned Greek scholar and Roman citizen on an intellectual sojourn of first-century philosophic proportions," he proceeded.

I found his waxing poetic to be distasteful.

"You are, of course, the Greek scholar, then?"

"And you are Watsonicus, the humble servant," he stated, completing my thought for me.

"Watsonicus? I have never heard of such nonsense," I sputtered.

"And please no verbal protestations, for after all, you will soon be deaf and dumb, my dear fellow."

"Deaf and dumb, as well? Why?"

"Unless you speak ancient Greek and Latin, Watsonicus," he reasoned, "when we leave our Druids behind, somewhere in Gaul, you shall have to abandon verbal language altogether."

As I said, I knew a little Latin from medical school but I could see he had me cornered. "Give me one good reason why I should go along with this charade," I spouted.

"If you do not like it, my dear fellow, why not just hail a hansom cab and be back at Baker Street in no time?" he inquired.

Conceding to no alternative, I begrudgingly said, "Well, it is not good, but it is a reason."

"The Druid influence extends into Northern Gaul, or France if you will, and I am convinced that it is in our best interests to rid ourselves of Drumb and his cronies at that point."

We walked along pleasantly enough, being led by Drumb and his cohorts, stopping for a noon meal of hardtack and dried meat. We had been given skins with delightful mead that was quite refreshing.

"By the way, old fellow," my friend remarked after we resumed our trek, "even though I have already effectively used the pistol, against my better judgment, I remember distinctly requesting the leaving behind of your service revolver."

"I thought you were insane, Holmes, or have you forgotten? I believed you to be in the mental state of a lunatic. Why would I listen to anything you had to say? I had no idea that you or that infernal machine of yours was actually in working order. I remain not so sure about you."

"It is imperative, Watsonicus, that we interact with these people of this time period as little as possible. The slightest activity on our part that could influence the smallest incident might have gigantic repercussions hundreds of years from now. It is like a rifle shot that misses its mark by inches at close range, yet finds itself to be off its target by yards at its furthest reach. Do you not understand my dear fellow? We must be careful."

After a moment he whispered a laugh and continued, "Who knows, Watsonicus, that stocky fellow in the blue hood up ahead might be one of your progenitors. It would not do to interfere with his activities, would it now?"

"Rubbish."

Holmes laughed. "Ah! Ah! Ah! Watsonicus, please try to control that tongue of yours, or I shall be forced to sell you to an unfortunate Parthinian noble who could not possibly know what he was in for, my dear fellow. You would, no doubt, be a ready wit employed in some wealthy Sheik's service, right?"

I pulled the hood of the robe over my head, squinted my eyes, and without saying a word, halted and sarcastically bowed deeply. Understanding my part, I took the bag from him and walked compliantly behind, adopting a very servile attitude. If I were going to be given a part to play in this drama, I was going to play it as best I could. I wondered if I should adopt a limp.

There was a cordial discomfort between the Druids and us, which allowed for very little exchange. I could almost see the thoughts spinning inside Drumb's head as he looked at us while whispering out of the side of his mouth to his minions. I maintained a cagey watch on him.

"I am very much afraid, Watsonicus, that we are going to have to get used to the rigors of first-century travel. It is certainly not as if we could hire a dogcart to fetch us forward, now could we, my dear fellow."

I had to agree, not being as young as I used to be. Although I normally took regular constitutionals, this sort continuous exertion was going to take some getting used to.

"How do we know Drumb is leading us in the right direction?"

"We should be right enough if my instincts are correct," my friend answered.

As we strode onward, the pathway opened up a bit, thus allowing for two-way traffic. Every so often, there was a tangential path that appeared to be equally well used and that went off into the surrounding forest. There were few travelers on the main route. We passed by a small horse-drawn wagon, driven by a bleak man, hauling bags of grain and leading two sheep by a leash tied to the back of the cart. Not a word was exchanged.

"I believe that this way will get us to our objective."

"Which is?"

"Some civilization, I hope," my friend said.

That would be pleasant, I thought, resigning myself to enjoying the journey. We kept on putting one foot in front of the other, talking occasionally, and noticing the pristine panorama. Around a particular bend, the roadway opened up to a village with smoke rising from almost every structure. Our party halted to take it all in.

"Do you know where we are?" I asked, practicing my deaf-and-dumb-role with minimal lip movement, while not looking directly at him. I felt something like a ridiculous ventriloquist.

"If I am not very much mistaken, we are on the outskirts of Londinium, or at least the settlement which will someday be the great metropolis. I cannot see the river from here, but I am sure it is not far off."

"The river?"

"The Thames, Watsonicus."

After hearing my first-century moniker, Watsonicus, yet again, I realized that I did not appreciate it nearly as much as he did. I was hoping that by ignoring it, it would go away.

As I looked around the scene, my eyes came to be fixed on a small group of armed guards. Holmes noticed my gaze and turned his head in accordance.

After a pause he said, "Roman soldiers."

6

THE FIRST CENTURY

I fell into a deep and dreamless sleep that night listening to the
most beautiful music I had ever heard: in a most unlikely location.

—DR. J. H. WATSON

Every event that I had experienced since we landed in the first century had brought me closer and closer to admitting, to myself, this truth; that I was indeed when I was. This was the final image that settled the issue of my whereabouts, or 'whenabouts' if I am allowed the latitude of coining a word, the image of those Roman soldiers. If ever there was a brutish-looking band of men, they were it. Although life seemed to go on peacefully around them, their presence dominated the foreground. They were burly, irregular, rough, and not so well appointed as one might think, carrying with them short swords and clubs. Some had throwing spears, while others had bows and arrows.

"Roman soldiers," I whispered quietly, echoing my friend's

statement from the shadow within the hood over my head.

"I wonder, Watsonicus, what fully armed support troops are doing here on the frontier?"

"What do you mean?"

"Upon observation, I do believe these troops to be support legionaries. Most likely they are auxiliaries of a smaller unit, used to bolster the regular army. Or possibly even mercenaries."

"Mercenaries?"

"Yes, willing to fight for the highest bidder. After all, this is the border of the empire at this point in time, so I would imagine heavy infantry troops of the official army would be deployed elsewhere. The historical conquest of Southern Britain does not take place until the reign of Claudius some twenty years from now."

"How do you know that, Holmes?" I asked doubtfully.

"History offers a myriad of fascinating subject matters, my dear fellow."

I have never known Mr. Sherlock Holmes to be a devoted student of history. He often told me about his reluctance to fill his head with such data as would be useless to him in his line of work. However, if he felt that any information might be germane to the specific object of his investigation, I am sure he would have no hesitation to find out all he could about it. His capacity for retaining minutiae was unparalleled.

Drumb vocalized something harsh in the direction of the armed troops.

These professional soldiers took themselves seriously, and one of them pointed directly our way and yelled some unearthly utterance. With sword drawn, he advanced deliberately toward us as the others followed.

Drumb took charge. He haughtily and hastily hatched a plot

against my companion and me.

The Arch Druid's bravado was to his credit. He boldly walked directly up to the soldiers who were coming toward us and spoke in the local dialect. He had, apparently, some authority. The fact that he also slipped them something did not go unnoticed by me.

Holmes must have instinctively suspected the worst because he slyly took both the crystal and revolver out of the bag and gave them to me as he sidled up to my left.

"Tuck these under your tunic and keep them in secret," he whispered under his breath.

I did so. "What for?"

"Not now, Watsonicus, not now," he trailed off.

Abruptly, Drumb turned toward us, pointing at me and then to my cohort while flinging utterances that did not sound complimentary. The mercenaries stopped short, looked among themselves, back at Holmes, and finally at me. Several of them lunged toward us. We could not respond quickly enough, as they were on top of us, and in number, faster than I could say 'Jack Robinson'.

One among the group pointed beyond a few makeshift wagons down the village road. We were forced in that direction through the marketplace, being closely escorted by the troops, walking among the mobile storefronts.

Holmes protested in Latin, which gave the warriors pause to consider. They consulted together yet again, but to no avail; the mercenaries drove us onward. We had no choice. They had us firmly in hand.

"Come, Watsonicus, let us be patient as we poke and pry our way around ancient London."

"What is this all about?" I inquired.

"A case of mistaken identity, perhaps, or worse," Holmes stated, glaring at the Arch Druid.

"I wonder what Drumb is up to?"

"We shall see, Watsonicus, we shall see."

"Should we make a bolt for it?"

"Not yet," he responded.

The street was occupied with the commerce of the day. As we passed by various vendors, we could see one, in particular, with a wooden plank upon which there were a dozen vials of some sort of medicinal looking elixir on display. The proprietor of this roadside establishment was in the grizzly process of pulling several teeth from the mouth of a client who was sitting on a stool to one side of the lane. Between screams of pain and swigs of a dark brown liquid, the patient spat out a profuse amount of blood then opened his jaws for more.

"The chap back there was some sort of street physician, Watsonicus. What do you think of the medicine practiced in the first century, my dear fellow?"

"Barbaric!" I said under my breath.

"I wonder what he would think of the medicine practiced in the twentieth century, eh, Doctor?"

One of the mercenaries uttered an oath and cuffed Holmes on the back of the head as if to quiet him.

This was, indeed, a predicament for concern. We went on in silence.

We wove our way through the paths of what would someday be the great city. Alive with activity and people attempting to eke out a meager living off the land and each other, it all made for an interesting street scene. I observed that haggling over a business deal was common. Very often a raucous exchange between proprietor and customer would break out into fisticuffs. While walking past a butchery, I noted one specific incident. Two men seemed to be fighting over a large bone that was hanging on display at a makeshift storefront. It looked like the leg bone of a large cow. No one stopped the fight, but a group of onlookers merely gawked at the event as if it were entertainment.

Leafy green vegetables for sale were neatly stacked by the way, and when humans were not looking, the cart-drawing animals would help themselves to the produce. If the animals were caught eating some of the inventory, they got a quick rap on the head for their indiscretion.

Children were running about, kicking back and forth some sort of leather-covered ball filled with who knows what. Street vendors were selling everything from nuts to wool. There was an ordered chaos to it all. It smelled of human stench.

The Druids and we were distinctive in our dress. The giant, Drumb, seemed to readily adopt a superior attitude that took people off guard and caused them to be a bit more docile toward him. He consistently commanded respect. With the soldiers and the Druids strong-arming us, Holmes and I were, indeed, strangers in a strange land.

We arrived at the edge of the great river, Thames. A couple of small flat barges were attached by tether to its banks. Beside one of the barges knelt a rough-looking fellow who seemed to be doing some sort of maintenance on his vessel.

We drew near to the fellow, and when he noticed us out of the periphery of his view, he stood up and turned to reveal a haggard, bearded face and a torso with only one arm. His left arm had apparently been amputated directly above the elbow. However, he moved surprisingly nimbly without it. He did not try to hide the scar at the end of the stump.

Drumb stopped us, and our escorts motioned us to wait as he moved forward.

The man and Drumb talked as if they were old friends. After a short exchange, the one-armed chap's eyes got very big as a broad, tooth-stained smile crossed his face to reveal a mouth within the hairy visage. His smile was infectious. With his one hand, he waved us toward him. I was a bit wary, but seeing as how we did not have a choice, Holmes tilted his head in that direction. The man started bowing and scraping, as he invited us to follow him. We followed to the bank of the river, where he herded some of us onto his barge, while the others took a similar raft. Releasing the tether, the man picked up a long oar and pushed us off the shore until we started to drift smoothly downstream. He made it look so easy despite what would seem to be a great disability. Before long, he stopped by a small bank-side earthen hovel to get some supplies. This was obviously the one-armed man's home.

It was late in the day and so it was decided, without any consultation, that we should spend the night there.

I will try to do justice to a description of our accommodations. Outside to the left of the burrowed shanty was a circular pen made from tree limbs and woven thatch. Inside the corral were a few head of sheep and goats, baying at our arrival. Off to the other side was a small patch of tilled soil. Although presently fallow, I am sure, in season, this manicured ground grew the necessary foodstuff for the owner. The area around the domicile was cleared and nicely maintained. The abode itself was built into the bank of the river and augmented with muddy clay packed into a thatch-and-stick framework. Grass and wild berry bushes were growing on the roof of the lair. In the middle of the one-room house, as was common in this time period, was a fire pit with a corresponding hole overhead in the earthen ceiling to allow for the escaping smoke. For that evening's repast we had, in silence, some kind of gamy meat roasted on a spit over the open fire and a pasty mush that could only be described as tasteless. We were wordlessly separated and herded into sleeping positions. Our mixed band of travelers took up the entire floor of the hut. We slept in a crosspatch pattern on the hard packed terra firma, very uncomfortable.

We were rousted up in the morning, and without any breakfast, shuffled onto the aforementioned barges and off again down the river.

It was myself, two soldiers, a couple of blue-hoods, and the one armed man on our raft, while Holmes, Drumb, the rest of the troopers, and crew followed on another vessel.

It was actually a fairly acceptable way to travel if you did not mind a bit of the Thames splashing up on you and oozing through the pitched cracks in the wood every once in a while. The craft we were on was really just a series of rough-cut logs bound together with heavy hemp rope. After a short time I was offered another 'hard cake', a delicacy for which the novelty had already worn off.

For some reason, they had separated my companion and myself. Because of the harsh treatment I was receiving, I was a bit miffed with Mr. Sherlock Holmes for bringing me along on this religious wild-goose chase of his. I had half a mind to take the crystal I had secreted away and transport myself back to the civilization of modern London, leaving my companion behind, if I could but affect an escape on my own and return to the time vehicle. I entertained the notion of doing just that. At the moment, however, that possibility seemed far-fetched.

We wound down a river that was blanketed on both banks by a thick forest and interrupted occasionally, on one side or the other, by small tracts of cultivated land with tiny thatched houses placed near the water. I also noticed a network of animal-drawn barges being relayed back upstream in what seemed to be a clever system to recycle the vessels.

The adroit one-armed man, making the most of the trip, had a few bundles of sheared wool, apparently to take to market, upon the vessel with us passengers. As one may imagine, by reclining on them, it made the trip for us detainees a bit more passable.

We traveled this way for several days, spending the nights tied up hand and foot on shore and falling asleep under the stars, most uncomfortable. Although all of us journeyed together, they made it a point to keep my companion and myself apart from each other as much as possible. I did not yet fully understand the purpose of this trip downstream. It was most disconcerting to realize that the soldiers and Druids kept looking at me like I was somewhere between a leper and a condemned criminal. I could not for the life of me understand the reason.

Talking to myself, I asked my alter ego, Watsonicus, what he thought of my circumstances and then shook my head. Finding myself sleeping on the hard ground with a rock for a pillow made matters worse. I could just envision Sherlock Holmes chuckling at my dreary accommodations. I felt I was too old for this sort of thing.

Our first evening out and those thereafter, we were treated to a concert. The one armed man took out, from under his sleeping mat, a small sack that he opened up to expose a little music pipe. He picked up the pipe and started to play the instrument in the sweetest way imaginable. Using only his one hand he cleverly adjusted his fingering to produce the most lovely, lilting sounds I have ever heard. As the evening turned into night, I curled up on the ground, closing my eyes and listening to the melodious sounds of the pipe. Some of the strains were soft and sweet, while others were sad and sonorous. I fell into a deep and dreamless sleep, listening to the most beautiful music I had ever heard, in a most unlikely location.

The next thing I knew, I was opening my eyes and waking up to a fresh day, then we were off again down the river. I managed to keep the crystal and revolver hidden beneath my voluminous robe by the use of an adequate interior pocket. Thinking this whole affair was absurd, I was constantly on the lookout for an opportunity to escape, but I could discover none.

So far, the weather was surprisingly fair; by contrast, the Arch Druid and his minions were dark and brooding, and the soldiers were intimidating. Our guide was very resourceful when it came to providing for our wants. By a combination of foodstuffs he brought with him, and edible berries and the like he found along the way, he was able enough to satisfy our needs.

I did find myself, though, wistfully contemplating Mrs. Hudson's kidney pie and Yorkshire pudding, something I never dreamt I would be thinking about wistfully. It would not be the last time on this trip I would savor a thought about one of Mrs. Hudson's meals.

Soon thereafter, a heavy fog beset us that lingered for days and caused the voyage to become cold, damp, and depressing. Yet another few days of dreary weather, then the soup broke, suddenly revealing a point of land to our right, a slight crisp breeze in our faces, and the English Channel ahead of us. Our appreciation at being out in the open sunlight was evident in the jubilant squeals of our one-armed guide. On the point of land aforementioned, there was a cheery settlement that appeared to be a coastal fishing village on the Strait of Dover.

After a while, we arrived at a makeshift dock on which several boats were tethered. By the time we actually disembarked, it was dark, but the village had not yet gone to sleep. Drumb seemed to know his way around, because he immediately led the way with great pomp. The troops, unceremoniously collared and pushed us to a large earthen building in the center of the assemblage of houses. Holmes acquiesced. We were not given a very long leash.

We found ourselves inside a cozy home in a quaint little first-century fishing village. It was obvious from their greeting that the Arch Druid and the owner of this domicile were well acquainted.

The abode was a well-lit wood and mud structure with a gentle fire and commodious appointments for these times. Over a simple meal, Holmes, Drumb, and a small committee of official-looking men gathered and conversed in Latin. The exchange became rather heated and reminded me of a legal hearing to determine jurisdiction of some sort. Since it was not in keeping with my servant status to make the master's business my own, I quietly sat and enjoyed the warm pleasant atmosphere of the cottage, while the host's wife puttered around keeping house and the one-armed man softly played his fife.

After about an hour and a half, Holmes rose and signaled me to follow him outside. I did. Once out of doors, he started to stride about the village as if to stretch his legs. He lit his briar. The rather pronounced shape of Holmes' pipe and the smell of his aromatic shag of tobacco caused a minor furor among the inhabitants. One of the mercenary soldiers lagged behind, keeping us watchfully in his sight.

My friend spoke first. "There is much to tell. The one-armed man who brought you downstream is named Gurralt. I caught the wastrel in the middle of our second night out attempting to rummage through my bag. In the faint light of the half moon, I saw him reaching over me and lifting the satchel from my side. I let him think

I was asleep. I could discern that he was especially dismayed with the lack of finding what he was looking for; it was almost as if he knew something was missing from the bag. I snatched it back, of course, before I ran him off. He might seem innocent enough, but I suspect there is a bit of the scoundrel in him, if I am not very much mistaken. Keep an eye on him."

"Do you think Drumb put him up to it?" I speculated.

"I have my suspicions," he answered.

Holmes continued, "Our host for this evening is, I suppose, what you would call the leader of the governing council. The committee Drumb and I were with before consisted of the local mayor, doctor, teacher, priest, and judge. As well as being the most learned men in these parts, at least by present-day standards, they also have the power to administrate. Drumb has claimed that you, my dear fellow, are a stolen slave and that I am nothing more than a charlatan and thief. We are currently under what I suppose you would call house arrest. Even though I have no proof of ownership for you, I have asserted that you belong to me and that I am a Roman citizen and, as such, have a right of hearing before Caesar himself under Roman law."

"House arrest?"

"Well, maybe more accurately, protective custody."

"I am a stolen slave? Look at this predicament we are in; it is intolerable!"

"The council seems to be a fair and judicious enough body, although they felt obligated to outdo me on almost every point of knowledge during our hearing. I believe, when all is said and done, that I have convinced them I am a learned Grecian scholar on a sojourn of extreme importance, exploring various cultures and religions, thus expanding my already vast body of human knowledge."

There was a slight stop as my friend's brow furrowed. "Come to think of it, that is closer to the truth than even I thought it was; except for the part of the Grecian scholar, of course."

"I must tell you that I am not for this venture. I have been privately entertaining the notion of returning to the time device and getting back home as soon as possible," I admitted.

"My dear Watsonicus, this is of the utmost importance. We must press on to finally disprove or prove firsthand once and for all the claims of Jesus of Nazareth. Do you not see the absolute value of this quest?"

"I confess I do not. And you wound me to the quick with your cavalier attitude after all we have been through together. What about me...a stolen slave?"

Holmes relented and appended, "I apologize, my dear fellow, but this is a temporary setback, and it might even turn out for the best. Since I have no proof of ownership document for you, the council has no choice. They believe this dispute to be a petty controversy between Drumb and myself, so not worth an audience before Caesar. And, of course, they are correct, but at my insistence they are willing to authorize us to Rome, if need be, to clear up the matter. They are scribing a sealed letter of transit for the journey. Don't you see, Doctor, this move gets us just that much closer to our objective, Jerusalem."

"I suppose," I rebutted, "but I find myself torn between enthusiasm and apathy for this entire adventure."

"The council will commandeer a dependable local fisherman that will take us to the coast of Gallia," my friend concluded.

"Gallia?"

"...Gaul...France," the Grecian Scholar stated.

"Gaul? Ah, yes, France," I whispered my own echo.

"Yes, France," he emphasized.

"I am reluctant."

"We are going, Watsonicus."

"Watsonicus!" I repeated, "I wish you would stop using that infernal name! What should I call you then, Master...Sherlockodies?"

"Ah, I like it, my dear Watsonicus. Shall we have, then, all the more respect for the learned Greek scholar, Sherlockodies, who has so much knowledge of so many things?"

"Poppycock!" I jibed.

"Let us look around a bit and then turn in for the night," he added. "But before we do, would you please give me the crystal and the revolver, old man?"

I balked. "And why should I?"

"The satchel has already been searched and will no doubt be exempt from such a repeat process," he stated, casually, holding out his hand.

"I will, but under mild protest," I finally said, retrieving the items in question and slyly passing them on so as not to raise any suspicions from the trooper following us. "I want it noted, however, that I do have my reservations regarding this entire course of action and my involvement in it."

"Duly noted," he affirmed.

"And furthermore, Sherlockodies...," I added, stopping myself, "...that is all."

As we returned to our host's hut, we found the breeze blowing in from the Strait of Dover to be cold and dreary.

After some libations accompanied by more sweet music from Gurralt's pipe lulling us to sleep that evening, I had a most bizarre experience. During the night, I received a strange impression that somebody or something was whispering a definite suggestion into my ear at very close range. It was difficult to make sense of it all because of my deep-sleep state. In reality, I numbly staggered to my feet without the least bit of self-consciousness and moved, devoid of my own volition, to collect the time machine crystal from Holmes. Soon thereafter, I woke up with a start to full self-awareness. I found Mr. Sherlock Holmes by my side holding a lit match and staring at me with an unbelievable expression. When I discovered my hand to be holding the time-machine crystal, I clarified the vivid impression. I had been told, by someone or something, to give the crystal to the Arch Druid, Drumb. Apparently I had walked like a somnambulist into the adjoining room, without waking a soul except the detective, to accomplish this task. This impression was most powerful, I concluded, almost supernatural.

"Strange, indeed. I wonder if it was not some kind of hypnotic suggestion or some such thing, perhaps something in the drink. This is most alarming, old fellow; we must redouble our efforts to be more watchful. There are forces at work here that need to be discerned and defeated," Holmes whispered, taking back the crystal. I went back to my mat but did not sleep at all the rest of the night.

In the morning, the council members introduced us to a local fisherman who grudgingly agreed to take us across the Channel. After incidental conversation and goodbyes to Gurralt and the other guides, Holmes freely gave out some silver and gold coins. The reader will recall, of course, the acquisition by Mr. Holmes, before our departure from the twentieth century, of numerous examples of the ancient coinage from a Portobello Road numismatist. From the men's delighted reactions, I supposed these coins to be of considerable value.

We set sail for the continent with the Druids and three brutish mercenary soldiers, Sherlockodies and Watsonicus, a pair of litigants, as it were, under protective custody on their way to court together.

"The pompous council was informative in their lack of knowledge," Holmes told me later. "When I asked them about the situation in the far reaches of the Empire, they knew very little. They told me they had never heard of any Jesus of Nazareth or any rumblings of a messianic religious figurehead emerging in that part of the world. They added that they were not surprised because they seldom get visitors who divulge anything of import and news travels extremely slowly. That makes me wonder about our status in this time period. What if we are here at the wrong time? I hope I was correct in my extrapolation of history."

At this point let me take the time to paint a canvas of what travel is like during this first century. While I do not want to bore the reader, I do want to attempt to complete the picture. Getting about in this time was haphazard at best. Although, up to this juncture, we had moved along consistently, it was not always to be the case. Walking, boating, or hitchhiking, we found ourselves to be at the whim of Mother Nature and whatever means of transportation was available. My friend's pocketbook had spoken fairly well for him as opportunists responded quickly to the coin of the realm, which seemed to be hard to come by. I could only wonder as to how long his cash resources would hold out. He spread the wealth around without much restraint.

"Why do you not attempt to bribe the mercenaries yourself?" I muttered in hushed tones.

"Too late for that. Unfortunately, Drumb has them securely contracted," Holmes said softly. He then whispered, "The Arch Druid is biding his time in order to calculate his next move, as are we."

Sailing across the English Channel was cold and dull. The wind was continuous, and the sea was high. I settled down into the bow of the boat as the fishermen tacked against the breeze, which was blowing westerly. The going was slow and that, coupled with my indifferent attitude, made the travel by sea extremely distasteful. The constant up and down movement rendered me seasick, and I had no recourse but to curl up and close my eyes.

"A sea biscuit, Watsonicus?" offered my friend, smugly, holding a small flat cake out to me. I looked at him as if he were mad. My stomach was in a knot. His smile was most annoying. "Well, perhaps later. By my calculations, we must average between fifteen and seventeen miles each day, be it either by sea or land, if we are to arrive at our appointed location on time. That might prove to be quite a formidable task. I hope not."

Being very nauseated, I responded by pulling my hood over my face.

Five days passed. Holmes and I took turns sleeping and keeping a wary eye out for any potential misbehavior. Drumb was watching us at a distance; I did not like it.

This sort of travel reminded me of my stint in the Fifth Northumberland Fusiliers as assistant surgeon during the second Afghan war. The hardships of the living conditions were more than a bit rough, but we always managed to buck up under the circumstances. I took the liberty of recording the above-mentioned experience in a case I titled: *A Study in Scarlet*—my first collaboration with the great detective. When I was younger, of course, these types of expeditions had been much easier on the body. There is something to be said, I suppose, for the indomitable English spirit, after all. We always did manage things in stride. What is it, "Only mad dogs and Englishmen…" or some such thing? I remembered this phrase as my head was over the port side of the boat.

This crossing of the English Channel grew long and tiresome due to the repetitive tacking back and forth against the prominent wind. During the fifth night at sea, I was on watch when the cloud cover cleared. By the light of a half moon, I noticed in front of us an imposing black sea wall. The sailors were talking among themselves and seemed relieved. They turned to starboard and started to run parallel to the coast, looking for a place to land the fishing boat. As the sky began to lighten, they took to the oars and started a vigorous stroke to shore. I awoke my companion, as I noticed the guards were already awake and keeping a watchful eye on us. Upon nearing the sand, there was a particularly large wave that almost capsized us. Were it not for the deftness of our captain and crew we would have had a wet arrival on the French, or should I say Gaul, coast.

After we were deposited on the beach, my friend paid off the fishermen, despite the protests of Drumb. The crew was well pleased but the Arch Druid apparently felt as if their services should have been rendered freely. As the sailors turned to push off, they were chattering among themselves and seemed joyous at the prospect of a brief sail homeward with the wind at their backs.

Although it felt good to be out of the boat and on dry land, the company oppressed me. We set a goodly pace by foot for days on end, only resting only for short spells in the height of the sun. Along the way, an occasional wagon or travelers of varying description passed us. Very few words were exchanged among sojourners on the road, as their minds were on their destinations and private concerns.

We passed by a large, meandering gray river with a crude fishing village on an island in the middle of the watercourse. Holmes, as we trekked on, sidled up to me, tilted his head in that direction and whispered, "Regard the Ile de la Cite, from which the great city of Paris will develop."

I was amazed, to say the least, at seeing the tiny hamlet that would someday be referred to as the cosmopolitan City of Lights—Paris, France.

We were not allowed to savor the moment as we were pushed onward.

It was past dusk, days later, when we spotted up ahead what one would think to be a welcoming roadside inn. The windows, holes in the mud walls with crude open shutters to be exact, projected an eerie and yet warm glow from within. There was a wooden plaque on the side of the building with some writing I could not decipher.

We entered, Druids first, then the two of us followed with the soldiers behind, to discover what appeared to be a hostel for the overnight traveler. It was a welcome sight. Apparently, we made for an impressive band of hooded travelers with armed bodyguards on an important quest, because we easily negotiated first-rate warm beds with rough wool blankets and a good hot meal. Something other than hardtack was extremely encouraging to my present state of mind and stomach. Holmes paid for it all that night ahead of time before the repast; he did not want to be obligated to Drumb in the least.

Holmes and Drumb had a virulent row after supper over what I could not imagine. In the heat of the mounting argument, the huge Arch Druid's face became bright red. He gave vent to his anger and easily tipped over the large common room table. In his tempestuous rage, he tossed stools about and had to be physically restrained by both the troopers and his own Druid entourage. Holmes stood there calmly, staring down his adversary. This made Drumb even more agitated, but he finally stormed off to bed, extremely upset. He was not a man to be trifled with. He had a short fuse and an erratic temper.

"What was that all about? Is he mad?"

"Believe it or not, the Arch Druid had his eye on the remaining potatoes and he was excessively upset that I took the last of them. Quite a mercurial chap, is he not, unpredictable? I am afraid something must be done," Holmes whispered back.

"Yes, but what?"

My friend did not give an answer but rather put his index finger to his lips and flicked his head in the direction of the guest rooms as I followed.

My companion woke me up in the middle of the night, and surreptitiously, we were off without the Druids or the hired thugs. A guard had been placed at the front door, so the detective and I slipped out a rear passage quietly through the stable of livestock and into the dark forest. Holmes reminded me then, as he had told me earlier, that we were leaving the Druid sphere of influence. The time had come to make it on our own.

"Hopefully, those men-at-arms will regard this trek to Rome as folly and not worth the effort. Perhaps they will reconsider the venture altogether. Let us trust that we can at least make them second-guess the wisdom of their continued endeavor to the court of Caesar. Drumb, of course, will not give up so easily. I am afraid he is both determined and ruthless. I very much suspect, Watsonicus, that we might be wanted men."

Things were getting even more disagreeable, as we were now escapees evading the law. We went on in haste and silence due to the deaf-and-dumb humble servant role I was now playing. In the light of daybreak, our getaway was enhanced by a convenient traveling farmer who just happened to be going our direction. He was hauling bags of what appeared to be seed of some kind. We looked like we could use a lift, so he halted. When he gestured to us to hop aboard his wagon, we gladly settled in among the overstuffed coarse sacks of grain.

Although fearful of how upset Drumb no doubt was at being left behind, I had to admit that it felt good to be out of custody and sans the ominous presence of the Druids and guards constantly about.

After trundling some distance, the farmer stopped at a fork in the road and pointed north-easterly. Holmes nudged me and we disembarked. Before the driver went his way and we went southward on foot, out of gratitude, my companion took out his purse and offered some coins to the fellow. The farmer looked at us, smiled, waved off the money saying something in his dialect and left on his way without remuneration. We continued on ours.

"Well," I said, "there is a decent fellow for you."

"Yes, it seems that we are being looked out for, eh, Doctor?"

"Looked out for?"

"Yes."

"There you go again."

"Where am I going?" my companion asked.

"You are implying that the good fortune we just experienced was somehow providential."

"Am I?"

Holmes produced an intake of breath, about to say something more, but I continued without letting him blather, "Do you not think that people on their own can display a certain degree of morality and goodness without the existence of God?"

"Well..." he began.

I stopped him, "We see kind, natural acts of benevolence and mercy from mankind, occasionally from even some very unscrupulous characters. I must, when all is said and done, strive to see the good in people. You, apparently, do not. Why cannot the desire that folks have for order, justice, and common decency be an outworking of natural evolution? Why must a Creator–God, be the source of all goodness and generosity? To my way of thinking it would undoubtedly make sense that these very traits would be important in order for a civilized society to exist. We have certainly learned to get along with each other to the benefit of all."

"I am not so sure about that."

I stared icily at him, "If I may continue, my dear fellow, it would be not unlike a school of fish that finds benefit and advantage in living in a group. I scratch your back and you scratch mine, for survival. The herd instinct could be a very powerful inclination and brought about like all our other instincts, perhaps even introduced into the species via evolutionary genetic makeup or a learned attribute passed down through generations."

"Well, Watsonicus, I remain an open-minded skeptic on this topic. I would submit to you that, indeed, if you were interested only in mutual back-scratching, there might be a limited benefit to helping your fellow man, but not a long term one."

"How so?"

"If natural selection and survival of the fittest were the final arbiters of life, as Darwin says, then logic would dictate that the strongest, fastest, smartest individuals would survive while the weaker ones would eventually fall to the wayside. Self-preservation then, when push comes to shove, would win out over group-preservation. Fish school only when the individual realizes some selfish advantage in doing so. There might be some symbiotic relationships that would be mutually beneficial for a temporary period of time, but the very prime directive of natural selection is that self-preservation, *survival of the fittest*, is the dominant trait, while something else like group-preservation would be recessive. Not unlike the right-handed trait dominates the left-handed one or brown eyes dominate blue. If, for example, the lone wolf finds advantage in being alone, he will submit himself to such an existence, will he not? He will naturally and predictably balk at rushing in to the aid of a fellow wolf if it spells, for him, certain death."

"Go on." I crinkled my forehead.

"If, then, people who live more isolated lives—say in the country—live longer and have more children, why would cities be growing? It certainly gives us pause for thought. If the murder rate is greater in the city, why would people, over the long haul, gravitate to the metropolis? Self-security and isolation would ultimately win out over brotherhood and exposure, especially when we witness man's inhumanity to man. I can then extrapolate that, perhaps, the hankering for community might be greater than the risks associated with socialization. It is reasonable and possible that being a human being could include the desire for togetherness as an innate attribute that is reflective of a creator who just might greatly desire heartfelt community with his creation. Evolutionary theory, then, does not fully account for the self-evident realities we find in humankind. I think one of the problems with Mr. Darwin's theory is that he studied animals and not people."

I knitted my brow in thought.

"For the sake of argument, allow me to add further, Watsonicus, this question. Why does the passerby dash into the burning building to save the mother and child?"

"Why, then?" I appealed.

"Well, the desire to help a fellow human being might be superficially engendered by the herd instinct to which you referred. Not unlike we are driven by other instincts such as motherhood, procreation, or survival."

"Yes, these traits are very motivating." I insisted.

"Indeed, but I would submit to you the following. There are two

124

particular feelings that might arise within the marrow of the pedestrian as he hears the cries for help emanating from the upper floor of the burning house. There would be the instinctive desire to preserve himself and remain in the street far away from the danger. There would also be the instinctive desire to help someone in desperate need. But this fellow standing there would also realize within his soul, beside the two conflicting impulses, that there would be a third thing happening, that he ought to help both mother and child by rushing to their rescue. This is something that he should do. There is a moral law embedded in the heart of man that arbitrates between and is different from the two driving forces of herd instinct and self preservation. That is the inkling that should be encouraged in all of us. That is the cue that very often drives us, you and me, my dear fellow. At some risk to ourselves, we strive to solve a crime, rescue the victim, and see that justice is done. That moral fiber elevates us from the wolf-pack mentality. That conscience, if you will, is our guide."

The great detective then forged ahead, "I also see the possibility, Doctor, of a selfish man being driven to give a cup of water to a thirsty man out of guilt, pride, or duty, not out of altruism. Can a person do the right thing for the wrong reason? Yes, the calculating dictator who allows his poor subjects to keep just enough of their food to prevent them from rebelling is a case in point; the slave owner who is magnanimous to his bondservants in order to keep them productive and from turning on him in hatred is another. Can someone do the wrong thing for the right reason? Yes, as the Crusades and the Inquisition are bound to illustrate."

"Ah," I suddenly declared, "you bring up a telling point about the consequences of religious institutions and their effect on history and humankind."

"Amplify, dear fellow," Holmes encouraged.

"Well, the Crusades and the Inquisition were indeed horrible! The philosophy of the theists has given us nothing but wars and strife for centuries. Religion has been used to promote violence and destruction throughout history, do you not agree?"

The Greek scholar considered, "A deeper look into the matter would seem to indicate that self-serving, deluded men, in the name of Religion, have used and abused the institution of the Church to the shame and betrayal of the very ideals that are held in reverence by it. Let me say, Watsonicus, that much more good than evil has been done in the name and spirit of the Church. In Britain and America, for example, who started the vast majority of colleges and universities? Who has founded all of the hospitals and orphanages? The Church established religions and their adherents, that is who, my dear fellow."

Knowing this to be true, I turned reflective and silent as we slogged on by foot.

There was another incident of note during our southward trek. If the reader will permit a sidetrack at this time, I will relate the occurrence. Brigands beset Holmes and me.

I suppose it was due to the fact that we traveled rapidly and without words that we had grown dull in our disposition. We were caught off guard. It was on a meandering roadway through a dreary forest, dusted with a light layer of frost from the previous night, that the highwaymen decided to strike.

We were walking along, myself slightly behind, heads down and buried inside the hoods of our tunics, pensive, when we heard a shout at close range. Looking up, we noticed that we were already surrounded by at least a half-dozen cutthroats that seemingly appeared from nowhere. As they wielded their imposing swords, they shouted out to us in a strange tongue. My companion and I looked at them and then at each other in stunned silence. There was a short hesitation.

All of a sudden Holmes started to gesticulate wildly and to voice his desire, in a shrill weird tone, for me to do his bidding. "Do precisely what I say, Watson. Place the bag down slowly, and carefully extract the pistol." He continued his histrionics.

I started to do this, but before I could accomplish the task, the men were upon us like a pack of wolves with weapons at our throats. We were helpless.

With both of us powerless, one of the presumed leaders of the thieves got down on her knees and began to empty the satchel one item at a time. It took me a moment to determine her gender but after a bit of observation it was obvious. She was a slight yet wiry maid, of indistinguishable age, with bad teeth. That seemed to be a common feature of almost all people of this era. She had brunette hair twisted and pulled back to expose her dark eyes and the dirty rough features of her face. If she were tough enough to keep the company of this gang of cutthroats she was, indeed, a formidable woman.

When she came upon an item that held her interest for some reason, she would look at it for a while and then, when the item lost its allure, cast it onto the ground; a pair of shoes, a magnifying glass, a pipe and matches, my trousers, etc. Holmes and I stopped breathing when the brigand came to the revolver. She picked it up and held it high to give it the once over; she smelled it, tasted it, bit it, and then started to fondle it. She then grabbed it by the barrel and made a gesture as if using it like a club. She snorted a deep throaty laugh, which brought a contagious chuckle to her cronies. Then she tossed it onto the ground to her left.

We breathed again as she stuck her head back into the satchel; all elbows and hands, she was. After struggling for a while, in one swooping move, she raised her torso to display her discovery. She had found the time machine crystal and the bag of coins. She stood up in triumph with one item in each hand as if the crown jewels were in her possession. She held the loot aloft and shouted for the glory of greed. The others joined in.

Taking advantage of the distraction, Holmes immediately took center stage. Falling to his knees, throwing back his hood, and wailing inconsolable sounds, he picked up large handfuls of muddy road dirt and mashed them down on his head and face. It was a grotesque scene that repeated itself as he did this several times. The thieves were entranced, as was I. What possible purpose could be served by this behavior? After a while, I could see what he was up to because he had worked his way toward the pistol as everyone watched his bizarre activity. When he was in position, all of a sudden he scooped up the revolver with one motion and fired a shot skyward.

The report of the pistol shattered the quiet of the forest as the bullet glanced off a small overhanging tree limb, causing a secondary furor of splintered wood. The highwaymen grabbed their ears and scurried off in panic in all directions, except for one brave soul. A rather tall, swarthy one with a great black beard drew back his blade and charged my friend with a vengeance. Calmly, Holmes allowed the robber to approach him and then, at the last possible moment, fired a shot at the sword just above the hilt, effectively knocking the weapon cleanly from his hand. The wide-eyed thief turned and ran, bellowing something over his shoulder as he went off screeching like a monkey.

In the confusion, the one with the bag of coins and the crystal, not letting go of the booty, pelted off hard to the east as if her life depended on it. She did not get very far when her foot got tangled up in some exposed tree roots and she stumbled. This fortunate incident caused her to let go of the crystal in order to free her left hand to break her fall. By that time, Holmes and I were unflagging in our pursuit. Instead of stopping to retrieve the crystal structure, which fell among the shrubs, she scurried off clutching the coin purse.

"Shoot her!" I shouted involuntarily. "It is not too late!" But Holmes did not. He watched her go.

Holmes fished around in the undergrowth and finally raised the crystal.

"Why did you not shoot?" I insisted.

"We cannot allow ourselves to interfere in this time period to that great an extent, Watson. Although it may seem far-fetched to us now, that very woman might be a necessary progenitor of Joan of Arc or some such personage. I simply cannot take that chance."

"What if she turned out to be an ancestor to Jack the Ripper?" I posed.

"All the same, Watson, we are not here to alter the past and possibly the future. We are here to investigate history and find out the truth. We must tread as lightly as possible."

After a silence in which we listened to the breeze, I asked, "What are we going to do now, with no money? The only course of action is to head back to the time machine."

"We shall have to press on, my dear fellow," he regrouped. "Look at this fine sword we have acquired."

Feeling it to be an unfair barter, I reluctantly repacked the satchel, and we then moved on.

"It is a fortunate thing for us that they did not make off with the crystal structure, eh, Watsonicus?" my friend said, after a bit.

"I should say," I responded.

"Surely she would have thought it to be a priceless gem of some sort," my companion speculated. "Which, of course, it is, I suppose." After another thought, "We would, no doubt, dread to face the prospect of spending the remainder of our days here in the first century."

"No doubt. Oh, for a plate of Mrs. Hudson's ham and eggs and a cup of hot Earl Grey," I moaned, after the thought.

"Hot toast with quince marmalade," my friend reflected.

I sighed.

"I am afraid I owe you an apology, Doctor. It seems that your pistol, so far, has stood us in rather good stead more than once during this excursion. With such consequences, I may, in the future and according to the results, give you selected permission to disobey my explicit orders," he relented and bowed graciously.

I returned his bow and noticed his face.

"You look a fright," I said, regarding his muddy head.

"All in the course of a good day's work, my dear fellow. Did I appear deranged?"

"Indeed. Quite convincing, I thought," I said, smiling.

Holmes smiled back. He enjoyed receiving a favorable review.

"To my way of thinking, the incident that just occurred has the earmark of enemy action. It certainly fits into the modus operandi of Drumb; using others to do his dirty work for him," my friend observed.

"Harumph! To my way of thinking," I returned, "it was just one big smacking example of the destructive, chaotic ways of man, a random happening. These highwaymen have no regard for others, order, and justice. They are merely looking out for themselves, opportunistically. Propriety and law are not the watchwords of the day, but indeed, basic greed would seem to prevail over common decency."

Holmes regarded me skeptically and said, "I see strategy behind this event."

"I do not," was my return. "I see bad luck and nothing more. How can you state that this capricious attempt at robbery was strategic? I suppose you will now imply that this event bolsters your theories of divine purpose? No, man, chance merely put us in the wrong place at the wrong time. What of your so-called pattern of the good and virtuous order? We were merely random victims, and to be most honest with you, I do not like it. I much prefer the predictable, orderly existence of twentieth-century London!"

"If our many adventures in crime have taught us one thing, Watsonicus, they have taught us to proceed on the basis of, as you put it, predictability and order. Foreseeable, measurable results that are derived from calculable reason are the very core of our investigative process. That is how crimes are solved. Permit me to illustrate the point."

"Proceed," I allowed.

"The very laws of chemistry, as you will admit, depend on anticipated results. Predictable chemical reactions are the very basis of all life. If the world around us were the outcome of a confused and arbitrary beginning, we would have no right to expect or predict anything. Disarray begets disarray. Order begets order. It becomes absurd for us to live orderly, predictable lives if we believe that all about us comes from chaos. I assure you that there is some sort of reason behind these most recent events, even though we do not fully understand it now."

That thought had not occurred to me. As we continued our trek, I reminded myself of the nature of what we had already experienced in this era. I supposed we were fortunate for having traversed this time period in the trial-by-fire fashion that we had. I looked over my shoulder to see if a squad of mercenary soldiers or a band of thieves was pursuing us. There was only a vacant road.

With no more money and with Druids, hired troopers, and thieves surely at our heels, I must confess that I was not surprised at what was bound to occur. What was soon to transpire would utterly dishearten my cohort. This entire venture was about to come crashing down on us.

Inexorably, things turned from bad to worse. My traveling companion was soon to be proven prophetic when he had earlier suggested my potential stay in a Sheik's service. As you can imagine, becoming a eunuch in an Arabian harem held very little fascination for me.

7

A Dead End

I selected and acted upon the best information I had, but I suppose there are some things obscured by time that ultimately cannot be fathomed.

—MR. S. HOLMES

As the weather soured into a wet and chilling winter, we traveled on. While the days became weeks, we made our way resolutely yet methodically across Gaul and into northern Italy. The roads were rutted with mud yet relatively passable, so that, coupled with an occasional free handout along the way, made the travel almost bearable.

Although the Druids and soldiers were behind us, it was impossible to rid myself of the notion that Drumb would not willingly abandon the whole affair. We pressed on while continuously looking over our shoulders. The empty road behind us was nerve-racking. The Arch Druid's absence was, somehow, even more menacing. Often we would travel far from the path and live off the land, which made the going rougher but the contact with potential trouble minimal.

Asking no questions and telling no lies, we melded in with a band of hot-blooded gypsies who were migrating south for the winter. This proved to be an experience for which there are few adequate words. Needless to say, they made for a unique set of traveling companions: jugglers, pickpockets, street performers, storytellers and scoundrels to be sure. There were also a few talented contortionists and some acrobats in the lot, who when thrown into the mix, brought delight to the locals as we passed through. It was a good cover. Holmes with his sleight of hand and me with some mumbo-jumbo medicine, were accepted as part of the group. We were in with misfits like ourselves, so others steered clear of us.

The gypsy outcasts, apparently by design, moved from village to village, not unlike a traveling circus. This circus was complete with clowns, musicians, and belly dancers, as well as a freak show that included disfigured dwarves, mutant babies, and a giant hairless albino. This combination made the whole scene both attractive and repulsive at the same time. Our cavalcade of wayfarers would stop in a hamlet for only one day and one night. We would work the crowd and then move onto the next little burg. The locals enjoyed seeing us come, and they enjoyed seeing us go.

The band also had a flock of exotic animals for the amusement of the various townsfolk along the way. Among the menagerie of beasts that accompanied us were a few giraffes and even some elephants. The presence of these pachyderms engendered another history lesson from my companion.

"Well, Watsonicus," the detective whispered to me, "think of it. This might be the very path by which the great military commander Hannibal, a scant two hundred fifty years ago, marched his forces from Hispania over the Pyrenees and through the Alps to conquer the Romans in northern Italy during the Second Punic Wars. If the medieval artistic renderings of this event are accurate, Hannibal used elephants for his mounted troop transports."

Holmes pointed to the looming mountains to the east of us as he continued lecturing me in his schoolmaster mode. "Hannibal Barca, from the cognate 'Baal is merciful to me' will be remembered as a politician–statesman from Carthage and a military tactical genius who kept the Romans frustrated and on their heels for several years. If our history books correctly do us service, Hannibal later committed suicide rather than submit to the iron hand of Rome. Fascinating, is it not, Watsonicus, feeling the very pulse of history?"

I gave him no answer, thinking it to be a rhetorical question.

The reader will excuse me if I resist the temptation to fully recount our gypsy experience as the complete retelling of it would prove to be too great a digression.

Veering to the south, circumventing the Alps, we went easterly to avoid the oncoming harshness of a northern European winter. Skirting southward and hugging the northern Mediterranean coast, we left the gypsies behind and hastily went on through several small settlements, among which were the beginnings of the twentieth-century towns of Genoa and Florence.

We gradually found ourselves proceeding easterly, along a very sophisticated thoroughfare. The roadway we were traversing upon was indeed wide and handsome; there was easily room for two chariots to pass in opposite directions. It was well maintained with hewn stones as neat little curbs on either side of the avenue. The roadway was made level and smooth by the well-engineered filling in of the valleys along the way and the precise road cuts to whittle down the hills. There were even regular convenience stops by the pathway for the traveler to change mounts and acquire refreshment. All of these advanced features were well conceived and well executed, much to the credit of the authorities.

"Well, this is certainly an improvement, eh, Sherlockodies?"

"Yes, my dear fellow, I do very much suspect that we are, indeed, on the Appian Way and nearing the great city of Rome itself," my friend conjectured.

He was correct. Holmes found his way around Rome with moderate ease, but because of our possible jeopardy in the city of Caesar, my companion insisted on not lingering very long. He was keeping his sights on the land of Judea to the east. Yet because this venture of his, this self-described quest, drove him to leave no stone unturned to find the truth, he quickly visited the local temples and shrines to see if there was anything of note. There were various edifices dedicated to many of their own gods, as if they were attempting to placate all of the possible heavenly combinations. The temples of Jupiter and Neptune were most impressive. There were also sanctuaries to the goddesses Venus and Roma. We noted a colossal structure that appeared to be under construction, and we were told it was a temple being built for the Divine Augustus Caesar. There were also several forums dedicated to great personages, as well as a few theaters and, of course, the formidable Senate itself. The renowned Coliseum and Arch of Titus were, of course, yet to be built. This was a city, to be sure, dedicated to itself and its own ongoing importance. Rome was so magnificent and proud that one could readily imagine how simple it was to have ingrained within the very heart and soul of the people the concept of invincibility and longevity. There was a tangible attitude shared by the urban elite and virtually all of its citizenry, which manifested itself in the conviction that the greatness of Rome would, without doubt, increase and continue forever. Looking at this mindset from my perspective caused me to ponder the reality of any society's conceited blindness and how it could so easily fall prey to the ravages of time and history in the first as well as the twentieth century. How the mighty have fallen and inevitably will fall.

"Nothing, Watsonicus; merely idol worship of the first order. Caesar has set himself up as the very Son of God. This claim is engraved on every monument, stamped on every coin, and even drenched in the literature of the day. Caesar's image has also been forged on the hearts and minds of the people, legitimizing his assertion throughout the empire. Interestingly, this self-pronouncement of divinity is also synchronized with the prophetic Oriental assertion of the coming Messiah."

Although the splendor of Rome was on the surface incomparable, I was bound to agree with him regarding the ephemeral nature of the great empire. No sign of Drumb made me pensive. I purposefully tried to dispel any false sense of security. Soldiers, naturally, were on every street corner. Holmes initiated several low-keyed inquiries about the happenings in the east but could find out very little. This news, or lack of it, seemed to disturb him visibly. We continued our quest without delay. To say the least, Holmes was a man with a mission.

"We must pursue the truth at all costs, my dear fellow. We must press on eastward."

Making our way to the east coast of Italy, we hired on to a boat that was headed across the Adriatic Sea. We swabbed the decks and fed the livestock.

Leaving the ship behind, we continued on foot. Moving across Macedonia and Achaea we traversed through the Grecian countryside, passing by Mt. Olympus, the legendary mountain of the gods, to the idealized city of Athens, the very seat of western civilization. Although the Roman authority was unquestioned and absolute, the Hellenistic influence continued widespread and pronounced. There was a remarkable reverence that the Roman intelligentsia continued to hold for Grecian thought and culture.

Athens, the city itself, was so named because it was dedicated to the goddess Athena. Most of the larger cities across the landscape of Greece were dedicated to their various gods. Upon arriving in Athens, Holmes was greatly distressed to see a city full of idols. Walking through the agora, the marketplace, my companion would eagerly converse and engage with groups of what I later found out to be Stoic and Epicurean philosophers who happened to be wandering the streets. These educated upper-crust types apparently had nothing better to do but engage in intellectual encounters. Seemingly, they lived for, relished in, and aspired to such stimulating debates about various beliefs and philosophies and regarded discussions about knowledge, morals, and ethics to be of paramount importance. My friend and I were invited to the Temple Parthenon. This great structure was the chief shrine of Athena, the Greek goddess of wisdom, skills, and warfare, and the protectress of cities. It was built on the Acropolis in the heart of the city and was a flawless example of Doric architecture.

At a meeting of the Areopagus, which was the highest council of the land, both intellectual and judicial, my friend exchanged much conversation with both foreigners and locals who seemed to sit around doing nothing but listening to and purporting new ideas and fresh philosophies. Each learned scholar would, in turn, stand up and deliver a long discourse that eluded me but held the interest of my traveling companion. Holmes, in his place, was allowed to stand up and deliver a speech that appeared to boggle the minds of the attending elite. After a few hours of subsequent debate and reasoning, my friend got up and signaled to me, and we abruptly departed, leaving the august group of philosophers behind with opened mouths.

Upon leaving and walking down from Mars Hill, Holmes commented, "I find it amazing that the great Temple itself is ringed with altars to the various gods. Even under the guise of sophistication and intellect, it is merely the same thing, Watsonicus: idol worship of unashamed magnitude. There is even an altar dedicated to the unknown god, just in case they happened to miss one; covering all their bases, as the Americans would say." He added, with a chuckle, "I shocked most of them, I think, with some additions to the Pythagorean theorem for which they were totally unprepared. I do not think they are quite ready for certain advanced calculus concepts."

"Do you think that was wise, considering your own admonition to tread lightly in this time period?"

He said nothing in return, but kept moving.

Pressing on to the eastern coast of the Grecian peninsula, we attempted to find gainful employment onboard a ship that was headed east. That not being possible, my companion decided to secretly stow away on a boat headed across the Aegean Sea to Ephesus. This was where, and when, our troubles escalated.

We felt like tightly packed clothing in a steamer trunk, hiding ourselves in the forward hold of the stout freighter that we had sneaked aboard in the middle of the previous night. Holmes and I were discovered when I tried, unsuccessfully, to stifle a sneeze caused by the proximity of a herd of goats and the several dozen chickens that provided eggs and fresh poultry for the wealthy chief of an important Arabic clan. He was the owner of the ship and currently on board. Instantly, we were cornered by the crew, who gruffly dragged us up some stairs to the upper deck. Without hesitation, we were then tied, hands behind our backs, and forced to stand there. I looked to my friend and hoped for something good to happen, as I did not know what else to do.

While we were waiting, Holmes somehow loosened his bindings, and pausing for the right moment, then lunged for the satchel. The watchful sailors grabbed the detective before he could reach inside the bag. He put up a tremendous struggle, but they eventually got the best of him. I would have aided him were I not bound hand and foot. Having had enough of the stowaway and his shenanigans, the sailors summarily threw Holmes overboard and, without looking at its contents, flung the satchel after him. I was stunned at the suddenness of this action.

In immediate shock due to my former roommate's sudden removal, I struggled to catch a glimpse of him bobbing in the water. Not seeing him did nothing to ease my anxiety regarding his disposition. He was an excellent swimmer, but his ability to make the safety of land at this point in the voyage seemed impossible. Predictably, I found myself experiencing severe dread about his unexpected and abrupt departure. I thought of the various brushes with death he had experienced and how he inevitably eluded the grim reaper time and time again. I wondered if, this time, he was going to experience his demise or yet another miracle. I was crushed, but I scarcely had time to think about his fate before mine was cast.

Straightaway, I was hauled into the presence of a very posh-looking potentate, a big, fat fellow with a voluminous gray-black beard. In fact, everything about him was large and round. From the satiny turban on top of his circular head to his corpulent shoes, he was a giant sphere.

His quarters were amidships and reflected the heavy, ornate decorative tastes that are preferred by such types. In his suite, there were many rich, luxurious fabrics, oriental rugs and pillows of exquisite material. Servants were constantly fanning and doting on him while he leaned back in repose, surrounded by a bevy of veiled beauties. Luscious bowls of fruit and cakes were at his disposal, as two of the women peeled grapes for him while another wiped his lips following each and every mouthful. After a while, he called me over, but I feigned deafness. One of his servants pushed me as I sprawled out on a rug, right before him. He proceeded to clap his hands, which caused the servants to scurry and the platters of food to be gone. After he inspected me at close range, not unlike a potential horse buyer looks at an old plug, he poked me, looked at my teeth, and smelled my body. Being apparently satisfied with his new find, he signaled to his man, and I was whisked off to be washed up and put into service as assistant to the head eunuch who watched over the harem.

I supposed, because of my age and apparent deaf and dumb status, the Sheik decided that it was acceptable for me to be in the delicate arena of helping to serve his many wives. I could only hope that he would not take any drastic measures to assure my limited involvement with his consorts. I, of course, not wanting anything to do with the aforementioned drastic measures, was on my best behavior. My natural aversion to the possibility of becoming a castrato motivated me greatly.

The food was good, the accommodations were acceptable, but the lack of freedom was a dark burden to my disposition. The following days turned into weeks, and I sorely mourned my traveling companion. Although I remained hopeful, I often wondered if I would ever see him again; as time wagged on, that eventuality seemed less and less likely. My concern for him deepened. I was beginning to believe that he was forever lost in the depths of the Mediterranean. The end of Mr. Sherlock Holmes made me shake my head with profound sadness and also made me regret my few disparaging remarks toward him.

He would never solve his final mystery. I cried bitterly at the thought of it.

As I settled into my new position, I resigned myself to it by saying that things could only get better from this point. After all, the certainty of my owner was now no longer in question. I belonged to the Sheik forever, and that was that. I began to think that even escape would do me no good. Where would I go and what would I do?

That Aegean crossing was difficult, dangerous, cold, and wet, especially that time of year. After our arrival in Ephesus, we went easterly, overland by caravan, and that movement aided us in making our way through Phrygia, Turkey, and Syria by a bit more time-consuming means. Stopping at the whim of the Sheik to spend a day at an oasis in a tented camp was not uncommon. We sometimes traveled at night.

The weather turned toward the good as winter relented to the advance of spring, and when all was said and done, I supposed that I had successfully avoided any Druidic entanglements. I kept trying to look on the bright side.

We reached the great city of Damascus, where the Sheik opted to stay for some while. I learned he had many friends in this part of the world and was quite the big man about town, in more ways than one. By this time, making the best of a bad situation, I had become friendly with many of the women in the harem, as well as my fellow slaves. Of course, I was careful not to become too familiar with the Sheik's many wives and to attend to my duties with a vigilance that won me praise and commendation from my supervisor. I even managed to do a little doctoring among the staff, and management that was greatly appreciated.

All this, however, would never substitute for one more day back in London at 221b Baker Street with my friend sitting across the table and a plate of Mrs. Hudson's sausage and eggs looking back at me. I was now convinced that I would never see him, my home, my own time, my practice, or that breakfast again. Doctor Watson would die, alone, some nineteen hundred years before his time.

On one particularly pleasant early spring evening, the Sheik was throwing a magnificent banquet with what I speculated to be a group of prominent persons from the city in attendance. There was dancing, entertainment, and food galore. There was also no lack of drink, and the Sheik became rather sotted with wine. He was quite taken with the adoring crowd and started to strut around dancing and, thus, in a good-natured way, began to challenge others around him to feats of strength. One skinny fellow in particular, a tall, doltish-looking bearded chap of obviously shallow mentality, was quite intoxicated himself and taunted his host in return. There arose a friendly competition. Words were exchanged, and the two men lay down prone on the floor, and facing each other, placed their right elbows onto pillows in front of them. Grasping their corresponding hands , they tried to determine who was the stronger of the two. This arm-wrestling competition was now the center of attention, with several of the partygoers placing wagers on one of the men or the other. I could not see how the doltish-looking man would stand a chance, but during the course of their engagement, he seemed to hold his own.

There was much hooting and howling on both sides of the question, as all in attendance were encouraging the contestants who were trying to best each other. It was a long and tension-packed struggle, with the Sheik calling more than once to one of his consorts to bring him refreshment. She squeezed wine from a goatskin into his mouth, the sight of which delighted all. The other chap asked for the same and got it. All the attendees exhorted the two contenders as the wrestlers continued for a protracted period, back and forth. Finally, with the greatest of efforts, the skinny fellow gave it his all and forced my master's hand to the mat. Simultaneous howls of disappointment and triumph filled the tent as a great cheer of applause blanketed the scene.

The winning doltish fellow stood up, rubbed his arm, and then resolutely turned and pointed to me, of all people. Looking in my direction, the Sheik waved his hand over his head. I was now, apparently, the possession of someone else. I had been the prize wagered and won by the victor. The skinny chap grabbed me by the arm, and bowing to everyone in the room, while kissing his own fingertips and waving, pulled me outside the tent. Next we were off into the night. He had a pair of camels waiting, and without so much as a how-do-you-do or have-an-apple, we mounted the beasts and started to ride. All of this happened so quickly that it took me some time to absorb it completely.

I was off again into the future, out of control. What in the world would happen next? As we were going along and my eyes adjusted to the scant light of the moon, I noticed a carpetbag slung over the back of my new owner's animal. It looked familiar somehow, but I could not place where I had seen it before. All of a sudden it hit me.

"Holmes!?"

He turned his head and removed his turban to smile his unmistakable smile.

"Watsonicus, you have been delinquent in your duties to your rightful master, Sherlockodies, and you, therefore, owe him a substantial term of allegiance."

My reaction to being reunited with my friend was not dissimilar to a mother finding her lost child after a long and anxious search. There would, no doubt, be immediate joy and exaltation at the reunion of the two, parent and child back together, but then the emotion would instantly transform into anger, with the mother chastising her child for putting her through such an awful ordeal.

"Is it really you?" I shouted for joy.

"It is I, my dear fellow, skillfully disguised, I might add, as Abdul the influential Persian silk merchant."

"How on earth did you survive being cast into the Mediterranean?" I sputtered, with eyes wide open.

"Nothing to it, old chap. You have, no doubt, noticed the clasp-locked configuration that fastens the top of the rubber-lined satchel together? It makes a 'zzzzip' sound when you use it. Quite a clever invention, actually, by a fellow named Judson in Chicago. Those interlocking metal tabs are almost airtight, thus making the bag a useful temporary flotation device. This allowed me to stay adrift long enough to take advantage of the appearance of a convenient Grecian fishing trawler. I predict that some day this type of fastening mechanism will be worldwide in its use."

"Unbelievable! I am elated! How did you know where I was?"

"Quite straightforward, Watsonicus. The flamboyant Sheik and his entourage left large footprints as they wound their way eastward."

The transition came, as the emotion shifted from joy to displeasure. "How could you desert me like that, to the fate of a slave; what a nightmare you have put me through! I might have been made a eunuch or some such thing, or even worse! Of all the unconscionable things! I was worried sick about you. I had given you up for dead. How shall I ever forgive you for this? Somehow, I wish you hadn't rescued me."

"I could hand you back to the Sheik."

"That will not be necessary!" I stuttered, and then continued after a thought. "What would you have done if he would had bested you at the arm-wrestling competition?"

"I would have given him the camel you are riding on, Doctor," he smirked.

"I do not know which is better, riding beside you on a camel or tending to a harem of beautiful courtesans," I thought out loud.

"If you do not know the answer to that one, dear fellow, I am not going to be the one to tell you."

We exchanged a long look with no words.

I made a mental note to myself regarding the rapidity with which circumstances can change on a journey like this.

Apparently the political times were changing as well. For once we entered Caesarea-Philippi and continued heading south, we began to hear rumblings of a messianic figure in the Palestine area, a prophet or holy man of some kind, or as some whispered, a deliverer. This, to be sure, was a title that the ruling authorities did not like.

We had heretofore been traveling through the heart of the conquered Roman Empire, where the environment was more stable and the people resigned to their lot in life to a greater degree. Now we were entering the frontier, a place fraught with discord. There was much more restlessness in this part of the world where Roman soldiers seemed to be more numerous, more alert, and far more aggressive. Realizing the disquiet in the air made for a palpable tension. This environment noticeably reinvigorated my companion and prompted us onward with increased zeal.

As we entered the Province of Palestine, we began to see increased traffic upon the roadway. Finding out that many fellow travelers were on a pilgrimage to the sacred city of Jerusalem for the ancient Jewish seven-day Festival of Unleavened Bread heightened our sense of destiny. The first day of the festival was to be marked by the feast of Passover, which commemorated the deliverance of the children of Israel from the hands of the Egyptians. My traveling companion recounted some bits of Jewish history as we went along.

The reader will, I hope, once again forgive me if I indulge in a little bit of impressionism. Although I have never had a preference for the things of yesteryear, actually living in it and seeing the flesh-and-blood of it all lent a new and weighty meaning to the dusty past. As Holmes put it, "We cannot escape history, Watsonicus." I also do not wish to exaggerate, but I honestly must confess to the ominous foreboding I sensed. Because I am writing this in recollection I will admit to having the advantage of retrospection, which offers some significant insight into my experiences. Yet I will state that to some degree, at the time, I subjectively and somehow intuitively caught the aura of the gravity of events that were soon to surround me. Reacting rather like a leaf being lifted up inside the middle of a swirling cyclone, the sense of adventure began to build. There was something like an electric charge in the air. What I was soon to discover was a crescendo of monumental proportions, time and history coming together at the hinge of a great occurrence. Not intending to overstate my feelings, I was somehow in the midst of events that would transcend the very nature of human experience.

After all, the death and so-called resurrection of Christ is one of the major historical happenings in all of western civilization. I am, of course, a doctor, and it is not my intention to wax poetic about the ethereal substance of a material event. Being of a scientific bent, it is not within my nature to do so, but that conviction, if you will, of import and destiny surged through my heart and mind like never before. I kept these impressions to myself and did not relate these feelings to my companion.

Holmes told me he had won the camels, clothing, and the little money he had in a game of chance in Galatia. However, after he described the way he played it, I could see that it was not chance. He bent the odds in his favor. Now, however, having once again run out of coins, we came to Tyre and my friend shared with me his notion to sell all of his possessions and pocket the returns. The camels and the clothing on our backs were all we had. He sold the things for what I thought to be very little. "We have not the time to quibble, Watsonicus, we are on a mission." He divided the proceeds with me, as meager as they were. I asked him why he did that.

He replied, "Just in case we get split up again, old man, I wanted you to have a bit to keep up the spirits. If, for any reason, we should be separated, remain in Jerusalem until I find you. Is that clear, Watsonicus?"

What he said was clear enough, but I wondered what he meant by it. Yet, as I remember, I gave the statement very little thought at the time. One reason why I was unable to delve into the meaning of the previous cryptic saying is that an approaching band of fully armed Roman Soldiers caught my eye. They were pushing and threatening everyone in their way. They were intimidating, to say the least.

"I suppose a bully is a bully in any time period, eh, Watsonicus?"

I nodded in agreement. We held our breath and stepped aside as we hid our faces under our hoods to avoid confrontation. After all, we were still, I supposed, wanted men under protective custody. They passed us by. We breathed again.

My friend had been, while on the road, a constant busybody, calmly talking with whomever he could to find out about current events. Slowly, over the past few days, he had begun to realize that, indeed, he appeared to be arriving at the place and time he desired to visit.

"Watsonicus, I believe we have done it! My calculations and research have paid off to the point of near certainty. We have almost arrived, a bit later than I was hoping we might, but nonetheless we are soon to be on location, my dear fellow. The trail is fresh." He did not realize at that time that he was soon to be extremely disappointed. There is a large difference between seeing something with your heart and seeing the same thing with your head.

I do not recall a time when I have seen Mr. Sherlock Holmes as excited as he was in anticipation of being able to investigate the scene of the crime. I use the phrase 'scene of the crime' on purpose as the reader will soon discover for himself. In one sense, the events that were to unfold over the following days, at the hands of the so-called authorities, were tantamount to a brutal and uncalled-for miscarriage of justice. I will admit that I did not think this at the time, but now in retrospect, it was an event, as my friend would say, that was masterfully and mysteriously appointed. One could reflect and perceive, I suppose, to a very substantial extent, the workings of both physical and spiritual forces.

We strode over a rise in the path to discover a panoramic view of a bustling city. After a pause, Holmes informed me quietly, "Jerusalem."

A recent, healthy, spring rain had made the road much less dusty.

As I followed, Holmes began to hum a familiar strain of Mozart that he was wont to play on his fiddle come an autumn evening in front of a roaring fire at 221b Baker Street, London, England, nineteenth century. All of that seemed so far away and dreamlike now. He was a little annoying in this blissful reverie. Appearing to have all but forgotten about the troubles we had managed to evade, he shifted his concentration onto the task ahead. I was not so easily distracted. Even though we had not seen the Druids for months, now, I quietly found myself keeping an eye peeled for Drumb and his hired fighters. The notion that the Arch Druid could possibly turn up aroused in me no little concern.

Descending slightly from a rocky mountain with olive trees on it, we entered the city with much anticipation. Jerusalem was a metropolis by first-century standards, both Hellenistic and Hebrew at the same time. A few main roads within the city were wide and easy to pass, but most of the streets were narrow and crowded with vendors. Jerusalem was aesthetically monotonous and without variation. Every edifice was of the same dull, light-brown hue.

After mixing and mingling with the townsfolk the rest of the afternoon, we noticed nothing unusual going on in the neighborhoods except a city getting ready for a yearly festival.

We spent the night with a small group of sojourners, like ourselves, who had set up temporary housing on the outskirts of the city by a small seasonal creek. The authorities apparently allowed that sort of village during this time of year.

I was beginning, once again, to lose track of the days we had spent so far on our journey; in addition, not having bathed or shaved for the longest time was most grating on my demeanor. I expressed my displeasure to my master regarding this state of affairs.

Finally giving up trying to communicate without words, I said pointedly, "Excuse me my dear Sherlockodies or Abdul or whatever your name is, do you suppose we could take some time to wash off a bit?"

"I am glad you brought that up, Watsonicus. I have been meaning to speak with you about your personal hygiene. It is most indecorous."

The weather was pleasant enough for the season. That evening we walked off the path, through the campers, to discover a secluded, still pool on the above-mentioned stream. "It is just what the doctor ordered," stated my friend.

The water was murky but acceptable. After a silent bath and swim, with a bit of laundry dashed in, we settled down in front of a meager fire to sup on some lovely hardtack we had purchased; our standard evening meal. The sun was setting now as our creek-washed clothes were drying on several rocks. I almost wished I were back with the Sheik.

"We should be all right here, blending in with this makeshift village of worshippers on pilgrimage," he said.

Leaning back and loading his pipe for a smoke, the detective pulled a black, bound book from the satchel, a book to which I had seen him referring upon occasion.

"It is interesting, is it not, Watsonicus?" he chattered, after he had read for a while.

"What is that?" I said in a monotonous voice.

"This is a copy of the *King James Version* of the Holy Writ, originally issued in 1611. It was authorized by the King himself, translated and printed to exact specifications. The four unique and yet strikingly similar versions of the life of Jesus are most compelling. Incorporated into these Gospel renderings is moving and substantial narration of the words and actions of this Jesus of Nazareth...the so-called Christ. His life and purpose seem to be at the heart of these writings."

"Of course, my dear fellow, I have a rudimentary knowledge of the Bible and its contents but I must admit that I have never had much interest in its content. I also never knew you to be attracted to the Bible or religious things in general for that matter," I retorted.

"Well, I brought along this book as a reference, in hopes of verifying for myself the events to which the writers of much of the first four accounts in the New Testament claim to give eyewitness testimony," he added.

"Eyewitness?" I questioned.

"Yes. It will be very interesting to discover, Watsonicus, to what extent the span of time between the first century and 1611 will taint the language and meaning of the text. If we have arrived at the correct destination, we should be able to answer this and other questions for ourselves."

"It is all lost in fable, surely. Over the course of centuries, various parties would most certainly compromise the text, though perhaps inadvertently, misconstruing passages or even deliberately changing the meanings of words or phrases, depending on the particular temperament of the day. You cannot blame people for wanting to make legends out of martyrs," I speculated, thinking it would be ridiculous to believe otherwise.

"Perhaps you are correct, Doctor, but I am not so sure. My research is inconclusive." Holding up the book, he went on, "This is either sheer foolishness or genius. It might very well be the best attested to and most consistent document in all of ancient writings or utter nonsense. It could contain the key to life itself or be mere useless bunk." The detective looked up at the stars.

"You call yourself a man of reason, do you not? If you ask me, it is absurd to even consider that this Jesus figure is the true way to find, if there is such a thing, the afterlife," I contended. "You are beginning to sound like a clergyman, not a detective."

"Am I?" Holmes questioned, getting an idea.

"Yes! You are not being logical. What about the millions of other people convinced that their religion is the correct one? They can't all be wrong, can they? What if their belief is right for them but not for others? Or had you thought of that?" I challenged.

"Well, my dear fellow, that is what we came on this trip to discover. Merely because one fails to believe in something does not make it untrue. Nor is sincere personal belief a validation of the truth. We seek objectivity: reason and data. Some things are true. Some things are not true. If something is true only for some people, it is not truth in the absolute sense. It is not the truth that I seek. Truth by definition is consistent with reality and the facts, and therefore, true to all."

He stood upon a nearby rock and started to grandly pontificate as if he were in the pulpit at the Cathedral of Canterbury or a lecture hall at Cambridge University or some such prominent place. "Let us not be like those ancient, or should I say contemporary, Greek philosophers, myself of course excepted, who would sit on top of Mars Hill and contemplate and theorize about the truth regarding the internal structure of leaves, or some such thing, without ever a thought of actually climbing down from their lofty platform and getting their hands dirty by tearing apart a leaf and looking at the thing for themselves a bit more closely to find out the truth of what actually constitutes the structure of a leaf. Thorough investigation first, and then honest conclusion, Watsonicus." His words and gestures echoed through the wilderness.

"What are you talking about...leaves and philosophers? I suppose you are mad or near about, so I repeat my dissatisfaction with your bringing me along on this flight of fancy of yours! I warned you time and time again that opium and cocaine use would eventually cause permanent damage to your brain and now I am proved correct!"

As nearby folks were staring in our direction, he continued, looking around and lowering his voice yet remaining in his didactic mode. "There is no wiggle room here, Doctor. Considering the claims that this Jesus made about himself, he is either, as I have said before, a self-deluded megalomaniacal lunatic, or calculating deceiver, or..." he paused as he climbed off his pulpit and became intently serious, "...just what he said he was: the way, the truth, the life." There was another thoughtful hesitation as he amended, "I can see no way around it. Jesus must be dealt with. He is the object of our quest."

"I did not have to traverse back to the first century to find out who the lunatic of all time is, Mr. Sherlock Holmes! What practical use could a two-thousand-year-old martyr serve in the twentieth century?" I put to him, as I also lowered my voice and looked around.

"Just, perhaps, all the use in the world, my dear fellow. This Jesus of Nazareth boldly declares, in Holy Writ, 'I am the bread of life'; he also calls himself the 'living water'. He claims to be able to confer rest if we come unto him. Is that reasonable? When he refers to himself as the bread and water of life, what does it mean? Will we never be hungry or thirsty again if we cast our fate with him? Is he insisting, in somewhat metaphoric language, that taking him in will result in eternal satisfaction, just like eating bread and drinking water results in earthly sustenance? Is he saying that we strive so hard after our daily bread to maintain this earthly life that we neglect our eternal well-being? Is there even such a thing as eternity? Is he attempting to make a timeless proposition to which all people can relate? These questions continue to disquiet me."

As he became silent, his tortured expression betrayed his anguish. I could see once again that this adventure was intensely personal to him. Pulling out of his inner restless thoughts, he riveted me with a penetrating squint.

"And you, my dear Doctor," he observed, changing the subject, "have seemed to veritably prosper under a diet of bread and water. You are looking much less rotund and more fit than your twentieth-century London counterpart."

Suddenly growing rather weary with the conversation, I pantomimed my tiredness and rolled over as if to sleep. As I lay there, I realized how exhausted I had become.

"'Come unto me, all ye that labor and are heavy laden, and I will give you rest," Holmes read quietly.

While I drifted off thinking of this conversation, I could hear a rustle of pages as Mr. Sherlock Holmes contemplated the ancient writings. That night, the last things I remembered were those very words of rest that echoed me to sleep, sweetening my dreams. I was temporarily moved to optimism by the prospect of perfect rest.

The following morning we went into the center of town and waited. What we were waiting for was beyond me. As the day wore on, I could see my friend becoming more agitated. It was relatively quiet in the city because it was the Jewish day of Sabbath. Finally in the late afternoon, my friend looked down at the ground and uttered five discouraging words, "What if I am wrong?" He was silent, deep in thought. It was during times like these that I would leave him alone and let him think. Remaining pensively there until well after nightfall, my friend and I finally dragged ourselves back to our temporary campsite, where I fell quickly to sleep listening to an increasingly obsessed Holmes muttering to himself and rustling through folded papers that he extracted from his *King James Bible*.

The next morning was the first day of the week. The town bustled. Silently we returned to the same spot as the day before. My friend made some inquiries and then afterwards sat down and was thoughtful for a few hours. Finally he said, "Watsonicus, I am the world's biggest fool. We are possibly off by a year or maybe two. Now, I am in doubt of my own research. I knew going into this affair that the scholarship was shaky at best. I selected and acted upon the best information I had, but I suppose there are some things obscured by time that ultimately cannot be fathomed." He ruminated, "If I am off by such a time frame, what are we to do? Our options, as I see it, are these: we either lay low here for a year or two, find the lay of the land, and wait for history to catch up to us; or go back to the machine and make a time jump to the next-best guess. What do you think?"

Either option was unappealing to me. I sat in stillness for the longest time, filled with impatient irritation. At last I spoke. Even though I had too much respect for him to be obnoxiously high-handed, I was at last proven right, and I was going to tell him.

"This is what comes, old man, of going off on an adventure that has little substance. I am glad you have finally seen the error of your ways and admitted your mistakes. There are simply no options to entertain; we must go back to the vehicle and return to our own time period at once, sooner if possible," I summed up. "If it is not already too late."

After a long, agonizing pause, my companion rose and started to move slowly back toward camp. I followed him smugly.

As I heard Holmes take a breath, about to speak, he was stopped by a sound that at first seemed unreal and far off. Yet when this noise was brought into clarity and pondered awhile, it was discovered to be near. It was a sound reminiscent of large volumes of rushing water.

8

SEPARATED AND LOST

Barely persisting in this subhuman existence
was one of the low points of my life.

—DR. J. H. WATSON

It was the sound of voices, many individual human voices surging in unison. They were crying out for joy and purpose. We listened. It was coming from the edge of the city.

We changed direction and walked toward the noise, winding our way through both narrow and wide streets. Getting closer to the source of the sound, where we assumed there to be a crowd, we noted others also converging. The shouting was nearer as we rounded a corner with many people at our elbows. Ahead of us, we could see a large mass of human beings advancing through a wide main street, which led into the city, and yelling out randomly what sounded like hosanna and then something in the local language I could not understand. The randomness of the cries turned into a spontaneous unified chant of those hosannas that grew in intensity. People around us were talking among themselves and asking questions. My companion translated for me.

"They are asking 'Who is this?'" he said. "Let us see if we can get an answer."

We came to the edge of the moving crowd as my friend made inquiries of those who were rapturously cheering. After a short but loud exchange with an excited middle-aged woman, my friend turned to me and cried out above the din of the exalted mass. "She said 'This is the prophet, Jesus, from Nazareth in Galilee'!" As I stood my full height trying to catch a glimpse of the man in the middle of the mob, I saw my friend pull out his *King James Bible* and quickly refer to a particular portion of it. He lifted himself up and screamed for joy, "We are not too late or early, my dear Watsonicus; we are exquisitely on time!"

I turned my attention to the center of the action as I was being jostled on all sides by an enthusiastic throng. At one point as I was being involuntarily moved along by the masses, I caught a view, through a break in the crowd, of a young-looking bearded man being ushered into the city, encircled by an adoring people and yet guarded by watchful intimates. He was riding on a donkey, while the enraptured mob was laying down palm branches before him. Some of the multitude were removing their cloaks and laying them down in the roadway ahead of the prophet. I assumed this gesture to be one of respect and honor. Seeing him through the throng, I perceived him to be the center of attention. He was placid amid the admiration. I marked the serenity of his demeanor as being singular in the midst of the uproar. I shall never forget my first impression of the man; he had a remarkably knowing look about him.

While I was trying to move in to get a closer look, the multitude grew larger as the street narrowed, so that I was effectively left behind in the wake of Jesus' triumphal entrance into Jerusalem. I had, of course, heard of this incident in history before, but this was nothing like my preconception. The enthusiasm and scope of the assemblage and the admiration it displayed was astounding. I felt as if this Jesus could easily and immediately be crowned as a king, if that was what he wanted.

The multitude went on ahead while I mindlessly followed. I will admit to being caught up in the moment. As the throng thinned out behind the brief parade, I noticed that Holmes was not at my side. I scanned the narrow passageway bordered on both sides by shops, but I could not see him anywhere. My searching turned to concern as I realized I was alone in the crowd. We had been journeying together for so long that without him I felt incomplete, isolated, even though there were people all around. I continued my search but came up empty. Forgetting my character, I shouted out, "Holmes!" more than once. No response, nothing. Stopping and looking around, as the street life started to take on some form of normalcy, I could discover him nowhere. The satchel was also missing; at least I did not have it. I was trying to remember the last time I did. My concern became panic. I realized I was again separated from Holmes and alone in the first century, in Jerusalem; I had no resources but a few coins and no hope of returning home.

While scouring the street scene for my companion, I was brusquely pushed aside by a squad of well-armed Roman soldiers racing after the fading throng. Following their exit, I looked for him the rest of the day with no success.

Every time I saw a hooded figure, my instinct made me look twice. I imagined I saw Drumb and the Druids as often as I did Mr. Sherlock Holmes. Thinking that I might find my friend that night at our temporary campsite, I returned expectantly. He was nowhere to be found, so I wandered about in hopes of spying him. Later, on my mat, I fell into a fitful sleep. I dreamed about an incident from my childhood, one I rarely bring to mind, when I was separated from my father while on holiday in Wales. It was most disturbing and anxiety provoking.

I woke the next morning, hoping the previous day's events were nothing more than a nightmare; I found circumstances to be otherwise. Wandering into town alone, with but a few coins to my name, I recalled the admonition of my friend to stay in Jerusalem. I grew increasingly angry at the prospect that he might very well have left me to my own devices on purpose for some reason beyond me. It would be like him to keep me in the dark regarding his intentions. Putting that distasteful notion aside, I tried to mingle with the natives while looking for the world's foremost consulting detective.

The action on that day revolved around the Temple of the Hebrews. Jesus spent much of the day teaching at the synagogue, and large groups of people would hang on his every word. I was content to remain on the perimeter of the admiring multitudes, while keeping a wary eye out for a peculiar Greek scholar.

There was quite a disturbance that day when Jesus, apparently in a fit of what I suspected to be righteous anger, threw out business people who were vending on the temple grounds. I could certainly understand this harsh response because I had noticed several times since my arrival in this time period that buyers and sellers often haggled over the exchange of goods almost to the point of fisticuffs, and this was no place for such confrontations.

Still my friend was nowhere to be found, and I went to sleep that night even more discouraged than the night before.

The next day followed much the same pattern, except for one

very distinct difference. Jesus of Nazareth was once again in the synagogue, but there was no overturning of tables or casting out of salesmen; instead, there was much teaching and debating with him in the middle of the assembly. Although I could not understand a word he was saying, his enthralling carriage was unmistakable. He laid his hands upon several people, offering blessings of some kind to them. There were those who seemed to be poor and wanting, and there were others that appeared to be lame or in the throes of illness. All those folks who came to him went away with renewed vigor and health. I could not fathom how he accomplished that effect on people. He patiently answered questions to the satisfaction of the crowd. He gave himself to all those around him. If I understand history correctly, many quality men have been martyred at the hands of corrupt officials, but I could not for the life of me figure why this man, Jesus, would be earmarked for such an execution.

Taking the time to fix upon the man in the center of the discussion, I discovered a pair of observations I shall attempt to pass on to the reader. The demeanor of the aforementioned Jesus of Nazareth communicated, singularly, a confident purpose. He was a man with a significant mission of some kind. Other than what I know of him from my childhood stories, being ostensibly the Son of God and having a rendezvous with a cross and a martyr's legacy, I got the distinct impression that he had his sights set on a unique target. Secondly, as I observed, there was something winsome about the way he dealt with people. As he interacted with them, both the wealthy and indigent, I discerned his marked compassion and the care he displayed toward those about. All did not share my view, however. Jesus was quite compelling, either one way or the other. There appeared to be no middle ground regarding people's reaction to him. He seemed to be adored by some yet, detested by others. I found this to be odd.

The third day, my companion was yet nowhere to be seen, as the day before. The frustration grew, as did the fear. I wondered which would be worse: running into Druids and mercenaries, dodging Roman guards, or starving to death. Seeing nothing but gloom and abandonment, I had run out of hope and funds. My stomach was telling me of its need to be nourished. The day dragged on with little to write about. I looked all around for Holmes with no results.

Finally by mid-afternoon, being tired, hungry, and broke, I put the hood of my tunic over my head, sat down at the foot of a wall which ran alongside a busy thoroughfare and held out my hand to appeal to the possible good graces of a generous passerby. Being so disposed, I did not particularly care, at this point, about adhering to my friend's command regarding noninterference in this time period. I was penurious and he was not about, anywhere. I became an alms petitioner.

Holmes and I had noticed the disparity in this time period, just like any other I suppose, between the haves and the have-nots. I chose this specific wall to solicit funds because there were, lined up with me, several beggars with what seemed to be much more need than me. I felt a bit ashamed and uncomfortable, looking around and identifying with the neglected and poverty stricken. But, apparently, this was the place of choice for those in want and I was, indeed, in want.

I was not there long before I heard a great uproar coming toward us from the north. A large crowd was on its way to us and I sensed a buoyant hope from my fellow wretches as we held out our hands for money with renewed enthusiasm. As the moving throng approached, I saw that Jesus of Nazareth was at the head. When he passed us beggars, he paused at each one to touch our heads and whisper a short blessing of some kind. Upon his caress I felt immediately revitalized. I looked into his eyes; the connection was unmistakably invigorating, deeply soothing. His followers were there to drop a few coins into my outstretched hand, as they did for the others also in need.

The gravity of my encounter with the Son of God did not come fully home to me until some time later. Being eminently human and in severe want of daily necessities puts a veil over the larger picture and makes it somehow more difficult to apprehend a loftier event such as the one to which I just alluded.

My elation at being now substantially and spiritually provided for was unfortunately short-lived. Directly after the crowd swept through, a brute squad of soldiers followed. They roughed up several beggars, chased more away, and snatched their money.

That, being bad enough, only magnified my worst allowable nightmare. What sight could possibly cause my blood to run even colder than it already was and my baleful fears to be totally realized? There before me, I beheld my darkest dread. Petrified was I to recognize a few familiar faces directing the mercenary soldiers. It was none other than Drumb and his minions, including the one-armed man, Gurralt. They had stubbornly traveled thousands of miles to exact their vengeance on me and my companion.

Joyous at seeing me, Drumb's adrenal gland shifted into unwavering activity. With a menacing scowl, the Arch Druid immediately pulled himself to his full height, which as I mentioned before was formidable, pointed in my direction, growled in his deep, guttural voice, and strode directly toward me. As he advanced, he screeched and stretched his arms, like a peacock spreading his feathers, effectively trebling his size. His commanding carriage and intimidating forcefulness caused everyone around, myself and the soldiers as well, to stop and privately quake in their individual

L. Frank James

footwear. His malevolent delight at approaching me was not comforting. After arriving over me, this giant of a man lost no time in literally lifting me, with one hand, by his incredible strength, off the hard packed ground. Slowly, with the front of my robe gathered up in his cruel, unrelenting, vice-like grip, he hoisted me so that I was at least a full foot off the surface of the earth, suspended, dangling like a child's toy. He held me tightly at the throat, so that I was half choking, for the longest time. The bully wailed at me verbally, spitting in my face and shaking me, while his contorted countenance got even more florid with rage. The revolting stench of garlic on his hot breath did not add to the pleasantness of the experience. I somehow kept my wits about me by being able to continue my deaf and dumb act. Finally, after achieving every terrorizing voice and gesture possible, he relented and threw me like a rag doll at the feet of the mercenaries. I was roughly searched, beaten, grilled, and summarily handed over to the authorities. Money changed hands. I was then conscripted to be a guest in the local prison for an indeterminate period of time. This was a prospect that I feared, but for which I was not prepared and in which I had no desire to partake. What is the cliché, 'out of the frying pan and into the fire'? The reemergence of Drumb offered no comfort to me at all. This cross-continent trek he had made with his entourage was extremely difficult and expensive. I would be running the risk of understating if I were to say the man was tenacious. In fact, I must admit that the newly recognized capabilities of the Arch Druid subsequently caused me to shudder and sleep to flee from me at the very thought of him. Apparently his sphere of influence was greater than my colleague had anticipated; I wondered if Holmes was aware of his presence in Jerusalem.

If there was a good side to the downturn of events, it was the fact that my room and board was now provided. A drafty jail cell and an

166

allotment of swill were my lot in life at present, and the prospects for rescue seemed remote. I was never reviewed nor processed, just rudely collared and tossed into custody. It was not a pleasant experience. I could certainly understand the attitude of the occupied peoples and their resentment of forces beyond their control. It was also significant to note my appreciation for, as inadequate as it might seem at times, our English common law system of justice. Nonetheless, this was where I was and where I was to stay for a while. I was not alone. There were a handful of wretches in the same cell with me. One in particular among us coughed as if he were in the late stages of pneumonia.

Finding a squalid corner and keeping up my deaf mute disguise seemed to be to my advantage, as it excused me from interacting with others. That, coupled with the fact that I could neither speak nor understand the local dialect, removed any pressure to communicate.

For the next two and a half days, I merely existed. Drumb was on the loose and not to be trifled with. If he came this far, he would surely stop at nothing to acquire the contents of the satchel, quash its owner, and exact his revenge. I felt as if, somehow, I had to break out of this prison cell and warn my companion of the impending danger, if he could be found at all. I could devise no method of escape and fell into an even deeper state of despair.

I thought more than once about my friend, Mr. Sherlock Holmes, and his lack of concern over the disposition of his chronicler and colleague, yours truly, Dr. J. H. Watson. In my isolation, I grew increasingly perturbed at his dragging me along on this adventure and then losing me as well. The accommodations, coupled with the dull passage of time, left me in a dismal and dark state of mind. Barely persisting in this subhuman existence was one of the low points of my life. The only joy that my mind could conjure was the fantasy that my traveling companion was detained someplace similar. I found myself, unreasonably, savoring this fancy.

At length, my fellow inmates and I could hear the winds of great moment. The hours slowly unfolded just outside our tiny window. We were incarcerated within the Praetorian complex. Silence fell across our little band of cutthroats and beggars inside, as a multitude collected in the near distance and shouted on several occasions as if orchestrated. Once, I heard the throng shout 'Barabbas!' over and over again; at another time, I heard them crying repeatedly in unison, something that I later found out to translate into 'Crucify him'! The ringing waves of mass voices that did ebb and swell escalated because of the mob-driven frenzy. There were intermittent jeering and clashes, indicating ongoing cycles of the surge and quelling of street unrest.

A detachment of Roman soldiers stormed into the cell complex, then identified and dragged out three of the inmates. Two of the prisoners were struggling and defiant, while the third was scared and quiet. I pitied them all.

Still the hours dragged on. After a long period of silence, a darkness grew over the face of the entire exterior, making it as dark as the blackest night inside our prison. It was difficult to determine the passing of time under such circumstances. There was no Big Ben upon which to rely.

At long last, in the brooding darkness, the earth suddenly shook, as if relieving some timeless agony and bringing forth terror across the fabric of existence. This reminded me of my own small mortality. Upheaval shot through the blackness. An earthquake! The creaking and groaning building in which we were imprisoned swayed back and forth like a massive tree in a great wind. Shards of brick and mortar came down as I covered my head. In the darkness, I heard prisoners scurrying to the bars in fear and hoping to discover a way out of this nightmare, but none was to be had. The earth finally stopped shaking, and there was a long period of silence. At one point, I fancied I heard in the distance the tear of a great cloth being rent; however, being in a preoccupied and confused state of mind, to the reality of that I would not attest.

Nothing was said or done within or without for three more dull days. There was an unmistakable pall in the air, as thick and dense as a dreary layer of black fog clinging to a soggy Hampstead Heath. The sun was not seen through the dank overcast sky. Because of my physical degradation and general depressed disposition, I had by this time fairly resigned myself to my lot in life, not disheartened but rather utterly surrendered. I was wanting of death. I had a dream. I dreamt that a beautiful angelic being was praying for me in front of a glistening crystal altar. I remembered my impression of Miss Hack-berry and the remarkable *Eye-of-God* narration related to me at 221b Baker Street by my companion. The contrast of that celestial image and my present surroundings made me fall into an even deeper depression, if that was possible.

There was little difference between day and night. Sometime during the middle of the third night, a fierce jostling abruptly awak-ened me. The earth was quaking again. I heard a grinding rumble and several sharp metallic poppings as chaos echoed all around. I sat still as tumult abounded. The earthquake seemed to last forever. I covered my head to protect against falling debris and spontaneously prayed for deliverance.

Suddenly I felt the closeness of another human being; I heard the word "Watsonicus!" in not so hushed tones. I was not dreaming.

"The game is afoot! We must hurry!" said the familiar, intense voice.

"Holmes!" I blurted. "Is that you…Where have you been?!"

I did not get the words out of my mouth before he had me up on my feet and dashing out through the fractured door of the cell. Able to see very little, I could feel people skittering everywhere like mice. The guards who were not running away in terror themselves were hopelessly trying to keep the escapees from fleeing. In the confusion, my friend led me quickly out of the complex without Roman interference.

"No time to explain now, dear fellow. I did not fully realize the potential magnitude of the temblor, but it was just the stroke of good fortune that we needed, strong enough to jar open the doors. It was a great probability, Watson, so I was purposefully standing outside the cellblock, attempting to devise a way to acquire your release, when the earthquake occurred. I had to strike the iron, as it were, before it froze!" he shouted, as he dragged me along at a break-neck pace.

I have never known anyone like Mr. Sherlock Holmes when it came to springing into action at a moment's notice. When his trained instincts took over, his energy and initiative were remarkable.

I immediately forgot my woes and my anger toward him while eagerly following him headlong into the night. "You mean to say that you knew the earthquake was going to happen?"

"I had it on good authority," he stated.

Because of my elation at being freed, I dropped that subject for the moment but was not fully satisfied with the answer. We wound our way through some narrow streets.

"But where are we going?" I voiced, as we ran along.

"Not far," he shouted over his shoulder.

"Drumb and his cronies are here. They had me thrown in jail!" I revealed.

"I am painfully aware of his presence in Jerusalem and disappointed in myself for not being constantly on guard. I am also afraid I have allowed myself to be distracted and in turn caused our visit to this time period to be perilously compromised. I hope you will forgive me if we are not ultimately successful in returning to the twentieth century, old man. But right now there is, I determine, a greater, more monumental matter upon which to focus our attention. This, Doctor, is the very object of our quest!"

"I do not much care," I shouted, as I ran after, "for the object of our quest."

He responded, "I do!"

"I want to go home!" I rebutted, as I followed.

"Me, too!" he replied, as he pelted off into the darkness.

9

The Scene of the Crime

*The simple scene I have just described to the devoted reader had the
instant, yet profound, impact of a conspicuously great moment.*

—Dr. J.H. Watson

I had thought more than once on our journey, about the dreaded
possibility of permanent residence here in this time period. However, I had quickly dismissed the notion because I had great faith
in Holmes and his ability to overcome any obstacle that would hin-
der our return to the London of the early twentieth century. But
presently, in his current mental state and judging by the tone of his
voice, I was forced to confront the very real feasibility of that dreadful outcome. I tried, with very little success, to dismiss as unthinkable the idea of living out my life in the first century.

As we continued dashing through the dark labyrinth, I could not
help but think how much more pleasant and fast our excursion
would be if we had a hansom cab at our ready. I ran behind him out

of habit, not will. What would I do without Sherlock Holmes?

Finally skirting a large brooding mound, we circled back to the right behind the hill to discover several frantic Roman soldiers sprinting directly toward us. Even though I could make out only shadows approaching us, the sound of the rattling uniforms gave away the identities of the oncoming hulks. The sound was quite distinctive. It was still quite dark, as there was only half a moon moving in and out from behind the patchy clouds offering a dull on-again and off-again illumination. I braced myself to be set upon by the ferocious half-crazed Roman horde, but to my amazement, they ran right past us. Some terror they had apparently just experienced overrode any sense of duty at that time. I turned around to watch them flee into the night. They seemed to be more afraid of us than we were of them.

"Not too far now, Watsonicus!"

We continued until we came to some large boulders that Holmes immediately started to climb as I followed behind. I was exhausted and experienced a slight case of vertigo. After a short assent, we reached a medium-sized packed-dirt plateau surrounded by large stones.

Even though I was in an emaciated state due to my recent lack of sleep, malnourishment, and incarceration, I had, for some unexplainable reason, energy to spare and went along with little protest. It must have been the excitement of the pursuit, or perhaps the joy of being unexpectedly released by the hands of my friend.

On the far side of the level area was a gaping hole in the side of the sheer rock face. To the right was a path, which wound away through a sparsely wooded plot of land that fell off gradually to our right.

"This is it!" Holmes said, with relish.

He instantly set to work as I have seen him do on so many occasions. Deftly pulling out the satchel he was carrying, he extracted a measuring tape and his magnifying glass as he went to work. At first he paced around the perimeter of the place like a cunning cat about to pounce on some poor unsuspecting prey. I noted some loose rocks around the site, probably there because of the recent earthquake. He had somehow acquired a small oil lamp to aid in his investigation. He delicately moved along, slowly working his way across the level area, stopping often and peering at the ground through his glass while making mental notes. Occasionally he would stop and lie down flat on his stomach to get a closer look, muttering to himself in either triumphant or displeased tones. Using his tape, he carefully measured at certain increments that were a mystery to me. At one point I heard him utter a phrase that sounded like 'herd of buffalo', or some such thing. He brooded over a lifeless mass clinging to the ground left of center. It was a Roman soldier, lying as if dead, off to the side. Holmes gave the body some careful attention. "Out cold!" he whispered loudly.

After a thorough examination of the entire site, he arrived at the sheer rock wall. I could now see, by the dim light of the lamp, that the hole was indeed a cave in the side of the rock face. Off some distance to the left of the opening was a huge round stone that was the same height as the entrance to the cave. Holmes went that direction and took great care to assess the size and heft of the stone and then scrutinized it carefully. It rested on a natural shelf that was elevated above the site. There was a sloped ramp that presumably was used to roll the huge rock down into place in front of the hole in the rock wall. If the stone was at one time covering the cave entrance, I could not imagine how it got back up the incline. Upon finding what appeared to be wrapped about the stone some sort of cord with a large seal of an imprint upon it, he inquired over it extensively. Being satisfied, he stood stock-still, deep in thought, before he turned his attention to the opening itself. He always prided himself in being able to find out much in the details overlooked by others. Peering for the longest time, astutely, over the exterior, he then moved directly to the inside of the hole.

Other than data, at this particular time, I could not detect what his prey might be. Holmes, like a showman, always savored the eccentricities he exhibited while deeply enthralled in the pursuit of his quarry. I have always suspected that he enjoyed the presence of onlookers at such a moment. He rose to the occasion.

My friend was inside the cave for a long time. I could not see him, but I could see the light from within fluctuate with what I presumed to be the throes of his investigation.

At this point, I detected the clouds overhead dissipating, as the faint orange-pink light of dawn continued its ageless pursuit of the night sky.

Finally he came out of the opening and paused there in thought as he snuffed out the lamp.

Without warning, off to the right, we both heard, simultaneously, the shuffle of feet headed our way on the hard packed pathway. This caused Holmes to hurl himself, posthaste, behind a large thick bush to the right of the mouth of the cave. I, as well, hunkered down.

As the sound of people coming closer made itself known, there was a sudden explosion of bright light upon the scene near the opening of the cave. I looked over the top of the rock behind which I was concealed, to see what the cause of such a phenomenon could be, but because of the intensity of the glow, I had to close my eyes and duck down behind my hiding place.

While my eyes adjusted to the influx of light, I lifted my head. The footsteps had arrived on site to indicate the presence of two women carrying baskets.

I count myself to be fortunate, during my span of years in concert with the great detective, that I have been allowed to observe many strange and astonishing sights, but in all my experiences with him, I have never seen such a tableau as presently presented itself. The reader will forgive any seemingly unbelievable aspect of the nature and purpose of the following description. I can only reiterate the excuse that I have given already; I am merely reporting what I saw. Some might consider these described events to be the absurd hallucinations of a recently escaped ex-convict, while others might consider them to be wonderful and exalted, but without there being an accurate recounting of these facts to which I was an eyewitness, no great conclusion can be drawn from this chronicle.

When I lifted my head above the rock behind which I hid, I saw two luminescent, spectral beings hovering atop the round stone. They were conversing with the two petrified women, who were holding baskets, at the entrance to the cave. These two larger-than-life angels, if you will, had on dazzling raiment of an unearthly quality, blazing gold wings, with a sparkling aura about them that seemed to command an automatic respectful awe. Their appearance was like lightning. They were indeed stunning to behold as they floated above the scene like brilliant jewels. If I had wished to speak at that time, it would have been impossible.

There was a small bit of conversation among them, after which the women turned abruptly and fled back down the path from which they came. The ethereal creatures then disappeared instantly before my very eyes. It was amazing.

There ensued a hushed quietude, after which I noticed my colleague slowly coming out from behind the bushes and giving some distracted investigative attention to the immediate area. He had obviously seen the same incredible spectacle I had.

Then directly behind the great detective, appearing from nowhere, was a plainly dressed, bearded man. The mere presence of this man caused my friend to turn and face him squarely. I could not recall, at first, if I recognized the man, but somehow he looked exalted and yet strangely familiar. There was a long moment when Holmes, with an absorbed expression, stared at the man. The man reciprocated with a steady focus. Not an audible word in any language passed between them initially. After what seemed to be the longest time of open-mouthed anticipation, deliberately, my companion went down to his knees and haltingly pushed forward the long fingers of his right hand to touch the foot of the bearded man who stood before him. Once that was accomplished, the man returned the favor and reached out his right hand and placed it on the head of the detective. With deliberate purpose, the bearded man then bent lower and whispered something into the ear of Mr. Sherlock Holmes. That was when it hit me. This was the same man who had blessed me in a similar way as I had, only a few days earlier, been begging for alms in the streets of the ancient city. After this gesture of blessing and without pause, the man pivoted and proceeded right down the path, directly after the women who had recently fled.

The simple scene I have just described to the devoted reader had the instant, yet profound, impact of a conspicuously great moment. The great detective had been face to face with Jesus of Nazareth.

Mr. Sherlock Holmes clinched his hands together and held them to his forehead for a spell. He then reached down his same right hand to the dirt below and, collecting a fist full, held it out and allowed the soil to fall from it like sand through an hourglass.

With new energy he arose with a bounce and turned toward me. I then observed something that I had never seen before. Not only was this a first in the annals of my experience with my companion, but also it was something I never even dreamed of seeing. As he was running in my direction, I could clearly see, in the early light of dawn, that tears of emotion were streaming down his face. I could not discern whether, they were tears of immense joy or profound sorrow, or perhaps a little of both. I was dumfound, to say the least. He was somehow changed, unmistakably. There was a new spirit about him. He then collected himself and shouted, "I am now satisfied, Watsonicus. The mystery is finally solved! We have not a moment to lose!"

I stood up and scrambled down through the rocks to intercept him. When we were joined once more, he grabbed the satchel and replaced in it his instruments of detecting.

As he pushed forward into the early morning light, he announced the following significant news, "I am exceedingly distraught to report to you, my dear fellow, that I have clumsily allowed the time machine crystal to slip through my fingers."

"It's gone?!"

"It has been stolen," he spurted out. "We simply must recover the thing, or we will never see twentieth-century London again. Quickly, follow me!"

I did.

10

THE PURSUIT

No miracles today, Watsonicus.

—MR. S. HOLMES

As the adrenaline from the night's adventure was starting to wear off, I realized how depleted I was in body and soul. Following hard after my companion, whose energy upon such occasions I knew to be boundless, caused me to protest his pace. "Look here, Holmes," I shouted after him. "I am spent from lack of rest and food. Cannot we pause a while and eat?"

"Yes, of course, old man, but only for a brief spell. Sorry about your short stay under the watchful eye of the local constabulary, but by the time I deduced your whereabouts, I had to wait for an opportune moment to spring you. While it was not the best place for you under the circumstances, I discovered the advantages of traveling about freely without a companion for a few days. Here, try this."

He produced from his bag the most delicious honey cakes and

dried meat I had ever eaten and fresh cold water. I ate ravenously and without comment, having no desire at that time to protest his ignorance of my whereabouts. I thought later about his attitude of allowing me to be on a shelf like so many dry goods, but at the moment my joy at being refreshed and reunited with my friend took precedence.

"We cannot linger, Watsonicus. Our quarry may have a two-day head start on us, and he is an extremely tenacious and resourceful sort. I have no doubt he is headed west, and if our prey has gone to Caesarea and then taken to water, we have not a moment to waste. However, if the thief has made a stop in Sidon, that might be to our advantage."

"Whom do we seek?" I inquired, with my mouth full.

"If I am not very much mistaken, Watsonicus, an adroit and persistent person whom we both know. Let us be off!"

"Drumb?" I added.

He was up and away without answering. I followed.

"Is anything missing beside the crystal?" I shouted after him, suddenly going cold over the prospect of Drumb in possession of my service revolver.

"No, Watsonicus, fortunately, but we must not dally!"

It was about a fifty-mile trip to Caesarea, which we made with very little waste of time. I did get a chance to recover physically as we traveled over half the way on a small tumbrel cart loaded with sacks of fodder. I did not complain, however, because I was only too glad to be able to sleep along the way in spite of being nestled in among the bags of coarse roughage. At least we were on dry land. My emotions were mixed. I felt pleased about the prospect of heading westward, back toward the time machine, but distressed about not having the essential key to work the thing.

I noticed that my friend was once again in the money. He dipped into his coin purse to locate the necessary fare for the driver.

"How did you come by this swag?" I asked.

"This," he said, holding up the moneybag of coins, "I have always had, Watsonicus. This was the bag of loot I held back for our return trip. It is very good fortune indeed that the brigands we ran into on our way here did not discover it tied securely 'round my waist belt. Be prepared, my dear fellow. That is always my credo."

We finally arrived in Caesarea, a man-made seaport. There were few natural harbors on this end of the Mediterranean, so the Roman authorities had a protective breakwater built out from the sandy beach. I dreaded any mention of an ocean voyage, but my companion assured me that with the coming of summer, the sea lanes were safe from storms once more.

After several inquiries, Holmes found a ship that was bound to Sidon on the Syrian coast. It was leaving soon, so we boarded immediately.

"I believe we are on the correct trail, Doctor, but we cannot assume that our thief is doddering along, whistling a joyous tune of victory."

"You know who the scoundrel is, then?" I asked, thinking I knew the answer.

"I have my suspicions, Watsonicus, but I will keep them to myself for the time being until I am certain. I will tell you this: I had the feeling for some time that we were being followed. I let my guard down for an instant while in Jerusalem, and this is the result. Never allow me to become so self-satisfied and distracted again, Doctor."

I nodded my head in the affirmative.

From Sidon, we sailed on, around to the north of Cyprus, to Myra. From Myra, we went to Patara and then on past Rhodes to the city of Cnidus. At every port, Holmes made inquiries which met with the same result. We apparently were not making up ground on our quarry. I wondered how far, by now, Drumb was ahead of us or even if we were going in the right direction. I could not imagine, besides the Druid, who else the thief could be. I reasoned that it had to be someone who had witnessed the battle of the magicians back in the Druid circle and believed that all of Sherlockodies' power lay in the crystal itself. Or would Drumb hire one of his Druids or a highwayman or someone else to do his dirty work? I could only speculate.

Holmes asked around with his usual questions and came to a decision. Because the weather continued to be fair and he was in fear of falling further behind, Holmes decided to head out to open sea and Crete.

"We must attempt to duplicate the trail left by our robber—at least as nearly as possible, Watsonicus. I just hope and pray we can make up some time on the rascal."

Since the sun was out and the sky was clear, we had a favorable wind and the water was smooth. I began to grow fond of sea travel. It was much easier than traveling by land, so with a ready concurrence from me, we sailed to the cape of Salmone. Once I had recovered from a slight case of seasickness, it was quite pleasant. That was, of course, until the storm occurred.

We were onboard an Egyptian vessel with a cargo of grain bound from Myra to Italy. Because of its heavy load and the two hundred and twenty passengers on board, the ship made headway with difficulty. We rounded the Cape of Salmone and made our way to Fair Havens on the southern coast of Crete without incident. Fair Havens was not a suitable port for anchorage, so with a gentle southwesterly zephyr, we headed west.

While we were attempting to stay near the shore, a tempestuous wind called a 'nor-easter' struck down from the sky. When the ship was caught and could not face the wind, we gave way to it and were driven miles off course, due south of the port of Phoenix on the southern coast of Crete. The sailors managed to get the ship momentarily under control, into the protected lee of a small island called Cauda. Fearing that we might be blown toward the dreaded shallows off the North African coast, they lowered the sails, but still we were driven south and westward. In order to lighten the load, the able-bodied crew began to dump cargo overboard the very next day.

The violent storm continued for two weeks without a single day of remission. We had not a clue as to where we were being blown. When there was some suspicion that land might be near, the sailors threw out the sea anchors and tried to hold on. The ship had been taking on water, but with the help of all on board, we were able to stave off the threat of sinking. There was some talk of abandoning ship, and if it were not for the calming leadership of Holmes and a few of the crew, all would have been lost.

The levelheaded among us persevered in hope of a cessation of the tempest. In the deep of the night, I fixed my gaze upon a remarkable sight. I espied Mr. Sherlock Holmes down in the hold alone, clutching a railing to steady himself. He was in a kneeling position and appeared to be praying, perhaps for the welfare of all on board. Dawn came and with it, a clear break in the storm. We could now see the coast of Malta not too far off our port side. The sight engendered great relief in all on board.

Holmes insisted on not pausing in Malta but immediately booked us on a vessel headed north to Syracuse and beyond, up the western coast of Italy.

On we went. At a port of call near Rome, acknowledging my entreaty, we proceeded inland and continued on dry terra firma, retracing our steps back through the capital city and then on toward the northwest. Holmes was, once again, a man on a mission. I had had enough of sea travel for a good long while. It felt pleasant to walk on Mother Earth, no matter what century it was.

My companion seemed to be leading us back to our landing point in this century. I could not fully see what the object of our journey could be. What would we accomplish in Londinium or at the time machine without the crystal? With every inquiry along the way, Holmes became more agitated and preoccupied as we continued to travel with insensate speed toward the west. There was a palpable sense that the trail pursued was not encouraging to my friend.

Day and night, by the fastest means available, Holmes drove on. He grew even more somber. I knew, from experience, in times like this it was best to leave him to himself.

"A sturdy brougham propelled by a pair of fit steeds would stand us in good stead, eh, Watsonicus?" he offered.

"I could not agree more," I concurred.

Days passed into weeks, as the trek turned dreary and dull with the sameness of pace. The reader will forgive me, at this point, for leaving out the details of the travel. Falling into a regimen of little sleep, moving by any means available, eating and back to sleep again made me dull of consciousness. It had the effect of blending the passing days together into what one might refer to as a blur. Certainly, the novelty of the journey had worn off at this juncture. We had stopped at a hostel in central Gaul for a few hours of sorely needed rest when my companion awakened me with a gleeful look in his eyes.

"The scent is fresh, Watsonicus. I interviewed the innkeeper and found him to be most illuminating. A man fitting the description of our suspect scurried through here not more than a day and a half ago. Up, man, we have not a moment to lose," Holmes stated.

With renewed vigor, my friend took up the scent, not unlike old Toby himself. Across the countryside we flew, leaving no available means of transport unused. From oxcart to riding donkeys bareback, we made the sort of time that allowed us to arrive on the northern coast of Gaul at an opportune moment.

Holmes had been, with increasing anticipation, expecting the appearance of someone or something up ahead of us. Every time we turned a corner to reveal a new section of the roadway before us, he would crane his head and squint his eyes in hopeful anticipation. As we came to a stretch of gently rolling grassy hills, we heard the distant sound of pounding waves.

Running toward the edge of the cliff, we arrived to look down upon a sandy cove. In this small lonely part of what would someday be called the Normandy Coast, we spied a tiny boat with two men at the ready, about to set sail through the light surf. I had expected to see Drumb with his minions, but instead I looked for the longest time at the men who dotted the otherwise deserted beach without the least recognition. One of them anxiously looked up to scan the top of the seawall and then stood perfectly still when his gaze came upon us. When he reached one hand, which was holding something I could not tell, above his brow to shield his eyes from the sun, I could now see that he hadn't another. He started to jump up and down, shouting wildly and kicking the sand in front of him. Suddenly he became known to me. It was none other than our one-armed guide and captain, Gurralt, who had conducted us down the Thames River to the English Channel on the first part of our journey toward Jerusalem. I now could see he held aloft in his only hand the crystal for the time machine. It was the same hand that had played the pipe so sweetly.

"I thought as much, Watson! We have not an instant to waste!"

Holmes immediately began to scramble down the tall embankment, while I followed hard at his heels. By the time we descended to the edge of the beach, my companion and I could see that the one-armed man and his confederate had hurriedly cast off and were by now well out beyond the shore break of waves.

"Blast!" my friend bellowed. "Quickly, Watson, we must find a launch!"

I lagged behind as he ran toward the west around a small point of land looking for a vessel of some sort. In retrospect, I was glad that under the pressure of the event he had dropped the moniker of 'Watsonicus.'

As fortune would have it, not too far around the aforementioned point of land was a little fishing enclave. Since it was the midday hour, there were a few heavy, open fishing boats at ease on the sandy shore. One in particular, a two-masted long boat, attracted the attention of my friend. There were three stout fishermen alongside, attending to their nets. I could see my friend speedily negotiating their services by wildly gesticulating and waving coins in their faces. By the time I arrived, the deal had been consummated, the nets had been abandoned, and the launch of the vessel was underway. I jumped on board as the waves began to lap up onto the gunwale.

The solidly built vessel we found ourselves in was weighty and awkward, but the three able-bodied seamen who attended the sails were well up to the task of handling the thing. Although the bulk of our boat and the weight of the cargo were hindrances, it was more than made up for by the amount of sheet we could lay to the wind.

With its double mast configuration, the boat was fast and proved that Holmes had made a good selection when it came to a suitable pursuit vehicle.

The crew laid to it very hard, considering they did not know the object of their voyage. They seemed to be caught up in the enthusiasm of the moment. As we sailed beyond the breakers, Holmes continued to wildly exhort their vehement efforts as he pointed northeast and drove them forward. With the sails completely deployed, the speed of the trawler dramatically increased.

On we sailed toward the general area of what Holmes thought to be our quarry's direction. The wind was capricious, but the deft handling of the sheets by the crew maximized our pace. It was somewhat encouraging to realize that Gurralt's boat was using the same wind that we were.

At the rise of every swell, we scanned the horizon looking for a dot upon the white-capped sea.

"Estimating the head start he has on us and his presumed destination, one would calculate the direction of our pursuit to be that way!" Holmes shouted, pointing across the Channel, as the wind seemed to shift to the north at his statement.

The devoted reader will be reminded, naturally, of the nautical pursuit I chronicled in the adventure of *The Sign of Four*. Whereas in that case, the boilers were stoked to the utmost, nearly to the point of explosion, in this case, the masts and sails were put to the test without a care for anything but the object of the chase. Once we got further out to the open water, the wind increased and we drove hard on. The vessel creaked and groaned under the strain of full sails and a running wind. The salty spray of the English Channel drenched us with stinging force. I held on for dear life as every wave threatened to throw me overboard.

Holmes' keen eyes were riveted to the horizon as he leaned forward, looking for the least sign of the boat ahead of us. With every rise of the sea, we refreshed ourselves with a new expectant gaze. The afternoon was clear and the sun was high as we cut through the billows with pitching pace. In the far distance ahead of us was the evidence of a low-laying fog bank that made me think of a familiar heavy London soup.

After a protracted period of time, I looked back to spy, behind us, the Continent disappearing rapidly from view.

All at once, I heard the voice of the great detective, which caused me to turn my head around.

"There he is!" Holmes shouted into the air. "And going like the devil! I shall never forgive myself if that boat of his proves to have the heels of us! Put everything into it, boys!"

Upon the crew's spotting the target, there was noisy chatter and a renewed effort. The trawler seemed to fly along the top of the water.

"We have twice the sail of him, lads. I only hope we can reach him before that cloud bank closes," Holmes added.

With one of the crew at the tiller and the other two trimming the sheets, we advanced on our thief with steady drive. I could now see the little scoundrel skittering about the tiny boat like a caged nervous rodent, jerking and jumping up and down for want of speed.

Slowly yet surely, we gained on him. I saw him paddling with his one hand and blowing into the sail as if these efforts would aid in his progress. Rapidly we advanced, as the bank of clouds was retreating before us but at a slower rate. On we drove, relentlessly bobbing up and down while thrusting forward, being battered with the piercing spray of the Dover Strait. I remember no seasickness at this juncture.

Gurralt's boat began to enter the foggy mass that was being mixed up and scattered by the brisk, forcing breeze. We were, by this time, almost to his aft. I was fearful of two distinct possibilities: one, that the mass of the thick mist would obscure and hide our prey, thus causing us to lose him; or two, that we would inadvertently ram the stern of the small craft, and that could possibly lead to the loss of man and treasure. Neither prospect was very attractive. We were close enough now to catch the wind and prevent it from filling the sails of the one-armed man's boat, which infuriated him even further.

Instead of either of my imagined possibilities, Holmes quickly and accurately motioned the crew to pull up alongside the slower boat. They accomplished this with a singular coordinated swoop of the tiller and luff of the sails.

Without hesitation, my companion doffed his heavy tunic, and wearing nothing but a loincloth, sprang over at least six feet of open sea to land on the deck of the nearby boat. Gurralt had picked up the crystal and clutched it out over the water on the far side of the craft. The detective was on him in an instant. Holmes with his two good arms got the better of him, but the younger, wiry raftsman was not to be easily taken. There was an agonizing struggle, which all of us observed for a time. The feeling, by all indications, was that the hirelings should let the primary parties fight it out without interference. Back and forth the two of them went on grappling while trying to maintain their balance on the pitching sea. Then, coming to my senses, I thought about trying to help my friend by entering the fray. I attempted to communicate to the crew to pull up closer to the other boat so I could board her and come to the aid of my cohort.

While the crew cast a rope toward the tiny boat, the sea heaved, catching the two wrestlers off guard. There was a large splash as they lost their balance and went over the side, clutching the prize in unison.

They came up for what was a brief, torrid contention of flailing limbs and splashing bubbles on the surface. After gulping for precious breath, they went down again. Both of them disappeared below, as the water above came together and erased any evidence of their existence or struggle.

The notion of time became worthless.

A thousand thoughts rushed through my brain as I stood transfixed looking into the sea. I could not move. Not knowing what to do, I did nothing. Was this, then, to be the final chapter in the life of the great detective? Was his last adventure to be left unrecorded for all of posterity? Was this mystery to end the way it started, in a watery shroud with no hope of rescue but by the hand of God? Was I ever to see my friend, my wise and trusted counselor, again? Would I ever see London again?

Still there was no sign of them. Surely, I thought, they would bounce up into the air at any instant. I remembered the lovely, lilting pipe-playing of the one-armed musician and what a contrast it was to the present scene. Perhaps God did not wish to interfere in the affairs of man this time. Perhaps God felt presumed upon and wanted no part of this ugly display of human folly and greed.

I tore off my tunic, took hold of a rope, and was just about to enter the cold water of the Dover Strait when suddenly my friend burst forth, breaking the surface of the water near the bow of our craft, with the crystal triumphantly in his grip. As he threw the prize on board, I shouted loudly, "You have it, man! You've got the crystal!"

Without hesitation, the detective took a deep gasp of air and sputtered, "Yes, but now I must get Gurralt!" Breathing deeply again, he went under.

After the longest time, Holmes, alone, finally came up out of the water totally spent and clutched the side of the bobbing boat while regaining his strength and composure. The one-armed man was nowhere to be seen.

"No miracles today, Watsonicus," he voiced at last, before he climbed on board.

11

The Effect

Mr. Sherlock Holmes' face contorted with harsh
memory as he continued his singular narration.

—Dr. J. H. Watson

With the wind directly behind us and the bank of clouds scattering before us, Holmes directed the crew to make for the shore of Briton. What a difference in travel time does a favorable breeze make. He was brooding in contemplation the rest of the voyage, as well as the entire remainder of the journey. As I have said before, this was not unfamiliar territory. He would often bask in a pensive mood for days on end, and once again, under such circumstances he was best left to himself.

I finally inquired, "Do you suppose that Gurralt was working on his own, or was Drumb behind the whole attempt?"

"I cannot imagine that simple Gurralt, on his own, would have the resources for such a pursuit; he must have had a backer. And if it is the likes of Drumb, you can be assured that he is not far behind. We must not linger, Watson," he forged on.

The ensuing trek back to the machine was rapid but uneventful. Finding the mouth of the Thames and working our way back upstream, walking or via the floating raft relay system, to which I alluded earlier in this narrative, seemed to be anticlimactic.

"We do not belong in this time, Watson. When all is said and done, I am afraid we might have irreverently interfered with issues beyond ourselves and of great moment quite enough, if not too much. I can only hope and pray that what we have precipitated will not alter the course of history to the least degree."

After some contemplation, I was inclined to agree with him.

Holmes looked behind and ahead, not being sure of the source or location of his concern. Arriving in Londinium, we barely paused to rest before we inexorably made our way down that small dirt path, through the bush, to relocate the time travel device. We barely somehow managed to avoid a squad of heavily armed troopers. Holmes had paused to collect a clay container of water from the river. This was above and beyond the skins of water we had for our personal use.

"What is that for?" I inquired.

"Just in case we need it to rejuvenate the battery that is, no doubt, onboard the machine," he responded.

Holmes' sense of direction and orientation was flawless. Maneuvering our way through the undergrowth, we found the goodly sized, familiar clearing with a huge, ashen fire pit in the center. There was, fortunately, no one about; it was the middle of the day. Walking through one of the large stone archways on the perimeter of the circle, we could not see the time machine anywhere. We paused to notice a pile of neatly organized rocks obscuring something on the other side. It looked like an altar. Clearing away some of the stones, we discovered the time travel device to be intact and untouched, except for a family of voles that had made a home on the floorboard of the vehicle.

"The Druids have apparently encased the vehicle with this rock structure as a ritual base or shrine of some sort. This is good, Doctor, as it served to protect the transport from the curious. Let us get to work," Holmes stated calmly.

A little over ten months, by our time keeping, had transpired since we had been at this very location in stunned disbelief. Now, desperately weary of travel, we removed most of the rocks, cleaned out the device and wordlessly climbed onboard, knowing that we needed to get back home as soon as we could. We had removed our tunics and donned our now rumpled and moldy twentieth-century clothing, in preparation for our arrival in the future. Pulling the crystal out of the bag caused Holmes to ponder the object for a heavy moment. Then fixing it into the appropriate socket, he took a deep breath and moved the levers. Nothing happened.

The detective tried the levers again and still nothing. He looked for and discovered a small door under the seat that, once opened, revealed a battery housing.

Upon inspection, he explained, "It is certainly a good thing for us that all the water had not yet evaporated, Watson. However, I should not imagine that much power is needed to activate the device."

After replenishing the reservoir, he replaced the battery and then tried the levers for a third time. Nothing happened.

What occurred next immediately drew our attention. It was the sudden appearance of a winded Drumb, two blue-hood Druids, and some mercenary soldiers storming through the pillars on the opposite side of the clearing. The imposing Arch Druid looked at us in stunned, wide-eyed shock. He twisted his head as he gulped for air. They, apparently, had been running for some great distance. After a brief pause of disbelief, Drumb screamed a horrifying cry and charged forward, brandishing a substantial hand-held club and grasping at the air with the other hand. The two blue-hoods followed with equal élan. The troopers stayed back, unsure of the opposition. This was more than just a now-or-never for Drumb; this was, for him, a gesture of unrestrained avarice. His greed for power, prestige, riches, and revenge drove him to pursue the Greek scholar, Sherlock-odies, and the magic crystal across the civilized world and back again. This was no small undertaking.

Without a pause while opening the satchel, the great detective removed the small oil lamp that he had used to cast a light upon the scene of the aforementioned great mystery, and hastily poured a few drops of oil onto the crystalline structure. Drumb was leading the Druid charge and was almost upon us when Holmes moved the levers.

There was a low, dull hum that emanated from the innermost parts of the device. From that subtle indicator, the machine reluctantly growled to life. There was, once again, a swirling haze that dazzled around us as the sense of falling forward reminded us to brace ourselves for the return ride.

At that exact moment, Drumb leaped over the cairn of rocks, grasped through the whirlwind and the framework of the device, and found the throat of Holmes. His empty hand hit its mark and clutched firmly at the detective's neck. Most of the Druid's massive right arm was inside the sphere created by the vortex, while the rest of his body was outside. The time machine attempted to speed forward as my friend refused to abandon the controls. There was a strained eternity during which neither man would relent, as the two adversaries matched their wills. Drumb, with a maniacal facial expression and gnarled hand, clutched for all his capacity at my companion's throat. This was in sharp contrast to Holmes' doggedly attempting to force the levers forward.

While the wrestling, between the two seemed to last forever, it was, in reality, a brief instant of time spent with neither man giving quarter. Then, suddenly, overcome by choking at the hand of the Arch Druid, the great detective began to swoon and abandoned the controls of the time vehicle as we came to an abrupt halt. With the smell of victory in the air, Drumb's vigor increased, and out of exaltation I suppose, he began to bash the framework of the time machine with his club. He vocally emitted the most macabre noise I have ever heard. The sound was somewhere between an otherworldly banshee and a gruesome hair-raising demonic wolf. Holmes could not loosen his opponent's iron grip. My companion's desperate struggle caused me to spring into unmeditated action. Without thinking, I grabbed at the strong right arm of the Arch Druid and found his remarkable grasp to be robust and immovable. Quickly, before the other druids were upon us, I let go of Drumb's arm, lunged for the control lever and pushed it forward. The time travel device jolted to life once again. The swirling haze vortex returned, as the machine lurched into the future. The momentum of the battle immediately shifted, while the expression on the face of the Arch Druid suddenly changed from victorious to totally defeated. He dropped the club from his other hand and grabbed at the opposite shoulder, jerking his bloody, nearly severed right arm back into his own time. For a split second, as the speed of the vehicle increased, we saw the twisted frame of the Arch Druid writhing on the ground in agony. His body could not tolerate being in two time periods at once. Something had to give; he lost his arm. A bizarre thought crossed my mind. I wondered if the number of one-armed men in the first century had to remain constant. As one ceased to exist, another one was formed. I will have forever chiseled on my memory that image of Drumb in absolute failure and ultimate pain. After an instant, the Druids and the detachment of guards disappeared, and then the large stone structures vanished. Time rushed ahead.

As Holmes recovered his composure, he cleared his throat and took command of the levers. He shouted above the din of the machine, "Watson, my dear fellow, you have saved us from a premature end!" Feeling the effects of motion sickness again, I did not have the will or desire to bask in his praise. He continued, "I shall be forever in your debt." I thought at that moment that it was only fitting, considering the number of times he had saved my neck.

This journey forward through time was, of course, the opposite of the trek already described earlier in this strange account. As we gained speed, ahead we could see the history of the immediate area come to life in a lapse of time that defied context. Villages and civilization grew around us as we bumped up and down in a haze of streaming natural and man-made cycles. Picking up speed, I could see my friend diligently at the controls, regarding the dials, carefully monitoring our progress through the centuries.

On we went as through the mist we could see the great city of London spring up around us. I was greatly anticipating our arrival back to the comforts of modern life and was gladly willing to leave the characters Drumb and Watsonicus behind.

Our object house materialized around us when Holmes slowed our forward progress. The laboratory again surrounded us as a tarpaulin once more obscured our view for an instant. We arrived precisely when he desired.

"If I am not very much mistaken, Watson, we are here approximately twenty minutes before we ever left, ten months ago by our time keeping," Holmes whispered, as he lit a match. "Quickly, let us be on our way."

I glanced at my pocket watch, and in the dull light, I could discern that the second hand was not moving. The workings were frozen in time, as it were. Perhaps it was due to neglect on my part, or maybe, to the abuse played upon it by time itself. I could not remember the last time I had attended to the piece with a good winding.

We removed and replaced the tarpaulin over the smoldering machine as we disembarked. Holmes placed the crystal device back onto the workbench but paused to contemplate.

"I wonder, Watson, if we might not retain the crystal against the advent of some sort of unforeseen necessity? Or perhaps it would be best in our hands to prevent any possible further defilement of history at the hand of a wrongdoer? And what about the future, is that a proper purview for mere mortals like ourselves?"

Holmes' questions were cut short by the realization that the house was coming to life. We again heard the dull thud of foot treads sounding from upstairs.

"Never mind, man, leave it. We must be off," Holmes murmured. Out of the house we flew, retracing our steps of ingress.

Once out onto the night streets of twentieth-century London, we strolled through the mist with silent wonder, if I may speak for my friend as well as myself. I could not determine which environment was more surreal, the one in which we found ourselves presently or the one from which we came. I was numbed to the process of evaluation. Through the fog, we heard approaching footsteps. Holmes pulled me aside to hide among the shadows on the opposite side of the road. Silently we stood vigil as the noise of approaching feet grew louder. We saw through the mist passing from our right to our left a bizarre sight. We saw ourselves, skulking toward the house that contained the time machine, about to embark on the investigation of a lifetime.

"Strange, indeed, Watson. My calculations seem to be about twelve minutes off," Holmes uttered.

"Those two have quite an adventure to look forward to, I would say."

"I, as well," my friend responded.

Exhausted, we spent the rest of the night at 221b Baker Street. I woke up late the next morning to resume my normal practice after, of course, a wonderful complete breakfast presented by Mrs. Hudson. I savored every bite. The marmalade was exquisite. Mrs. Hudson was bewildered at our appearance; she turned and walked away, speechless. A hot bath, a shave, and a brisk haircut, together with fresh clothing, made me appreciate the likes of modern London as never before. I refuse to ever complain again.

While Holmes immediately returned to his country home, it took me some days, naturally, to regain my regular regimen as well as my composure. In some ways, I fell back into the routine without skipping a beat, but in other areas the recent adventures weighed upon me to a ponderous extent. Forgive me for excerpting the Bard, but the distinct feeling that time was out of joint governed my every moment both awake and asleep. Those around me said I seemed distracted or preoccupied. They were, of course, correct. I desired, several times, to communicate with my friend but felt deeply that I needed time alone to attempt to make sense of it all. I was profoundly changed by this most recent adventure, but I did not know why.

It was about one month later when I received a telegram from my companion, requesting my company for the weekend at his place down in the Sussex Downs, a request to which I eagerly responded in the affirmative.

Closing early on Friday and catching the train from Victoria south, I arrived at the country home of the world's most famous consulting detective. I was just in time for a pleasant, late afternoon walk down to the sea and a sumptuous meal of roast mutton and new potatoes. It was during the walk on the sandy beach that my friend and I stood gazing out, silently, onto the placid body of water in front of us. I paused there for a portion of time, deep in thought, reflecting on recent events and our momentous encounter with the forces of nature and humankind. The vast plain of blue-brown water made me glad to be on dry land. In one very real sense, the happenings of not so long past, juxtaposed to the serene seascape that presently captured my attention, evoked a feeling of dreamlike distance and a slowing down of motion and incident. I was greatly moved, by what and toward what I could not say. It struck me that, perhaps, it was the very ephemeral nature of existence.

After our evening repast, we sat in front of a comfortable fire for a while in silence. I marked that Mr. Sherlock Holmes appeared a full ten years younger.

Holmes broke the taciturn stillness by taking his pipe from between his lips and making some weighty remarks, the subject of which had been heavy on my mind. He, as always, had a way of cutting through the cryptic and strange and turning them into commonplace.

"Have you had an opportunity to put any thought into our most lately occurring investigation, Doctor?"

"I have thought of little else, actually, but I will admit that the significance of this adventure escapes me. Traveling through time naturally seems like such an absurd recreation," I replied.

"Hardly a recreation, my dear fellow, but rather a means to an end."

"But to what end?"

"I wish it to be clearly noted," he indicated, "that this latest case of ours is not merely an adventure, as you have labeled most of our efforts in the past, but rather a quest. The difference being this: an adventure tends to be a diversion to occupy one's mind for amusement, while a quest, if you will allow, is a potentially life-changing search of a more epic, moral proportion. And if you will further allow, Watson, it occurs to me that this quest of ours has made necessary some diligent application of brainpower in attempting to put into cogent order the happenings to which we have recently been a party. After all, there is a universal utterance inside each of us that tells us something is amiss...and consistently we are driven to find the answers to that sense of defect." He suspended his thought for a moment before he added, "I am perpetually reminded of the nature of people when it comes to the fascination we have for a mystery. In the not too distant future, I intend to write a brief monograph on the subject matter. Mankind has an innate compulsion to discern clues from that which is around him and follow those telltale hints to their logical conclusions. It is fascinating, is it not? Folks have a curious longing to solve a mystery and find out the truth."

"Please continue," I said, getting him back on track.

"Yes, of course. First of all, you will remember that I was prompted by a singular case, the *Mystery of the Eye-of-God*, in which I was rescued in miraculous fashion from the depths of the Thames River. I have thought since, many times, of the precious Miss Hackberry and felt certain of her continuing prayers for me.

"Secondly, this challenged me to establish, to my own contentedness, the notion of a Creator–God as the grand architect of all that is seen and all that is invisible. As much as I wanted to believe in an accidental universe, I could not deny the structured pattern of everything that I observed and knew to be true. Can you imagine, Watson, wandering into the library of the British Museum to survey the immense number of volumes of science, philosophy, and knowledge so carefully catalogued and documented, and then believing that their arrangement and existence is one big fluke of time and chance? It is unthinkable. Humankind is more accurately explained by that which is higher than us, as opposed to the order of species that is lower. At least I was firmly persuaded to embrace the working assumption that a remarkable designer was the genesis of us and the cosmos. With that solidly in place, you will also recall that I seized the opportunity to research the extant historical record of the times and places surrounding the significant personage known as Jesus Christ. Is this Jesus of history truly the only emissary from God, and is he intimate with us? Thirdly, going back in time as an eyewitness, I analyzed the person of Jesus of Nazareth himself, and then, lastly, I investigated firsthand the occurrence of his alleged resurrection. All of these things, I might add in retrospect, I explored to my personal satisfaction and to a standard of investigative quality, you will observe, that far surpasses any casual glance at the issue. After all, in an American court of law, while trying a grave case involving a capital crime, the judge clearly instructs the jury to make its decision based on evidence that is beyond a reasonable doubt. The highest stakes possible, life and death, Watson, are judged by proof that is merely beyond a reasonable doubt. I put forward to you that the physical testimony I have exposed during this investigation clearly goes beyond that criteria and into the realm of virtual certainty. I have no doubt."

"I would not expect you to be satisfied with anything less."

"Indeed. I also have had opportunity to study, firsthand the ancient belief systems of Rome, Greece, and the Druids. You will, furthermore, take notice and be pleased to learn that I have reached a significant conclusion," Holmes appended, "Hume was wrong, Doctor, cause and effect are operational in the seen as well as the unseen arenas. The happenings of yestrerday impact us today and those who will follow us tomorrow."

"You have my undivided attention," I interjected seriously, as I leaned forward.

"Are the biographies and evidences of Jesus accurate both in the historical context as well as the spiritual realm? Is there a Jesus of history or a Jesus of faith? Are they both one and the same?"

"I have wondered that myself," I said.

"Besides our own subjective encounter with Christ, there are extensive secular writings, Watson, outside the primary sources of Holy Writ, that would lead one to an easy conclusion of the very real historical existence of the person, Jesus of Nazareth. Many ancient non-Christian sources, such as Josephus, make that abundantly clear."

Holmes continued, "With my studied knowledge of the indigenous languages, which I might add was surprisingly satisfactory, I gleaned much by a close scrutiny of the very words out of the mouth of Jesus, himself. As I listened closely to what he said and compared it to the written record, I discovered the Bible to be, indisputably, completely reliable. In fact, my dear fellow, you can be entirely at ease with the reality that his words were recorded by the writers of the New Testament with stunning accuracy. Word for word, as precise as any translation from one language to another can be."

"Remarkable!" I said.

"Quite. Given the span of time from the first century to the seventeenth, it can be accounted for only by divine inspiration."

Holmes had a penchant for stating his conclusions without equivocation.

The detective was on a roll as he pressed forward, "But what of his claims to divinity?"

"Yes," I spouted. "I will have to grant you that Jesus of Nazareth really existed, for I cannot deny my own eyes. That there was something extraordinarily winsome about him, I am also not willing to dismiss, for I have experienced it myself when he touched me. I will also grant you that he was in possession of some exceptional spiritual awareness, which he was, for some reason, willing to pass on to others. However, can you assert that he is anything more that just a good and wise teacher?"

"I defy you, Watson, to deduce from any source, including the words out of his own mouth, that Jesus of Nazareth was merely a good and wise teacher, without me from that very same source being able to disprove that he is simply that and no more."

"I do not quite follow you," I said.

"From what sources have you heard that Jesus is just a good and wise teacher?"

"Well, I have never given the notion much thought. I suppose from...people with theological authority...teachers, scholars, ministers...from thoughts and ideas passed down through the generations...Bible stories...common sense, really, a collection of information," I replied.

"People with theological authority also identify him as one of the Holy Trinity, teachers and scholars ascribe to him a special spiritual status far beyond the commonplace, ministers call him the Son of God, tradition has it that he sits in heaven at the right hand of God the Father, the Bible states that he is **the** only way to acquire eternal life and common sense assures us that he is unique."

"And so?" I inquired.

"His very words and deeds would lead almost anyone to conclude that he is possessed of wisdom and insight beyond the norm. Yet his very same words and deeds, as I have heard for myself, also axiomatically include his divinity and supernatural power. One should not claim one notion without entertaining the other. The evidence simply, does not allow for it. He said at one point that we are to do unto others the things that we would wish to be done unto us, a golden rule to which virtually everyone ascribes. However, he also claimed—I understood him quite distinctly—to be the way, the truth, and the life and that no one comes to the Father except through Him, the very Son of God. You will admit that that sort of exclusiveness is rather uncompromising, Watson. I believe it becomes intellectually unfair and illogical to whimsically pick and choose the phrases that are to one's own liking, while rejecting the others. It is much like a recalcitrant child who, upon the admonition of a parent, hears and acts only upon the instructive words he wishes to hear and act upon. The willful child has selective hearing, and he blithely ignores the unappealing advice but grasps eagerly the ideas that are to his own liking. He hears what he wants to hear and does what he wants to do, very often to his own detriment."

"Very well. I see your point, but I am not totally convinced. What of those stunts of his? Were they real, or were those so-called miracles he performed some sort of sleight of hand or prearranged ploy to evoke a following for a self-serving aggrandizement?" I asked.

"If that were so, then of course, the whole movement would never have stood the test of time. Jesus made the statement that he would rise from the dead after being entombed for three days. If he was a fake and he knew himself to be a fake, things would have turned out differently. Once he made the fatal miscalculation of allowing himself to die at the hands of the Roman authorities and there was no resurrection, his followers, realizing they had backed the wrong horse, as it were, would have dissipated out of fear for their own lives. They would have known that he was a fraud. But the fact of the matter is that almost all of Jesus' disciples died martyrs' deaths, true in faith to the very end. They faced tortures and executions for their beliefs, and yet they did not betray their master. One might certainly die for the truth. One might also willingly die for a lie, if one believes it to be true, but not for a lie that one knows to be a lie. There is a difference. That is a result, if history is to be our instructor, which never occurred. Instead, the storied facts of the advent of Jesus and his faithful followers remain the most enduring testament of the ancient world, not to mention the resulting effect upon mankind of such a legacy down through the centuries."

"I suppose your argument is well taken, but what if his legacy, as you call it, is based on madness? What if his power to perform incredible acts of healing, for example, was a result of a delusional transfer of self-will from an insane practitioner to an eagerly willing disordered recipient? The human mind, with all its properties, both material and spiritual, is after all, a powerful and mysterious entity," I rejoined.

"This, of course, is why I chose to investigate the conundrum myself. I would willingly respond to your question by alluding to the result of the inquiry, in the outcome of which there can be no doubt. Having the same questions as you, my dear fellow, and discovering the answers empirically and objectively, I rendered the problem soluble. Nothing less would do. I was there, Doctor. While you were in the safekeeping of the Roman guard, I followed Jesus quite closely.

At this statement, I shot forth, "Yes, how in the world did you know that I was in prison, anyway?"

"While following Christ, I saw you sitting beside the city wall, begging for alms. You obviously did not notice me within the throng because I was disguised as a Cypriot olive oil merchant. However, I was most gratified to espy you. You looked quite dejected. Naturally, being relieved to relocate my faithful servant, Watsonicus, I circled back to discover that a formidable squad of mercenary soldiers had already detained you. It was at that point that I decided to bide my time for the appropriate moment to spring you," Holmes remarked.

"Then you did not abandon me on purpose?" I asked, gleefully.

"Of course not, my dear fellow. I merely took advantage of an unfortunate situation," Holmes stated.

"I knew it!" I said triumphantly, standing up and running to him with outstretched arms.

He, placing his hand flatly between us and ignoring my expression, continued without a pause, "Please, sit down, old man, before you lapse into an embarrassing state of apoplexy."

I stopped. "Did you know Drumb was about?"

"Oh, yes, I was well aware of his presence and continuously on guard. My several disguises, however, kept me one step ahead of him. Except for a brief moment when I was discovered and let down my caution, I was completely concealed. The clever one-armed man was able to purloin the crystal-structure from under my very nose," Holmes confessed. "That would fit perfectly with the Arch Druid's mode of operation, finding a weak vessel who would do his dirty work for him, perhaps even utilizing a hypnotic trance of some kind. Once again, the innocent suffer at the hands of the ambitious." Holmes looked up, drew on his briar, and then asked, "Did not Drumb remind you of someone in particular?"

"Well, yes, now that you mention it, but whom I cannot say," I responded by furrowing my brow.

"For me, he brought to mind my former nemesis, the infamous Professor Moriarty," Holmes said.

"That's it!" I said, instantly. "That is who I have been trying to remember!"

"That is who I have been trying to forget, my dear fellow," Holmes shot back. "Yes, the same cunning intelligence, tenacity, and vicious disregard for others, if it suits his purposes. I should not be surprised if Drumb were to turn out to be a distant ancestor of the notorious Moriarty himself, but we shall never know."

I gave the matter some abstract thought.

Holmes waved his hand and proceeded, "Getting back to the object of our quest, I saw and heard the entire train of events, Watson, in keeping, I might add, with the historical record contained in the Bible. During more than one of his dissertations, Jesus claimed to have—and exhibited—power over the life and death of others. His healing demonstrations, I witnessed, were quite authentic. It is not difficult to discern a forgery. Not only that, but he also asserted his ability to predict his own death and resurrection, a sentiment for which, if it were not true, he should surely have been cast into a madhouse. No mere man has ever made a journey like that. He was, as well, capable of forecasting the betrayal by one of his very own beloved disciples. To this very day, the term 'Judas' is synonymous with treachery and treason. His knowledge of the future did not stop there. I will personally attest to the fulfillment of the Apostle Peter's disavowal of his master before the crowing of the rooster on that fateful morn.

"You know my methods, Watson. One forms a set of theories that fit the presumed conditions. One investigates the circumstances and gleans the factual data. Then one throws out all the inconsistent explanations, irrespective of their assumed feasibility, until the one true theory that fits all the data, regardless of how improbable it might seem, remains standing. This is the very case here," Homes continued.

"I witnessed the death of Jesus, Watson," my companion went on with his narrative as his demeanor changed from didactic to pensive, "and I observed, from a distance, his entombment. At the hands of the authorities and the behest of the religious leadership, he was executed unjustly, then taken by Joseph of Arimathea and committed to a cold, well-secured rock-hard grave. I investigated the site most thoroughly, as you observed. Although I was rescuing you from a Roman prison at the time and did not actually witness the miraculous rising from the dead, I can assure you that it is the only possible explanation.

"My pre-dawn investigation of Jesus' burial site was straightforward enough. He rose from the dead, I must tell you earnestly. I could plainly construe, from the footprint record, the string of events that occurred in front of the tomb even with the passing of three days. There had been a substantial detachment of Roman soldiers, I would say in the neighborhood of some eighteen to twenty, carefully standing guard at a meticulously secured and imposingly sealed grave. There were no other footprints outside the burial chamber. There were several distinguishing marks left by the many unique soldiers that I will not bore you with. Suffice it to say the patrol was composed of warriors who had seen their share of heavy fighting and more than sufficient for the purpose at hand, unless," he paused, "there was divine intervention."

"What did you observe when you went into the tomb itself?"

"I will tell you this, my dear fellow: it was a sight that, to this day, is exponentially beyond any scene I can now recall to mind. And that is saying a great deal, considering the strange incidents to which

I have been a party and you, Doctor, have taken the time to corroborate during our many years together."

"I second the motion on that." I quickly reviewed, mentally, the astonishing sight of angels that we witnessed that night. I fancied as I sat there and conjured that dominating spectral-like image in my own memory; the same facsimile was running through the mind of my companion. Our eyes met in a wordless exchange before he hastened to proceed.

"The interior of the rough hewn grave was stark and oppressive; the air was still and damp. There was no corpse, and there were only three sets of footprints inside to perceive. One set was distinctly that of a wealthy man. I had made a quick study of the various footwear used in that time period and noted immediately that distinctive tread of a newly fashioned, expensive shoe. The other two I recognized as simple sandals, well worn, patched, and common. I could presume that a rich man and perhaps two of his servants actually placed the body into the tomb. That I was the first person to have stepped inside the grave after the interment, I will adamantly avow. There was a stone slab in the middle of the vault that was cold and forsaken. As I bent over it, I saw strips of linen lying there, neatly arranged, as if they had been wrapped around the body in an orderly fashion and then suddenly abandoned by their occupant. I also noted the burial cloth that had been around the head of Jesus neatly folded by itself, separate from the linen. The faint pungent smell of embalming substances caused me to shudder and take a step backwards. The Jewish burial custom involved a mixture of myrrh, aloes, and other spices. To preserve the body, it was wrapped with the spices in linen strips. I sensed a palpable former presence in the cave, and yet it was markedly empty. The conclusion from my intense, albeit brief, investigation of the burial chamber itself was unavoidable: the body of Jesus had miraculously departed."

"What do you mean, departed?"

"I could not tell exactly what bizarre incident occurred, but at one particular point during the night there was, perhaps simultaneous with the earthquake, a shocking phenomenon, apparently both physical and ethereal. It must have been stunningly impressive. It could not have been ordinary because whatever it was frightened those battle-seasoned Roman soldiers into fleeing like schoolchildren at the sight of a baying hound. This elite detachment of official troopers could not have been bribed or cajoled in any way, because their very reputations and necks were on the line. Life was harsh for an unfaithful Roman guardsman at that time. A soldier's dereliction of duty was punishable by flogging. His right hand was cut off for desertion. Insubordination usually precipitated a beheading.

"I could see by the footprint record that the large stone was not physically rolled away by humans or animals up the arduous incline to the place where it rested. It would have taken several men and a couple of oxen a full day to cause that to happen. Furthermore, the seal that was set on the stone was intact and untouched, impossible if earthly methods of removal were employed. The cave was opened up by a dramatic force, the stone rolled away up the incline, and the body of Jesus wondrously evacuated. There were no barefoot prints anywhere upon the ground, and Jesus was buried without any footwear. To that I will personally attest. There were, I might add, some scorch marks on the rocks outside the tomb, which would be consistent with lightning strikes, but that is speculation on my part. The fallen rocks that were about, of course, indicated a great earth movement. That, I am sure, contributed to the spectacular event that occurred. Considering, too, the celestial beings that we were beholders of, I consider myself on safe ground to allow for the possibility of a heavenly apparition, which must have been astonishing and over-whelming. There can be no mistake about the evidence."

"By the way," I interrupted, "why were you standing outside my prison cell, and how did you know there was going to be an earth-quake at that precise time?"

"Elementary, my dear Watson: refer, at your convenience, to Matthew 28:2. You will find it well documented and quite reliable. I was only too pleased to discover, at the time, that the earthquake of three days previous had affected the integrity of the jail complex to the point that the ensuing tremor easily fractured the doors and restraining partitions, thus allowing the inmates, you included, to effect their escape."

"Amazing!" I said.

"Quite predictable, actually."

"Let me ask you, Holmes," I hesitated.

"What is it, old man?"

"There is something I have been wondering. If the object of your quest, as you call it, was to be an eyewitness to the actual event in question, why did you not stay at the burial site to do just that? Why did you plant yourself outside my jail cell to await the advent of the earthquake and the opportunity to liberate me?"

"That is a good question, Doctor. To be honest with you, I had the specific intent to stay at the site of the burial and see the event in person. After all, there is more than one way to spring a criminal from the local keep."

"I wish you would not refer to me as a criminal."

"Sorry, Watson, let me say, detainee."

"Thank you."

"I actually hovered around the locale of the tomb that night, in hiding, until I was clumsily discovered by an intoxicated trooper who came upon my secret niche by accident and sounded the alarm before I had a chance to silence him. There was simply nothing I could do but flee the scene, as I was chased through the city by a brute squad of Roman soldiers. I then, knowing they were on the lookout for me, decided to concentrate my efforts on freeing a particular prisoner, you. I was certain and free to be able to fully investigate the scene in question once it was freshly vacated by the guards. That, coupled with the fact that I had blunderingly lost the time machine crystal, dictated that I had to have you in hand to immediately retrieve the thing as soon as the mystery was solved to my satisfaction. I simply could not wait around afterward for an appropriate opportunity to emancipate you. In retrospect, however, I am willing to suppose that perhaps the actual resurrection was a sight that I was not destined to witness. Maybe I had bent the fabric of time beyond the pale, as the idiom has it, and attempted to see a sight that, for me at least, was irrevocably unacceptable."

Holmes exhaled before he went on, getting back to his train of thought. "I reiterate: I discovered, by the on-site investigation, that the mammoth stone had been rolled away by some sort of unearthly power that I could not ascertain. The inhabitant of the tomb departed by some unknown method, certainly not by foot, carriage, or animal, and all of it was extremely uncanny. There is no other explanation.

"The theory that his twelve followers stole the body, after the fact, to support their fallen master's claim, is unsubstantiated by the footprint record. The only viable interpretation is divine intervention," he asserted.

"How can you be sure that Jesus was really dead when he was placed inside his grave?"

Holmes' face grew troubled. "Once again, Watson, I appeal to the integrity of the first person when I state that I was there. There is a hill in Jerusalem called Golgotha—it is called the 'place of the skull' in Aramaic—where the Romans carried out their brutal executions.

"From a distance, I watched Jesus of Nazareth as he was arrested, without putting up a fight. In fact, he healed the wounded ear of an arresting soldier after one of his own twelve closest allies had tried to defend the man from Galilee by putting a sword to the guard. I got the distinct impression that this Jesus of Nazareth laid aside his own ability to defend himself and went willingly before his accusers for some greater purpose.

"After his arrest, he was brought before the religious high council, where he was interrogated. Because of the preexisting contempt they had for Jesus, the result of that inquisition was predictable. What do they call it in Australia, Watson, a 'kangaroo court,' I believe? By their own religious rules, the Hebrew authorities could not assume the burden of executing anyone during the sacred festival. He was then sent to the palace of the Roman governor, where he was again questioned."

Holmes added, "While I was passing from the chambers of the Sanhedrin—that is the Jewish high council—to the governor's compound, I noticed a man whom I recognized to be the Apostle Peter warming himself at a fire. I inquired of him as to the disposition of his master, but he denied any knowledge of him in most vehement terms, so I passed on.

"When directly questioned by the governor about his assertions of kingship, Jesus answered by reiterating the truth of his claims. At this, Pilate responded by asking, 'What is truth?'" Holmes paused.

"Indeed! Cannot the truth be relative to the individual?" I interrupted, again.

"There are two ways to slide easily through life, Watson: one is to believe everything, and the other is to doubt everything. I have devoted my whole life to unearthing the truth, the objective truth. It requires wholehearted effort. Although I have found it, at times, to be elusive, it is inevitably discoverable and always worth the effort. The truth, in any arena of life, be it concrete or ethereal, is not something to shy away from but rather, when found, to be enthusiastically embraced. It produces a freedom and satisfaction that is unparalleled. For example, imagine any system of justice that finds truth to be in the eye of the beholder. We would certainly rue the day, my dear fellow, that a perpetrator could subjectively hide behind his own point of view. Imagine! Everyone doing what is right in his own eyes: what chaos that would cause."

Holmes thought for a moment.

"I then saw the viceroy, Pilate, literally bring out a bowl of water to wash his hands of the matter as he remanded the prisoner for crucifixion. This he did, I presume, out of fear of the crowd, because they threatened to take the matter before Caesar himself.

"When he was brought forward, it appeared as if Jesus had been flogged and belittled in a most humiliating way. I noticed he had a crown of thorns on his head and bloody welts on his entire body as he was forced to carry his own cross to the place of the skull. He was brutalized beyond recognition, disfigured and degraded. The scene was excruciating.

"An execution at the hands of a detachment of cruel Roman soldiers is not a pretty sight, Watson. With all its inadequacies, the British system of common law and justice is far superior to the brutal and arbitrary way of doing things in the iron-fisted realm of the first century Roman Empire. To be crucified, I observed, was to be actually nailed with iron spikes, hands and feet to a rough-cut wooden structure shaped like a 'T'. Actually, the spikes were driven into the wrists of the convicted criminal to better support the weight of the body once it was vertical. This cross was then dropped into a pre-dug hole, forcing the condemned to hang by the sinews of his extremities. Being in such a state and in an upright position, I am sure, would soon cause the victim to lose the capacity to breathe, because of the weight of his own body pulling down on his torso. It must have been quite painful, to be sure.

"A sign was placed above his head and written in Greek, Latin, and Aramaic was the phrase, 'The King of the Jews.' One would suppose the purpose of such an epigram to be one of mockery."

Mr. Sherlock Holmes' face contorted with harsh memory as he continued his singular narration.

"There he was on display, Watson, hanging between two other condemned criminals, making no defense for himself and guilty of no transgression. I supposed it was his family and friends mixed into the multitude of curious onlookers that contemplated the morbid event. I did recognize some of his followers hovering on the fringe of the crowd, perhaps in fear for their own lives. Of course, there was Mary, his mother, unashamedly standing near the cross with tears of dismay streaming down her face. She, along with other women, mourned and wailed at the sight. The blessed Mother of God, the Madonna, was crying over her son, whom she loved so dearly, the love of a mother for her child, Doctor. At one point, shortly before his death, Jesus quietly said something to his mother that I could not discern, but apparently it was sufficient for the moment.

"Even as his garments were gambled over by greedy soldiers, I could not help but fix my gaze upon his eyes, Doctor," Holmes paused, as uncharacteristic emotion nearly overcame him.

"I could not escape Jesus' eyes. They seemed to follow me as I walked among the throng. His eyes were piercing and yet tired; as much as I attempted to elude them, they cornered me; they haunted me, while at the same time they invited me. There was a sense, I thought, that he was at ease with this ill-fated circumstance that had been dealt to him, and that he was simultaneously tortured by some sort of painfully monumental broken relationship. You know me, Watson. I am not generally given to idle intuitive interpretations of such situations, but this was indeed unique. I suppose it might have been his penetrating eyes that gave rise to this impression. And, as I have often said, intuition can be an essential element in any array of tools possessed by the working detective. I know it sounds seemingly unexplainable and rather outside the scope of my usual area of comfort, but I was witness to a special event that has no peer, a mystery like none other." There was a long silence before he proceeded.

"The sky became black with clouds, and the earth shook with a mighty convulsion, as if groaning and mourning a great loss. As I dared to get a bit closer, I noted that his side was pierced with a spear, dispensing a profuse amount of the thick dark red liquid blended with lymphatic fluid, a gory sight. Clotted blood mixed with dirt and sweat made the scene even uglier, if that is possible. His hands were nearly ripped from his forearms by the weight of his own body, and I vividly recall the acrid smell of urine mingled with the distinctive odor of vomit. And then, after an excruciatingly long period of time, he said in Aramaic, 'It is finished,' and he gave up his spirit and died. He remained nailed up on display for several hours. That is only an estimate on my part because, of course, I had no timepiece. His body was flaunted, no doubt, for the sake of the crowd and the gravity of the incident, while the Roman officials made sure of his death. This fact, my dear fellow, I declare earnestly to you. Those soldiers were expert at their craft. After which moment, I observed his body being removed and transported, ceremoniously by the well-to-do fellow named Joseph of Arimithea and his hired staff to the previously mentioned tomb for burial. None of the family and friends made that processional trek to the tomb. I did observe a few men and women and a chap named Nicodemus secretly following along at some distance, I suppose out of fear, grief, or both."

Another ponderous hesitation ensued as my companion was lost in heavy thought. He then went onward.

"That is why, Watson, when I saw that man from Galilee alive, three days later at the site of his very own burial, and gazed once again into his unmistakable eyes, I had the boldness to actually place my fingers upon his wounded foot. At that point, I was convinced, beyond the least shadow of a doubt, of the validity of his claims."

"What words did he whisper to you?" I gently inquired.

"That, my dear fellow, will remain my treasured secret. But I will tell you this: the words were good and precisely what I needed. Indeed, He is the truth, the light of illumination, and the path. His death and return to life give Him indisputable authority, and if His assertions about Himself are correct, I cannot remain immovable, but rather, I must come to my senses and mindfully participate in a reviving repentance and belief.

"This whole affair has made me painfully aware of my own deficiencies, and I discover that it has become necessary for me to listen to the message of Christ and personally comply with it. I must hand the reins of my life, as it were, over to this Jesus of Nazareth, both heart and mind. I can see no other option," he added, uncharacteristically humble. "Furthermore, I have no desire to entertain any other alternative. His faultless being, at one and the same time both utterly divine and quite human, I will gladly trade for my own woeful defects. The transaction of exchanging my imperfections for his spotlessness is to be done in the inner reaches of the heart and will,

Doctor, very intimate and very individual." He sighed.

"There had to be, Watson, some great reason for which I was miraculously rescued from a watery grave in the Thames River.

"The Almighty adores his creatures, you and I included, to the extent of allowing His only offspring to act as a sacrifice in our stead, so that we might be utterly reunited with Him throughout all of eternity. This truism is that Jesus lived the life that we should have lived and died the death that we should have died, in our place, so God can now receive us, not for our record but for His record and sake. It is a free gift. It is up to us to accept that free gift. We need that gift. We need to be redeemed."

"But why would anyone who is self-sufficient, in control, and competent feel the need to be delivered? I simply do not. If you feel that way, more power to you, but it seems to me to be a lot of silly twaddle. I find it a slap in the face to all that I believe," I confessed.

"If I search my soul deeply enough, Watson, I do not. When I look into the face of a perfect God, I realize myself to be totally inadequate. I admit that I am so destitute that Jesus had to die to save me. But I am so cherished that Jesus was happy to die to save me and Jesus Christ brings me to God. Let me put it in your parlance, Doctor. I have been given the diagnosis, and it is not good; but fortunately, I have also received the cure, and it is good.

"As a practitioner of the deductive arts, I am afraid this conclusion is not very scientific. And forgive me, old man, if I am devoid of my usual end-game explanation, but in my declining years, it is compelling nonetheless."

"And what do you mean by that?" I quizzed.

"I am painted into a corner, Doctor. God is a troublesome God. In my heart of hearts, I strongly resist the idea that I need to be rescued. I do not like the fact that when I look out over the world and all of creation, I must conclude a designer behind it all. I do not like the fact that, ultimately, I am not in control. I do not like it that I am finally incapable of saving myself. I resist it with every fiber of my being. I do not like what Jesus said to his Father, 'This is eternal life, that they may know You, the only true God, and Jesus Christ whom You have sent'. Jesus calls himself a stumbling block; I do not like this snag, but I cannot ignore it. I am a reluctant convert at best.

"I am not preaching to you, Watson. I am no better than anyone else, but I know this: I need to be extricated. I must be corrected in my thinking. I now believe that Jesus is accurate in declaring that there is an afterlife and that this present life in which we find ourselves is only important inasmuch as it determines where we spend that eternity. While you might suspect that I find such a paradoxical occurrence to be distasteful and directly opposed to my basic way of viewing this episode we call existence, in this case, I discover it to be immensely comforting. It is like a writ of pardon to a condemned man." Holmes hesitated, looking beyond me.

"I seize as my own, dear fellow, the following word picture: attempting to scale the imposing rocky heights of human meaning by using the tools of reason and understanding, I have struggled hard up the sheer cliff face of ignorance, only to pull myself over the final ridge of doubt to discover at the summit of the mount a circle of theologians that has been there for hundreds of years."

After a moment, he said, "I assure you, Watson, the reanimation of Jesus was **not** a magic trick, as one to be performed around a bonfire by the likes of Drumb or a cheap carnival showman like myself." He hung his head.

"How did you, inside that Druid circle, perform those magic tricks as you call them?" I queried.

"Simple, my dear fellow." Holmes picked up, off the table beside his chair, a box of strike matches, and holding two of them by his thumbs behind the middle fingers of each hand, twirled his palms in concert and deftly struck the match tips against each other. Holding out the backs of his hands toward me gave the illusion that fire was emanating from the tips of his middle fingers. I applauded.

"And the gunplay?" I eagerly inquired.

"The pistol shot was no more than a sharpshooter at a carnival sideshow might execute. I had noticed a particularly reflective facet on the crystal that allowed me to discern my target clearly. Using the crystal merely added to the mysterious aura that it had already engendered," he stated coolly, as he puffed on his pipe.

"The explosion and greenish-brown flames?" I asked.

"A simple fulminate of mercury compound mixed, quickly, with a dusting of copper sulfate did the trick. I combined the fulminic acid and powder into a small, breakable vial I had in the bag: very unstable stuff; you have to be careful. Smashing the container into the fire caused the predictable reaction, quite commonplace, actually."

"Astounding. How on earth did you know to bring along such items in your bag of tricks?" I wondered.

"Always be prepared for the unexpected, Doctor. I cannot remember how many times I have told you that," he smirked.

The great detective rose and poked absentmindedly at the suitable fire. The mystery was solved, and his burning doubts were quenched.

Following a bit of quiet contemplation on the evening's conversation, I carried forward, "I am afraid I cannot agree, Holmes. I staunchly reckon that any change of heart, as you might call it, on your part is unbecoming and improper. I do not believe in Jesus as you do, and I am dismayed that I must part ways with you on this subject matter."

I expected a retort, but none was forthcoming. Holmes said not a word but continued his fiddling with the blaze.

There, however, in the warmth of silence and with some further introspection, I confessed to myself that I had made an unspoken commitment to consider the relevance of these weighty issues to my own way of thinking.

My friend changed the topic. "I hope you don't mind, my dear fellow, but we will not be alone this weekend. I have taken the liberty of asking the lovely Miss Hackberry and her father to join us. They will be arriving tomorrow morning on the 11:15 from Victoria."

"I should very much like to meet this extraordinary woman and her father," I responded.

"We shall pass a pleasant Saturday afternoon and evening. Then, the following morning, I have planned for us to attend the Sunday morning service at the little church in the village. My Scottish neighbor, Mrs. MacNaughton, to the west, refers to it as the wee kirk. If I remember correctly, the Reverend's homily this week is titled, The Timelessness of Christ, certainly a fitting subject matter, eh, Watson?"

"Indeed," I responded.

"As the poet says: 'God's concept of time is perfect, purposeful and beyond my understanding'," Holmes went on.

"The vicar is an exceedingly amiable chap, not unlike you, Doctor. He also possesses a passable game of chess, an indulgence for which I have recently acquired a passion. I would like to explore the significance of chess as a metaphor to life, Watson. You will join us, then, I am sure?" he inquired.

"I would not miss it for all the time in the world," I answered.

The End

About the Author

Author L. Frank James Jr., was born into a Christian home in Pasadena, California. (The 'L' is for Leroy.) Having a rich Christian family heritage, he was raised in the church and was taught the Gospel of Jesus Christ from an early age.

Frank's early Christian background was heavily influenced by his Godly parents. As a lad, he would accompany his mother to Pentecostal prayer meetings, healing services, and special crusades and events that faith preachers would conduct in Southern California. His dad was a dedicated servant around the church, serving as a deacon, a trustee, and in the capacity of general ambassador to people and missions during his working days and even after his retirement from the business world.

At the age of eleven, at the behest of his mother, Frank knelt down beside her at the edge of his bed and asked Jesus into his heart. Of course, given to exaggeration, the next day when asked to describe the event, he characterized it as being "struck by a lightning bolt."

Frank had a speech impediment when he was young, causing him to stutter badly. Consequently, he was afraid to go to the lunch counter at John Marshall Jr. High School in Pasadena, because he would stammer too much while attempting to order a peanut butter and jelly sandwich. He underwent years of speech therapy with his teacher Mr. Gray who, himself as an adult, had a distinctive infantile 'R'.

When Brother Oral Roberts came through town, Frank's mother took him down to the evangelist's revival and healing tent ministry crusade. Brother Roberts placed his hands on Frank's head and prayed over him that the Lord would loosen his tongue. Though not healed right away, he is convinced that God answered that prayer through the medium of theater.

It was Frank's first year of high school when he chose to take a drama class as an elective. He vividly remembers standing on stage in the Little Theater at Pasadena High School and having to read a part in a play—a script that he had previously reviewed. Having the opportunity to rehearse what he would be saying before he auditioned, allowed him to read it perfectly, without stuttering. Consequently, this experience taught him that if he could preview and practice beforehand, he would be relieved from fretting, stammering, and groping for the words he needed to speak.

Drama and theatre attracted Frank during both his high school and college years. (He says that the only thing he could do was to stand up in front of people and make a fool of himself.) At Pasadena City College he was a Drama Major and graduated from Cal State LA with a bachelor's degree in Theatre.

His mother's death from cancer in 1975, caused Frank to begin to re-think the faith of his youth—he was assured that she had prayed for him during his backsliding years.

He met and married his bride, Charlotte, in 1977. They have five children: Barbara Lyon (Married to James Lyon), Patrick, David, and fifteen-year-old-twins, Martha and Beth. The family stayed in Southern California through 1988, allowing Frank to earn a Master of Fine Arts Degree in Theater from UCLA.

During the '80s Frank often worked in theater and tried to break into film and TV as an actor. He had a day job working at a billboard company and at night he would do theater—writing, producing, directing, and performing in local theatrical efforts.

Frank, Charlotte, and the kids moved to Northern California in 1989 to help plant Valley Springs Presbyterian Church in Roseville, CA. He held the position of Drama Director under David George, Senior Pastor, and is now the Pastoral Care provider.

Being a former member of the Screen Actors Guild (Frank hasn't actually paid dues for years) and AFTRA, officially puts him in the position of a lot of people—'Don't quit your day-job!' He originally obtained his SAG card when he landed a part as a security guard on *General Hospital*. (That's the high point of his TV career.) He taught high school drama and has a long list of acting and directing credits in community as well as professional theater.

Awards, activities, and recognition...

Robert Reed acting award UCLA—*Hamlet*

Birdsal acting award—*Remember Me*

Elly acting award—*The Dining Room*

Bank of America award—Best actor

Published Author: Plastow Publications—Church format sketches for Sunday morning worship events

Performed and directed with various touring companies: FACE (Fellowship of Artists for Cultural Exchange), mounted and toured with two shows for ELIC (English language Institute in China) to Mainland China

Performed & directed with 'Last Minute Productions'

Participated in worldwide mission trips to China, Kenya, Tanzania, Philippines and Mexico

Participated in theater—Paris, France—Theatre Du Terte

Selected Bibliography

Camus, Albert. *The Stranger*. New York: Alfred A. Knopf, 1988.

Chesterton, G.K. *The Everlasting Man*. San Francisco: Ignatius Press 1993.

Christie, Agatha. *The Unexpected Guest*. New York: St. Martin's Press, 1999.

————*The Secret of Chimneys*. New York: Dell Publishing, 1978.

Dickens, Charles. *A Christmas Carol*. Hertfordshire: Wordsworth Editions Limited, 1993.

Doyle, Arthur Conan. *A study in Scarlet*. New York: Penguin, 1982.

————*The Sign of Four*. New York: Penguin, 2001.

————*The Hound of the Baskervilles*. New York: Signet, 1986.

Eldredge, John. *Wild at Heart: Discovering the Secret of a Man's Soul*. Nashville: Thomas Nelson, 2001.

Eldredge, John and Staci Eldredge. *Captivating: Unveiling the Mystery of a Woman's Soul*. Nashville: Nelson Books, 2005.

Grisham, John. *The Testament*. New York: Dell, 1999.

Johnson, Phillip E. *Objections Sustained: Subversive Essays on Evolution, Law, and Culture*. Downers grove, IL: InterVarsity Press, 1998.

Lewis, C.S. *The Chronicles of Narnia*. New York: HarperCollins, 1983.

————*The Great Divorce: A Dream*. London: G. Bles, 1945.

————*Mere Christianity*. New York: HarperCollins, 2001.

————*The Perelandra Series*. New York: Scribner, 1996.

McDowell, Josh. *The New Evidence That Demands A Verdict: Fully Updated To Answer The Questions Challenging Christians Today.* Nashville: Nelson Reference, 1999.

Morison, Frank. *Who Moved the Stone?.* Grand Rapids: Zondervan, 1958.

Nordhoff, Charles and James Norman Hall. *Mutiny on the Bounty: A Novel.* New York: Little, Brown and Company, 1932

Paton, Alan. *Cry, the Beloved Country.* New York: Scribner, 1948.

Rand, Ayn. *The Fountainhead.* New York: Signet, 1952.

Ross, Hugh. *The Creator and the Cosmos: How the Latest Scientific Discoveries of the Century Reveal God.* Colorado Springs: NavPress, 1993.

Schaeffer, Francis A. *How Should We Then Live?: The Rise and Decline of Western Thought and Culture.* Wheaton: Crossway Books, 1983.

——— *True Spirituality.* Wheaton: Tyndale House Publishers, 1979.

Strobel, Lee. *The Case for a Creator: A Journalist Investigates Scientific Evidence That points Toward God.* Grand Rapids: Zondervan, 2004.

——— *The Case for Faith: A Journalist Investigates the Toughest Objections to Christianity.* Grand Rapids: Zondervan, 2000.

Tolkien, J.R.R. *The Lord of the Rings.* Great Britain: HarperCollins Publishers, 1994.

Vonnegut, Kurt. *The Sirens of Titan.* New York: Dell Publishing, a division of Bantam Doubleday Dell Publishing Group, 1959.

Wodehouse, P.G. *Life with Jeeves.* New York: Penguin, 1953.

——— *The Most of P.G. Wodehouse.* New York: Scribner, 2000.